To my fabulous Market
my wife, who has worked tirelessly to get my work out there.

Copyright © Rob Ashman 2020

*Rob Ashman has asserted his right under the Copyright Designs and Patents Act 1988
To be identified as the author of this work.*

This book is a work of fiction. Names, characters, businesses, places, events and incidents are either the product of the author's imagination, or used in a fictitious manner. Any resemblance to actual person living or dead, is purely coincidental.

Apart from any use permitted under UK copyright law, this publication may only be reproduced, stored or transmitted, in any form, or by any means, with prior permission in writing of the publisher, or, in the case of reprographic production, in accordance with the terms of licences issued by the Copyright Licencing Agency.

Also by Rob Ashman

The DS Malice series

Killing Pretties

The DI Roz Kray series

Faceless

This Little Piggy

Suspended Retribution

Jaded

The Mechanic Trilogy

Those that Remain

In Your Name

Pay the Penance

Prologue

'A man once told me I was good on the outside... evil on the inside. He's dead now. Which I suppose proves his point. I've learned that people are pre-programmed to be deceived and the more principled they are, the stronger their convictions. And the more heart-felt their beliefs, the easier it is.

Twinkle twinkle, little lies ...

'Reflect back to them what they want to see and it's like taking candy from a baby. They desperately want to believe others share their view of the world. Figure out what that is and they will do the rest.

How I see them in your eyes ...

'Society is just as bad. When the media create their own version of reality and politicians bend it to suit themselves... that is seen as acceptable. But, when an individual does the same it's greeted with howls of outrage and derision, and what is acceptable today may find itself on the banned list tomorrow. I've come to realise that there are no rights or wrongs, only colours of opinion at any given time.

Keep the truth inside your head ...

'Everyone walks around with an invisible set of user-instructions hanging around their neck. The trick is, working out how to read it. It's my one and only skill, but then I've reached the conclusion... it's the only one I need.'

And hope that no one winds up dead.

Chapter 1

Joseph's head bounces off the wall, causing his eyes to roll back in their sockets. He staggers backwards and his knees buckle. Frank swings him by the bath towel wound tight around his neck and heaves him to his feet, choking off his air supply.

Clements screams in Joseph's face.

'The money, where's the money?'

Joseph coughs a response. Clements nods to Frank who pivots his considerable bulk sending Joseph crashing into the wall again. There's a sharp snap as his shoulder fractures under the impact.

'Twelve grand over three months. Did you think we wouldn't notice?' yells Clements. 'Where is it?'

Joseph gargles. 'I don't know… what you're… on about.'

I check my watch; we've been going at this for ten minutes.

I must admit, I hate this part of the business but accept it is a bleak necessity. Joseph was a rising star, enthusiastic and resourceful. But success went to his head and he began to piss me off. I watch as he doubles over, his hands secured behind his back. He's coughing blood onto the carpet — that's a poxy cleaning job for later.

I cast my eyes around the room. It looks pretty much the same as the day I acquired it from my parents' estate; sparsely furnished with an old three-piece suite, a coffee table and a TV. The sofa and table have been shoved to one side to provide as much wall space as possible.

Frank is Clem's brother. A giant of a man with three redeeming qualities: he's fiercely loyal, would prefer to take instruction rather than think for himself and on a violence-scale of zero to ten, has the ability to go all the way up to twelve in the blink of an eye. He's a sadist with a smile, who wears the same expression on his face whether he's buying you a beer or breaking your thumbs.

Frank is the perfect blunt-edged instrument to Clem's smart business brain. He was never academic at school, studying — for him — was something you did with a centrefold in a magazine. But he takes his role of enforcer very seriously, so much so that he's taken to studying CIA enhanced interrogation techniques. The internet is a wonderful thing. He explained the process to me a few months ago while I made him a sandwich for lunch.

'The victim is pushed back against a flexible, false wall while wearing a neck collar to prevent whiplash and head injuries. The false wall amplifies the sound of the impact, tricking the victim into thinking he's being hurt more than he is.' Frank read the Wikipedia description out loud to me. 'Sounds like a winner, don't you think, Twinkle?'

As I listened, while spreading mayonnaise on a slice of bread, I knew this would not end well. The subtleties of the technique were way too complex for him to comprehend. The result of which is Joseph is being flung around by the neck and hurled into a breeze block and plasterboard wall. You can always trust Frank to enhance something that has already been enhanced. It's a good job the house is detached.

'I want my cash back.' Clements grabs hold of Joseph and shakes him. His mis-shaped head rolls back and forth and is a deep shade of purple. Clements turns to face me. 'Wat do you think, Twink?'

I shrug my shoulders.

Frank twists the towel and windmills Joseph around in an arc, slamming him face first into the wall. His nose goes squelch against the anaglypta paper, leaving a starburst of red.

More bloody cleaning.

The collision catapults him backwards with such force that not even Frank can prevent him hitting the carpet. He's lying on his back, his bloodshot eyes staring out of his blood-smeared face. One of his front teeth is protruding through his upper lip.

Frank tries to haul him to his feet but Joseph's body goes into spasm. White foam bubbles from his mouth.

'Get up!' Frank yanks on the towel but he's shaking and twitching like we've wired him up to the mains.

'Oh bollocks,' says Clements. 'Take it off.'

Frank unwinds the towel and tugs it free. Joseph is convulsing on the floor, spewing blood and foam on to his chin.

'I didn't mean to …' Frank pipes up.

'I know you didn't, Frank.' Clements drops to his knees and opens Joseph's eyelids wide with his thumbs. 'That's bloody annoying.'

'What is?' asks Frank.

'One pupil is bigger than the other.'

'What does that mean?'

Joseph lets out a rasp of air and then is still.

'It means, game over' says Clements.

'That's a real shame.'

'Yeah, but more than that, where's my bloody twelve grand?' Clements looks at his watch. 'Come on Twink, we're gonna be late. Frank, take care of this will you?'

Frank nods his head. 'I got it.'

I follow Clements out of the house, get into his car and we drive the three miles in silence. Silence that is punctuated every few minutes by Clements shaking his head while uttering under his breath, 'Bloody shame, that.'

We pull through the wrought iron gates, park the car and walk around the building to the back. The sound of the choir belting out Jesu, Joy of Man's Desiring drifts through the night air. I open a side-door to be greeted by ten smiling faces seated in a horseshoe around the room. The place has that familiar smell of old books and candles, with wood panelled walls and three large chandeliers hanging from the vaulted ceiling. The wall lights give the place a cosy glow.

'Sorry we're late.' I say removing my jacket. 'Is everyone okay?' There's a general murmuring of 'Yes' and a nodding of heads. Clements takes a seat among them and I stand at the front of the room. 'Let's take a minute in silent prayer.'

The eleven men bow their heads. I follow suit.

But I don't pray — never have. My mind toys with the events of the day.

Clements is right; it's a shame about Joseph. There are many cardinal sins in our profession: chief amongst them is 'Thou shalt not skim money off the top', which I suppose comes under the category of 'don't be a greedy bastard'. But in reality, we're all guilty of that and I don't have a problem with it. Clements, on the other hand, has a different view.

If only Joseph had admitted his transgression, he could have taken a good kicking and lived to fight another day; but he insisted on protesting his innocence. But then I suppose he couldn't do anything else. Joseph didn't skim money off the top... I did.

Chapter 2

My name is Twinkle, as in the children's lullaby. I was raped on my fourteenth birthday, my sixteenth birthday and on my twenty-first. To mark the occasions, I was given a bike, a phone and a jewellery set, but it's the rapes I remember the most.
I hate birthdays.

My family failed to protect me, as did the police, as did God. So, I decided looking after myself was down to me. You would have thought after the first rape I'd have worked it out. But I guess I'm a slow learner. I left home and ditched the church — still not sure which one was easiest to do — and went my own way.

That's when I met Dennis. Despite us bumping into each other in a bar in Spain, he was a guy from my home town and after travelling around Europe for a while we came boomeranging back.

The year we tied the knot it was like the film Four Weddings and a Funeral, only we had Four Funerals and a Wedding when all four parents died — breast, lung, bowel and pancreatic — in the game of cancer bingo we'd be shouting House! Out of the blue we had two houses in the same town, so we moved out of our accommodation to live in one and rented out the other.

Dennis the Menace I used to call him after the comic book character who also had a shock of black curly hair and a liking for stripy jumpers. His hair is now a thin covering though, since the chemo did its job. The poison they pumped into his body made him drop six stones but the steroids helped him to balloon to over seventeen. That all happened fourteen years ago. Now he's back to weighing nine stones, complete with weeping sores and split skin. My only saving grace is his speech is almost non-existent and, while I can understand him well enough, it does provide me with the excuse to ignore him.

My husband is now a wheelchair bound, double-incontinent slob. I would kill him but the incapacity benefit comes in handy to spend on other people who are prepared to look after the useless fuck. I mean, when I said my vows at the wedding no one said 'Til death do us part or until you become a stinking heap of useless male flesh'. Brain cancer was never part of the deal. The problem was he survived. At least our parents had the good grace to die.

It took two years for social services to get their act together and for the financial support to come through. At that time, Dennis could cope on his own at night, so I worked as a carer at a local nursing home. Fucking ironic, right? I would leave the house at half past nine at night to return at half six the next morning, then spend the day looking after him. It was a routine that turned me into a walking zombie. Days blurred into weeks, weeks into months. When the support finally came through, I collapsed. Six months later I met Clements and everything changed.

I turn to wave goodbye to Clem who's given me a lift home and then open the front door to find Zoe pulling her coat on in the hallway. She's been with us for ages now and always has a ready smile to brighten her otherwise unfortunate face. With her angular features and propensity to twitch and fidget, I always think she has a bird-like quality.

'Sorry I'm late,' I say, giving myself an unnecessary once-over in the mirror.

'Hi, Twink. It's no problem. How's your day?'

'Oh you know, not much to report.'

'Dennis has been fine; he's taken all his meds but hasn't eaten a great deal. I've made him a sandwich and left it in the fridge.'

'That's really kind of you, I'll see you tomorrow.'

'Night, Twink,' she says, her day's penance paid in full. The time is a little before nine o'clock, Rebecca won't be here for another hour to take over on the night shift. She's been coming to my house now for three months and I don't like her. She's too fucking interested for my liking, too thorough, too nice, too… genuine.

Up to now, the band of helpers who've tended to Dennis have all been what I call 'Plastic carers'. They do the right thing and say the right words but their façade is tissue thin. But that's okay, I applaud their deception.

Rebecca is different. I don't trust a person who cares that much about anything.

He likes her, fuck knows why!

I remove my coat and shoes, and take another look at my reflection. My bob-cut has long since ceased to be bob-like and my self-styled fringe is sharp enough to slice bread. I like it savage, it's a good look. All part of the charade.

I wander into the living room. Dennis flinches when he sees me. Zoe's dressed him in a blue tracksuit top and jogging bottoms — a ridiculous outfit for someone whose arms and legs don't work properly. I presume the starting blocks and running spikes are in his sports bag.

I turn on the TV and walk out to the kitchen to fix myself something to eat. The sandwich sitting on the middle shelf in the fridge under a skin of clingfilm looks dead tasty. I peel away the plastic and take a bite. Eww! Bloody mustard. It will have to be crackers and cheese then.

I return to the lounge to find David Attenborough banging on about melting glaciers or some shit and put the sandwich down on the arm of the chair. Dennis mumbles something. I pretend not to hear him. He does it again.

'Caaahhhh aaaa eeeggghh ta, eee ggrrunnngy,' he says, which roughly translated means, 'Can I eat that? I'm hungry.'

I watch the TV and crunch my crackers.

He gargles again, a series of incoherent noises. 'Can you move it closer.' I turn the sound up. 'Twink, move it.' His right arm is jerking around.

I stand up, take the cushions off the sofa and arrange them on the floor. Dennis goes into a shuddering mess, mumbling and grunting for all he's worth. I grab hold of the arm rest on his chair and lift him onto two wheels. He's gurgling and spitting in the air like a waterboard victim.

'I do wish you'd be quiet,' I say, flexing my arms and flipping the chair over. A plume of goo and snot erupts from his face as he lands on the cushions.

Crackers and cheese in the bath will be just the ticket. I drift out of the lounge and up the stairs. He's robbed me of my life. The least I can do is rob him of the next hour.

Chapter 3

Bodies move when they're dead. Soil settles after it's been dug. Three fingers protruded from the ground, one had been feasted on by an animal who'd found it not to their liking. The nail and tip were missing, leaving the bone gleaming white in the morning sunshine.

Detective Sergeant Malice had checked the weather forecast before leaving the house and decided a short-sleeved shirt was in order. He'd broken a new one out of the cellophane packet, removed the carboard and pins and put it straight on his back. He'd made a conscious decision to adopt the clean shirt routine ever since he began working with Detective Kelly Pietersen. It wasn't fair on her to share a car in the summer months with a colleague who, on occasions, could smell like someone who lived in a box under a bridge. It was a glorious morning for sure, but the nice weather-woman had said nothing about it being a lovely day to exhume a body.

Khenan Malice was the product of a Jamaican mother and English father. His family had come to Britain as part of the Windrush project and had made it their home. The marriage of a black woman to a white man had not gone down well in either camp and when he came along he was one of a kind in his neighbourhood.

'So, are you white or black?' his friends would ask.
'Both I suppose,' he would reply.
'Kinda coffee like?'
'Yeah, kinda.'
'That's cool. Let's go play footie.'

His mixed race had never been an issue until he reached his teenage years, then the racial divide bit him in the arse like a rabid dog. Having friends of both colours no longer worked. You had to pick a side. Malice chose black. Mainly because, where he lived, they were in the majority. Life was easier that way.

His beloved dreadlocks had long since hit the floor in his mother's kitchen to be replaced by a short crop-cut whenever he sat in the barber's chair. His passion for slugging it out in the boxing ring had honed his physique to be the envy of a bloke twenty years younger, though the lines on his face told a different story.

Malice trudged past the CSI vans and across an expanse of wasteland to the disused factory. The building was a cladded steel structure with heavy metal stanchions holding up a roof shot through with holes; so many holes it would have trouble fending off the effects of a brief rain shower. At the far end was a square of bright light coming from a half-open roller shutter door. As he approached, he could make out the strip of yellow tape stretched across the opening. A man in uniform was loitering to one side.

Malice's footsteps echoed around the cavernous space.

'Sir,' the officer said holding out a clipboard.

'Morning,' Malice said as he signed the register before donning a paper suit and pulling on a set of overshoes. He immediately began to sweat.

'Over here, Mally,' Catherine Anders, the Crime Scene Manager, called out when she clocked him in the doorway. 'I thought we'd wait until you got here.'

Beyond the tape was a plot of overgrown land that reached out to the perimeter fence. At the back was a large corrugated structure that used to be a bike shed.

Anders was standing next to it while two other people dressed in CSI gear were hunched over, staring at the ground.

'Thanks for that,' Malice ducked under the tape, then picked his way across the hardstanding. 'What have we got?'

'So far, we have this.' Anders squatted down next to three fingers protruding from the dirt. 'Two digits are intact. The index finger has been gnawed down to the first knuckle.'

'When did that happen?' Malice gestured towards the chewed finger.

'I'd say the damage was caused in the past week. We'll know more when we conduct a PM.'

Malice joined her and wrinkled his nose. 'Okay, let's go to work.'

Anders gave the nod and a team of white-suits descended with trowels and brushes. Within minutes they had exposed a brown shirt cuff, then a forearm, then a shoulder—after twenty minutes they had uncovered the body of a man, laying on his side in a shallow grave. High definition cameras recorded the process frame by frame.

He was dressed in a shirt, jeans and wearing some sort of trainer; the fabric of his clothing had perished to reveal the decayed flesh underneath.

'The body is reasonably well-preserved but the head has decomposed at a faster rate,' Anders said, shining a torch into the hole and peering at what they had uncovered.

'How long do you think he's been buried?' asked Malice.

'Difficult to tell. The ground has been kept pretty dry due to this.' She pointed a finger up at the tin roof, 'and the soil is close to PH neutral.'

'Could you hazard a guess?' Malice cocked his head over to one side.

Anders clucked her tongue against the roof of her mouth and touched the dead man's shoulder with a gloved finger.

'If you pushed me I would say between nine and twelve years.'

'Hey!' Detective Kelly Pietersen was hurrying towards them dressed in the same oversized gear. 'I got here as soon as I could. What have I missed?' Pietersen was in her late twenties; her dark shoulder length hair pulled back in a ponytail and tucked under the paper bonnet perched on her head. Her South African accent gave away her heritage.

Malice waved his hand over the body as if introducing a friend.

'It's reasonably well-preserved,' repeated Anders. 'We should get some good info from the post-mortem,'.

'Cause of death?' asked Pietersen, crouching down next to them; looking each one in the face.

'Bloody hell she doesn't hang about,' Anders said nodding towards the new arrival.

'Tell me about it.' Malice raised his eyebrows and blew out his cheeks.

'Yeah, okay,' huffed Pietersen. She shone an LED lamp onto the body and began peeling away the clothing with a gloved hand. 'How long has this place been derelict?'

'For as long as I can remember,' said Malice. 'The business went bust a long time ago.'

'I wonder why no one bought up the land?' mused Pietersen.

'Look around.'

Pietersen stood up and scanned her surroundings — the penny finally dropping. The building was flanked by the Claxton estate on the one side and the Bermondsey estate on the other.

'Point taken,' she said. 'Any property developer would have found their stuff on e-Bay the first night.'

'Exactly,' said Malice.

'I suppose whoever buried him here used this bike shed as cover.' Pietersen tugged at the roof and it wobbled on its mountings.

'It was still a risk carting the body across the yard.' Malice estimated the distance to the factory. 'There's got to be easier locations to dump a body.'

'How long–'

'Between nine and twelve years,' Anders butted in. 'Not sure if it was the cause of death but there's significant blunt force trauma to the base of the skull. Look how the bone is concave and splintered.' The beam of light highlighted the back of the man's head.

'That'll do it,' said Pietersen. 'So, he was murdered.'

'Looks that way,' Malice pulled on a glove, reached down and patted the front pockets of what was left of the man's jeans. He then put his hand underneath the body searching for a wallet or some form of I.D. He came away empty handed. 'Doesn't look like he has anything on him,'.

'What's that?' Pietersen removed a pen from her inside pocket and began prodding around in the dirt. She retrieved a thin, oblong piece of white plastic.

'Is it a credit card?' asked Malice.

'Don't think so. There's no magnetic strip running down the side.' Pietersen held it between her fingers and turned it in the sunshine.

'What the hell is it?' he asked.

'I can't be sure but it looks like a hotel key card,' Pietersen replied. She shook open an evidence bag and dropped it in. 'When can we expect the results of the post-mortem?'

Malice shot Anders a sideways glance. 'Told you,' he said.

'Give us a chance,' Anders snorted through her nose. 'The doctor hasn't pronounced the poor guy dead yet.'

'I know, but when do you think…?' Pietersen asked again.

'The morgue is pretty quiet at the moment, so I would expect us to have the preliminary findings later today.'

'Okay, there's nothing more we can do here,' said Malice standing up. 'Thanks for waiting, Catherine.'

'No problem.' Anders beckoned over the two men to finish off the painstaking task of removing the body. 'I'll be in touch as soon as we know anything.'

Malice and Pietersen made their way back to the roller shutter door. They stripped off the protective garments, deposited them into bags, signed the clipboard and handed them to the uniformed officer.

'Nice,' Pietersen said, looking him up and down as they walked back to the road.

'What?' replied Malice.

'Are you setting a new trend?'

'What do you mean?'

'Having horizontal creases in your shirt. It might catch on, you know?' She stifled a snigger behind her hand.

'I can't win. I put on a clean shirt and–'

'Can't be bothered to iron it?' She quipped.

'Sod off.'

'Or is your iron broken?'

'I can categorically say it's not broken.'

'You don't have one, do you?'

Malice shook his head, puffing a small laugh out of his nostrils. 'I might not.'

'Didn't your mum ever teach you how to iron?'

'No, but she taught me how to tell cheeky detectives to piss off.'

'I was only asking.' Pietersen was still smirking when they reached their cars. 'Waite is not going to be a happy Superintendent when we tell her.'

'Why's that?' Malice was only half-listening. His attention was drawn to a dark blue Mondeo parked across the street.

'She's not going to be keen on having a cold case on her books.'

'Yeah, maybe…' He watched the driver's window slide down to reveal a man with a dark stubbled chin and short dark hair wearing sunglasses. He was staring straight at them.

'The chances of catching whoever killed our guy is significantly diminished when…' Pietersen rambled on, patting her pockets for her keys. Malice was glaring at the driver when he heard the sound of an engine starting up. The car eased away from the kerb. '… I'm telling you, she won't be happy.' Pietersen continued, rifling through her bag. 'It has every potential to make her figures look bad.'

'Suppose so,' Malice replied, still staring at the driver.

'You're not listening,' Pietersen said.

Malice clenched his fists. The hair on the back of his neck was standing to attention.

The man was smiling. Then he stuck out the thumb of his left hand and drew it across his throat.

Chapter 4

Malice had been enjoying a new lease of life. For the first time in God knows how many years he was no longer a bent copper. Taking down Lubos Vasco and his gang and relieving them of their hard-earned cash had significantly improved his finances. And his mood.

He had enough money to ensure his ex-wife and daughter were secure while setting aside a sizeable nest-egg for himself. Though neither of these changes in fortune had helped him to negotiate the choppy waters of maintaining a civil relationship with Hayley, his ex-wife. The harder he tried the more he found himself in the dog-house.

However, despite his new lease of life he had a niggle in his head — the man in the blue Mondeo. He'd been so shocked when the guy drew his thumb across his neck he failed to clock his registration number. A rookie mistake for which Malice had been giving himself a well-deserved kicking.

Pietersen entered the meeting room. With an over-sized round table and two chairs, the place was already uncomfortably full. She shuffled to one side, closed the door and handed Malice a coffee.

'You don't own an iron ...' she said, cracking a smile.

'Pack it in or I'm gonna be rude.'

Malice pulled the desk phone towards him, hit the speaker button and tapped in the digits. The synthetic warble of a phone ringing the other end filled the room.

'Candice Harris,' a voice answered.

'Hey, Candice, it's Mally and Kelly Pietersen. Thanks for your email.'

'That's okay. You said you needed a fast update on the body we received this morning.'

'I appreciate the quick response.' Malice liked Harris. She was his favourite Home Office Pathologist.

'Hi Candice,' Pietersen said.

'Hi Kelly, are you keeping him in line?' said Harris.

'Are you joking?'

'Ha, tough job, eh?' Harris laughed.

'I am here, you know?' Malice leaned into the speaker.

'I think he needs more coffee,' Harris quipped.

'I've already administered a third cup,' laughed Pietersen.

'Can we press on?' Malice slumped back and took a slug of coffee.

'Okay,' said Harris with a rustling of papers. 'Our vic is male, mid-to-late-thirties, about five feet ten inches tall and of medium build with dark hair. He wasn't carrying any form of I.D, in fact he had no belongings with him at all. The most likely cause of death is major blunt force trauma to the base of the skull which resulted in a twenty-five-millimetre diameter indent.'

'About the size of a hammer head,' said Malice.

'The extremities of the wound were bevelled so it could be in keeping with that being the murder weapon.'

'Are we looking at a possible mugging?' said Malice.

'How long had he been in the ground?' asked Pietersen.

'Hang on,' Harris protested. 'There are no signs of defensive wounds on his hands or arms. I reckon he's been buried about ten years, I'll be firmer on the date when I do more tests. His teeth are in good condition so when you tell me where to look I can use dental records to formally identify him. I've sent a DNA sample away for analysis but if he's not in our data base it won't help.'

'So we're looking for someone who went missing ten years ago,' Pietersen mused to herself, repeatedly clicking the top of her pen.

'I can do a little better than that. You owe me a coffee for what comes next.'

'I can run to that,' Malice replied.

'The vic's shirt wasn't brown, it was yellow and it contained a number of thrips.'

'What the hell are thrips?' Pietersen asked.

'They're more commonly known as thunderbugs or thunder flies or storm flies.'

Malice and Pietersen glanced at each other and shrugged their shoulders in unison.

'You'll have to give us a clue,' she said.

'Thrips are small black creatures about one to two millimetres in length that can be found in abundance in rural areas during the summer months. There are six-thousand different species each one attracted to certain crops. When the crops are harvested they become airborne, landing on everything from people to picture frames. And here's the thing … they're drawn to bright colours. Our vic was wearing a yellow shirt and, so far, I've found six of the little critters in the material. I will know more when I've identified which type. But I think it's safe to look at him being killed in the summer months.'

'Anything else, Candice?' asked Malice.

'That's it for now, and don't forget, you owe me a coffee.' Harris hung up.

'That's narrowed down our time window,' said Pietersen.

'June, July and August of 2009.'

'Better iron your shirt when you take her for that coffee.'

'Fu–'

'Mally! My office,' Superintendent Samantha Waite yelled down the hallway.

Pietersen looked at him. 'Told you she wouldn't be happy.'

Malice edged past Pietersen and only just managed to squeeze himself through the partly opened door. He paced down the corridor to Waite's office.

'Bloody hell, you're popular,' he said walking in to find his boss sitting behind a mountain of paperwork.

'What half of this has got to do with policing is beyond me,' she replied, flapping her hands in the air.

'You wanted to see me.'

'Yes, I understand a body has been uncovered near the Claxton estate.'

'We got the preliminary report and it looks like it's been buried for around ten years. The cause of death is most likely to be a blow to the back of the head with something like a hammer.'

'Do you have an I.D.? A murder weapon?'

'Nothing, guv.'

'Bollocks.' She shook her head and shuffled paper around on the desk.

'The likelihood is the person was from out of town and we found what looks like a hotel key card at the site. The lab found thrips in the victim's clothing and–'

'Whatever the fuck they are?' Waite interrupted and got up from her desk, pulling her jacket from the back of the chair. 'Look I gotta go, what are the next steps? I don't want this hanging around for any longer than is necessary. You know how notoriously difficult cold cases are to solve. If we're not careful it will soak up time and resources we don't have.'

'As I was saying, ma'am, the vic had no personal possessions so we're working on the assumption that this was a mugging. The evidence would suggest he was from a rural location and was visiting the area and the hotel key would corroborate that theory. We've identified twenty-six hotels and guesthouses in the vicinity where the body was found. Twelve of these are B&Bs who don't use key cards choosing instead to use traditional keys. And eight weren't in business in 2009. That leaves six for us to have a pop at.'

'What's the approach?' She slipped into her jacket and gathered up a mound of paper.

'The victim may have left without settling his bill.'

'Or… he might have been killed *after* checking out; or the card could have been in his pocket for weeks; or…'

'Yes, guv, they're all possibilities. I know it feels a little like we're trying to find a needle in a haystack, but we have to start somewhere.'

'Okay, keep me posted. And the moment this begins to grow arms and legs I want to hear about it. We can do without it turning into a pantomime.'

I'll do my fucking best, ma'am.

'Will do, guv.'

Waite bustled past him and disappeared out the door. Malice followed behind until he reached the stairs then ran down to reception and out into the car park. Pietersen was waiting at the main entrance.

'I thought you'd gone?' he said, his brow creasing.

'I wanted to know how it went with Waite.'

'Not too bad, though she put down a firm marker that the minute this gets out of hand she wants to know about it.'

'Bet she does — she's not going to like having this on her books.'

They both turned and walked to their cars.

'Three hotels for you and three for me,' Malice said as he unlocked his car.

'See you back at the station later,' Pietersen called out as she slid into the driver's seat and started up the pool car. It misfired. 'Come on, you crock of shit.'

Malice could hear her berating the fact she wasn't driving her Porsche. He chuckled to himself and pulled out of the car park before her. He looked both ways as he drifted into the flow of traffic.

And then — out of the corner of his eye — he spotted a blue Mondeo.

Chapter 5

I smooth the creases out of my dress and primp my hair in the bedroom mirror. A bit of lippy and a brush of mascara and I'm ready to go. I'm looking forward to this afternoon. I love being a lying bitch.

The person staring back is unrecognisable from my younger self. I'd always adored the old black and white mob films and fancied myself as a gangster's moll. I admit it was never a great career aspiration for a young girl but I gave it my best shot. It soon became apparent that I had neither the glamour nor the poise to pull it off, so I turned to punk and tattoos to fill the gap. The punk scene gave me confidence and tattoos gave me the power of self-expression.

My days of safety pins and ripped clothing are a distant memory but I've been inked twenty-seven times, each one commemorating a special event. Clem has names for all of them and his favourites are the ones that are not on public display. I guess I kind of made it as a moll. After all, the difference between *gangster* and *drug-runner* is a matter of semantics.

'Bye, Zoe, see you tonight,' I call out as I dash down the stairs and into the hallway. The front door slams behind me and I set off in my car. Dennis has avoided me this morning, well… as much as a person who relies on others to move him around can avoid anyone. He's still sulking about me tipping him onto the cushions. Don't know why, he should be used to it by now.

The traffic is light and in no time I'm pulling through the gates. The car park is full – testimony to our clientele being mostly retired. I make my way around to the side and enter the building using the back door. I could use the front entrance, but I love the aroma of books and candles as it once again wraps around me. I take a moment to breathe in the exquisite scent.

Another door opens and he strides in, his arms outstretched. Reverend Peter Collins — or as I like to call him, *Ketchup*, due to the abundance of the condiment daubed on his ties — is a complete tosser.

'Twinkle, twinkle little star, How I wonder what you are?' he sings, smiling like a crazy person. He always greets me the same way and it makes my skin crawl. 'I thought I saw your car. You need to be out front, not back here. Come on, come on.'

My uncle used to murmur his own version of the children's rhyme.

Twinkle, twinkle little lies,
How I see them in your eyes …

I remember him whispering it in my ear when he used to come into my bedroom to stick his cock in me. Every time Ketchup utters the words it catapults me back there. The shame, the embarrassment and the pain all come flooding back.

Ketchup takes me by the arm and breaks my train of thought, leading me through a door into the vast space beyond. The coolness of the grey stone building chills my cheeks. The floor is a kaleidoscope of reds, greens and blues from the sunlight streaming through the stained glass windows. We walk along the central aisle to the front where the café is located and I can hear the muted conversations of earnest people.

The café consists of a long counter with a refrigerated glass cabinet displaying home-made cakes and buns. Behind that is a commercial coffee-making machine and two fridges. Tables and chairs are dotted around.

'Look who I found lurking in the back!' Ketchup announces to the gathering. 'Twinkle, Twinkle little star!'

I'm going to punch you in the throat.

Twenty faces turn to greet me.

'Hi, everyone,' I say, with the enthusiasm of discovering I have a yeast infection.

'Hi, Twink,' they chirp back.

'This is a splendid turn-out.' Ketchup flaps his hands in the air like he's swatting flies.

'Hello, Twink, it's lovely to see you.' A woman strides up to me, wearing a plain blue dress and matching spectacles, and gives me an unnecessary hug. She looks vaguely familiar but I can't be bothered to place her. 'What you do here is wonderful.' She looks like she's going to burst into tears.

'Thank you,' I reply, peeling her off me.

'Everyone, take a seat,' Ketchup calls out. 'We're gathered here today because we're celebrating a significant milestone. We've reached our target of three thousand pounds!' His voice reaches a crescendo towards the end of the sentence and the group clap and whoop like an American gameshow audience. 'In fact, we are currently sitting at three thousand and eleven pounds, fifty-eight pence.' A ripple of laughter echoes around the walls and off the ceiling. 'This coffee shop was the brainchild of our beloved Twinkle. She had the vision to recognise that if chains on the high street could charge four pounds for a coffee, we could do a better job for a lot less. I guess you could say she took on the big boys and beat them one cup at a time. That was three years ago and our café has served this community ever since. A lifeline to many who have fallen on hard times. It has also been a major source of fundraising where we have hit our target every year thanks to the efforts of Twinkle and her team. This year is no exception, except this year we've reached our goal in seven months!' He pauses for another round of applause and pointless whooping. 'It is my great pleasure to invite Twinkle and her team to do the honours by moving the pointer on our totaliser.'

I inwardly roll my eyes and then get to my feet and shuffle to the front to stand next to him. Four other women join me. We're stood there like fucking lemons.

'Go on then, Twink,' a man in the audience calls out. He's the one who smells of cigarettes and piss.

I smile and slide the cardboard arrow up the thermometer to the red line. The audience do some more whooping. Their days must be boring if this is what gets their rocks off.

'Don't forget the eleven pounds and fifty-eight pence!' Someone shouts. I fake another smile and nudge the pointer up.

Then I glance over the heads of the people to see Sherbet loitering at the back door. He's a young man who's worked with us for years and has an addiction… to Sherbet Fountains.

'Wonderful, wonderful,' Ketchup crows the words into the air. 'Time for tea and cake, I reckon.'

The four women at my side spring into action. I hang back, keeping half an eye on Sherbet. The look on his face isn't good.

'Twink,' Ketchup strides up to me. 'A coffee perhaps?'

'Maybe another time, I have some things to do with the OutReach group.'

'Always on the go, Twinkle. You're amazing,' he says as he grips my hand and gives it a squeeze. I smile and tug myself free from his clammy palm.

'Excuse me.' I wander over to Sherbet and nod for him to go into the back room. As soon as I close the door behind us he starts babbling.

'It's Clem. We got hit. He was on his way to–'

'Sherbet,' I reach up and place my hands on his shoulders. 'Slow down. What's happened to Clem?'

'That's what I was saying. We were out on a supply run and they came from nowhere. I was travelling with Frank and we'd got split up and then–'

'Sherbet,' I shake him. 'Look at me. Calm down and tell me what's happened.'

'They hit us.'

'Who hit you?'

'I don't know.'

'Where's Clem?'

Sherbet looked down at his shoes, then back up at me.

'In the hospital.'

Chapter 6

The green line on the monitor blips in time with Clem's heart-rate. His forehead is heavily bandaged as is the right-side of his face. His left eye is black and swollen. Bags of saline and antibiotics hang from a metal pole, their tubes running into the needles stuck in the back of his hand. He's in a coma.

We're in a side-ward and I can see nurses filing past the window in the door. My leg has gone dead from sitting on this plastic chair for so long.

When I arrived, the nurse had reeled off a list of Clem's injuries and when she reached the point where she said 'stab wound to the abdomen' I tuned out and consoled myself with a summary... he's in a bad way.

'What happens next?' I'd asked.

'We wait,' was her reply.

On the way to the hospital Sherbet had briefed me as best he could and I sent him home. The less he's seen in public, the better. I gaze across at Clem and slip my hand into his.

We've been together for twelve years. Well, when I say together mean that's when our business relationship began. He was the twenty-two year old son of Malawian parents, thirteen years my junior. I was recovering from being a walking zombie having clocked up two years of looking after Dennis.

We met in a pub and sealed the deal a couple of weeks later over a pint of beer and a curry. Oh, and he screwed me to a standstill to consummate our arrangement.

Nowadays, what we do has a fancy name — county lines — where dealers move into a new area and recruit a drug user with a house or flat. They supply them with their drug of choice for free in exchange for the use of their premises from which they run their operation. A process known as cuckooing.

We didn't have a name for what we did back then, it just seemed like common sense. The cities were being squeezed and rather than fight back it was easier to use the city as a base and explore pastures new. Clem wanted to extend his network. I had a house and needed money. Our business venture took off. We had something for everyone: from bored housewives to thrill seekers, from business executives to low life, they came flocking. It was un-tapped demand.

Clem had the vision. I had the three-storey house. My tenants were lovely but they had to go. Next, we recruited a team of runners, people who would handle the customer end of the business. And we needed a cover. That's where the clever bit comes into play. What better place to hide your darkest misdemeanours but in a church.

So, I went back to the congregation and was greeted like the prodigal daughter returned. Which I suppose I was. The OutReach programme took a little while to get off the ground but it served as a ready training and recruiting ground for our runners. It also earned me the nickname of Saint Twinkle. I laugh my tits off every time that idiot calls me it. It's amazing how much sin you can hide under a veneer of repentance.

I told myself I would quit when I had enough money to leave Dennis and sail into the sunset. Now I have enough money to buy my own yacht and moor it up while I go shopping for another. I hadn't accounted for the addictive nature of what we do.

Clem said he'd quit when he had enough to buy his parents a nice house. A noble act that backfired when they sold the four-bed detached property that he'd gifted them and buggered off back to Malawi where their money would go further. He never got over their betrayal.

I squeeze his hand. His skin feels warm to the touch.

We don't consider ourselves in a relationship, rather what we have is an extension of our business arrangement. Youngsters would call it friends with benefits. I call it cock on tap.

The door swings open and Aaron almost falls over his feet in his haste to enter the room.

'Wow, careful,' I say to him. Aaron is one of our OutReach boys.

'Twink, we've…' his voice tails away when he claps eyes on Clements. His mouth gapes open. 'Holy shit.'

'Aaron what is it?'

'I … umm …' his eyes dart from me to Clem and back again.

'Aaron, talk to me.'

'Fuck.'

'Aaron, why are you here?'

'Frank called and told me to get you. He's got something you need to see. He said it's urgent.'

'Did he say *something* or *someone*?'

Aaron screws his face up.

'It could have been someone,' he says.

A ball of panic wells up in my chest.

Fuck.

'Where is he now?'

'Frank said you'd know.'

'Text him and let him know I'm on my way.' I lean over and kiss Clem on the forehead.

'Shall I come with you?'

'No, Aaron… why don't you stay here and keep Clem company for a while?' I reach into my bag and take out my purse. I fish out four pound coins. 'Get yourself a coke.'

'Jesus Christ, Twink. I mean look at him …'

'I know Aaron. I have to go.'

'But Twink, what will happen to Clements?' He has a firm grip on my arm.

'He'll get better.'

'But look at the state of him.'

'I know it doesn't look good, but he's in the right place.' I wrestle my arm free. 'I need to go.'

'Is he going to be okay?'

'Yes, he'll be fine,' I lie and hurry from the room before Aaron has any more questions.

I need to get to Frank before he kills someone.

Chapter 7

Pietersen breezed through the automatic doors to the Wolsey Grange Hotel and Spa, past the coffee shop and stopped at reception. A young man dressed in a blue waistcoat and white shirt was manning the desk.

'Can I help you?' he said, smiling his best corporate smile.

Pietersen flashed her warrant card.

'Is there anyone here who might be able to answer a few questions about this hotel, from ten years ago?' she said, looking around at the flashy decor.

'Not sure any of the current staff were here then. I'll get my manager.'

He beetled off into a back office. Pietersen could hear the sound of muted voices.

After a while a woman appeared dressed in the same style waistcoat and trousers.

'Hi, my name is Amanda Reading, I'm the General Manager. Tim said you have some questions relating to ten years ago?' She came from behind the desk and shook Pietersen's hand.

'I'm DC Kelly Pietersen. It's a bit of an odd one, I'm afraid. We're looking into a missing person case and we suspect he might have stayed in a hotel in the area. We also suspect he might have left without settling his bill.'

'That is out of the ordinary. What I can tell you is, this hotel was in business at that time, though I only came here six years ago.'

'Did it operate a key card system?'

'I'm pretty sure it would have done. In 2009 they were pretty much industry standard for larger hotels.'

'I'm looking at a time window of June, July and August. Do you keep records from around that time?'

'We will do... follow me.' Reading turned and ambled over to the lifts. 'Mr Wolsey isn't in today but I think what you need will be in his office.'

'Mr Wolsey, as in ...?'

'Yes, that's right. We are a family run concern with a chain of eight hotels. Mr Wolsey takes a hands-on approach and insists on having an office at every location. His father was in the hotel business all his life and when the opportunity came along to buy a hotel, he jumped at the chance. He's a smart-cookie and it's a good place to work.' Reading pressed the button for the third floor and the doors closed. 'Don't suppose you have a name of the person you're looking for?'

'No, that's the problem.'

The doors pinged open onto a long corridor with grey patterned carpet and taupe painted walls. The place smelled of air freshener. Three maid-trolleys were parked up ahead.

'This is Mr Wolsey's office,' Reading said, pulling a bunch of keys from her belt and unlocked a door marked Private.

'How can you tell if this person stayed at your hotel?'

'Every hotel in the chain files monthly reports relating to how their particular part of the business has performed. It covers operations, commercial, HR, sales, financial — the usual stuff you would expect to see. If a guest fails to settle their bill when they checkout we have a process of trying to contact them and if necessary take the monies owed from their credit card.'

'Providing they have given you the details.'

'Exactly. Pre-authorising cards is standard practice these days but ten years ago it was less so.'

'That means if a person failed to settle their bill it would show up as a bad debt in the accounts.'

'Correct. I'm not sure what protocols were in place at that time but if we're unable to recover the money it will appear as a distressed sale and the debt is then aged as time goes by. The milestones tend to be thirty-days, sixty-days, ninety-days and one hundred and twenty days. If after that we've not been able to recover the cash we either instruct our legal team or we write the debt off.'

'But you only need to keep records for seven years?'

'That's an Inland Revenue requirement, but Mr Wolsey has an entirely different take on record keeping.'

Reading opened the door onto an office packed to the ceiling with ledgers and files. Mounds of paperwork and folders were stacked on top of a long bookcase which itself was rammed with letters and reports.

'Do we have to...?' Pietersen pointed a finger around the room.

'Hopefully not.' Reading pushed a stack of papers to one side on the big oak desk, took a seat and powered up a computer. The ancient hardware clanked and whizzed in protest at being woken up. 'The system is old. The intention is to upgrade to a new one and integrate it with the current operating system, but that costs money. And I think Mr Wolsey likes all this.' She clicked the mouse and the computer complained again. 'It might take a while.'

Pietersen wiped the palm of her hand across a chair, clearing it of a layer of dust and then sat down.

'That's okay,' she said. 'I can wait.'

Three miles away, Malice was having no such luck. The story at the first two hotels was the same: 'Yes, we used key cards back in 2009; no, we don't keep records from that time; you might want to consult Companies House.'

Bollocks.

He was walking through the reception of the third hotel when he clocked a man dressed in a pin-striped suit wearing a badge that read 'General Manager'. He skirted past the front desk and made a bee-line straight for him.

Malice took out his warrant card.

'Do you think I could have a word?' he said. The man nearly jumped out of his well-tailored suit.

'Has there been another complaint?'

'No, nothing like that.'

'Because we dealt with the noise issue at the time and the damage has been–'

'Mr Jacobs,' Malice read his name badge. 'This is not about a noise issue. We are trying to trace a missing person that might have stayed at your hotel.'

'Oh, I see.' Jacobs regained his composure. 'How can I help?'

The next few minutes went well. Yes, they used key cards back in 2009; yes, they still had records on file and yes, he could see them now.

Result.

'Here we go,' Reading said, turning the screen so Pietersen could see. 'We had two runners in the time window you mentioned. But only one of them hit the 120-day mark. The person checked in on the 18th of June, 2009 for three nights and left an unpaid bill of £157.10.'

'Did you chase it up?'

'It doesn't say but it looks like we wrote the debt off. The entry doesn't appear in November's financial results for the same year.'

'Do you have a name?'

'Give me a minute, the details are in the supplementary section. Ah, here it is…'

Malice had been given a coffee and was now sitting in a comfortable office staring out of the window, while Jacobs trawled through financial reports and computer records.

The downtime allowed his mind to wander. The blue Mondeo worried him. More to the point, the man in the driver's seat who drew his thumb across his throat worried him. Given Malice's history of illicit activities there could be any number of people looking to do him harm. Chief amongst them could be a relative or business associate of Lubos Vasco, whose body was currently burned to a crisp and still unidentified. Along with three of his henchmen.

It did pose Malice with a problem — there were far too many candidates. He had a bad feeling and needed to get back to the station.

'This is the period of time in question,' Jacobs finally looked up from his laptop, breaking Malice's train of thought. 'Our reporting is different now and much more granular. But we have an entry here referring to an unpaid bill.'

Who the hell uses the term 'granular', isn't that something to do with sugar?

Malice put down his coffee and skirted around to the other side of the desk to peer over Jacobs shoulder.

'What does it say?' he asked.

'A guest left without setting a bill of £184.70. The monies were never recovered.'

'Do you have a date?'

'Give me a second,' Jacobs said, clicking away. 'Yes, here it is. Checked in 18th of June, 2009 and stayed for three nights.'

'Do you have a name?'

'Yep, it's here somewhere…'

Chapter 8

The atmosphere in the office had taken a turn for the worse — or, it would be more accurate to say — the demeanour of Superintendent Waite had.
'First you tell me it's like looking for a needle in a haystack, then you come back having found two!' Waite had her arms folded, staring at the evidence board.

'It wasn't what we were expecting either, ma'am. John Horton and Timothy Maxwell both failed to check out of their hotels and both left unpaid bills.' Malice jabbed a finger at their names on the board underneath two mugshots. Horton had a gaunt face with hooded eyes while Maxwell looked like he'd eaten all the pies.

'Their hotels were two miles apart. Each one checked in for three nights on the same day in June 2009,' added Pietersen, scribbling the dates and hotel names on the board.

'That's a lot of coincidences,' Waite sighed, shaking her head.

'Horton was thirty-seven years of age when he was reported missing and Maxwell was thirty-six,' Pietersen said consulting her notes. 'Maxwell has no surviving relatives and Horton has a wife but no kids. He also came up on our system as having been involved in a fight in a pub. There were no charges.'

'When was that?' asked Waite.

'Back in 1993.'

'Who reported them missing?' Waite asked.

Pietersen consulted her notes again. 'Maxwell was reported missing by a work colleague and Horton by his wife.'

'So, which one is taking up shelf space in the morgue?' asked Waite.

'We don't know,' replied Malice, staring at the mugshots. 'We've provided Candice Harris with their details and she's going to pull the dental records if she can find them. If the files are there, she's confident we'll get a positive I.D.'

'The other strange thing is, ma'am,' Pietersen chipped in. 'Horton and Maxwell lived ten miles apart in the same town. There's a strong possibility they might have known each other.'

'We also have to consider, ma'am, there might be another body out there,' said Malice.

'Or, that one of them killed the other and did a disappearing act,' added Pietersen.

'But why draw attention to yourself by not checking out?' Malice muttered under his breath, tapping the side of his head with his finger.

'Shit. That's all we need.' Waite got to her feet and wandered off. 'Keep me posted.'

Malice and Pietersen shot each other a look.

'That could have been worse,' she said.

'Yeah.'

'To pick up the boss's point — irrespective of which one is lying in the morgue — we've got a murder victim *and* a missing person on our plate now.'

'Agreed. It might take Candice a while to track down the records so we may as well make a start with what we got.'

'I have one more hotel to tick off the list. Why don't I pay them a visit while you do some digging?' said Pietersen reaching for her coat.

'Okay, I'll pull the missing persons files and see what else I can find.'

She scooped up her bag and walked away.

'I'll try not to come back with a third needle,' she called over her shoulder.

Malice looked at the board and scratched the stubble on his chin. He spun his chair around and tapped away on his laptop, feeding the registration of the blue Mondeo into the PNC system. It came up blank; not stolen or wanted. Next, he brought up the DVLA database. The vehicle was registered to a Bradley Craven.

Who the hell are you?

After a couple of minutes Malice slumped back in his chair, tapping the tips of his fingers against each other.

Well, well, well ...

Malice spun his wheels in the car park and sped out of the station gates. His eyes were everywhere — no sign of the blue Mondeo. The traffic was heavy and not even the constant stop, start broke his concentration.

'Bradley Craven, Bradley Craven,' he repeated over and over.

At the roundabout he hung a left and headed out of town on the dual carriageway. After ten minutes he pulled off into a side road, through a barrier and entered a vast car park. The building in front of him had the words Chiswick Hotel emblazoned above the door. He switched off the engine and waited.

'You're a little off your patch, Bradley Craven,' he mused to himself. The minutes ticked by. 'Have you been handed a contract? But if so, why go to the trouble of warning me?'

There was a tap on the window and Pietersen opened the passenger door. Malice snapped his head back in gear.

'How did you get on?' he asked.

'No third needle I'm pleased to say. Their records didn't go back that far.' Pietersen fastened her seat belt.

'Waite will be relieved.'

'I got your text. Why do we need to leave my car here?'

'Because we'll pick it up on the way back.' Malice started the engine.

'What did you find out?'

'There's good news and bad news.'

'Let's have the good news.'

'I tracked down John Horton's wife, Wendy. She only lives thirty miles away and can see us today.'

'That's great, let's get going. What's the bad news?'

'She was sectioned under the mental health act and lives in a secure hospital.'

Chapter 9

I run from the car, leaving the door wide open and dash across the cobbled yard. The place has long since ceased to operate as a working farm and the main house is in a poor state of repair, but it's ideal for our purposes. Clem bought it at an auction seven years ago. He had no interest in farming but the ramshackle outhouses and five acres of land provide us with the perfect location to hide drugs and cash.

Right now, I'm not here to pick up supplies. I'm here to prevent it becoming a murder scene.

The barn off to the left is where Clem would deal with his most awkward business partners. I slide through the door to find Frank doing what he does best. It would appear that in his rush he's forgotten all about the finer points of his CIA research. A man is hanging by his wrists from the rafters. Stripped to the waist, his torso streaked with bruises and oozing blood. His head is slumped forwards. His long hair matted against his shoulders. Frank hurls a bucket of water over him and picks up a four-by-two length of wood. The man gasps as the water slams into his body again.

'Frank, no!' I yell. 'Stop.'

Frank wheels around. I've seen that look on his face before. I'm just in time.

'This is one of the fuckers who did Clem. The bastard.' He turns and smashes the plank into the man's ribs.

'Agghhh.' There is a sickening crack and he swings wildly at the end of the rope.

'The fucking …' Frank steadies himself and takes aim.

'Frank!' I dash over and grab his arm. 'If you kill him he's no good to us.'

'But look what they did to Clem.' He yanks his arm free. I seize the end of the wood.

'Listen to me. You need to stop.'

Frank's waving the weapon around trying to shake me off.

'For fuck's sake, Twink. They put Clem in hospital.'

'I know they did, but this is not the answer.' He's flailing me around like a child's toy.

'I want to beat the fucker to a pulp,' Frank rages while shoving me to one side. This is not the first time I've had to talk him down. He always says he would never hurt me, and every time a situation like this happens I pray to God he remembers. I hurl myself at him and grapple my arms around his heaving shoulders.

'Frank, you have to stop.' I scream in his ear.

He drops the batten, shrugs me off and skulks away.

'But did you see what they did to Clem?' He throws his arms in the air.

'Yes I did. Now cut him down and tell me what happened.'

'Cut him down. Why the fuck—'

'Do it Frank.'

He lumbers over, pulls a knife from his pocket and slices through the end of the rope tied to a wooden cross-member in the wall. The man crumples to the floor, unconscious.

'I don't see why—'

'Now sit down and talk to me.'

Frank drops, cross legged on the ground with his elbows on his knees, taking deep breaths. I follow suit.

'We were on a supply run. Clem was in the lead car and me and Sherbet were following behind, but we got split up because of some roadworks. They hit Clem's car when we were in the country lanes. By then, I was a good few miles behind, and when I got there they'd already dragged him out of the car. He was lying in the road and four of them were kicking the shit out of him. There was blood everywhere.'

'You were going to the pickup. So you had no product?'

'That's right. I had the cash with me. They were beating on Clem for nothing. Me and Sherbet ran at them and they scarpered. I didn't realise they'd stabbed him, I just saw red and chased after them.'

'What happened after that?'

'Sherbet stayed with Clem and tried to stop the bleeding. I caught up as they were piling into their car. They began to pull away and I managed to get the passenger door open and yank this fucker out by his hair.'

Frank cocks his thumb in the direction of the bloodied figure lying on the ground. 'I knocked the fucker out, carried him back to our car and dumped him in the boot. Brought him here. Sherbet stayed with Clem and called for an ambulance.'

'What story did he give them?'

'We agreed it would be a road rage attack. Him and Clem walking along the road, guys jump out, Clem gets stabbed. You know the sort of thing.'

'That's smart. Has Sherbet given a statement to the police?'

'I assume so. I told him to get a message through to you.'

'I got it at the hospital. Clem's in a bad way.'

'Jesus ...' Frank wipes the tears from his eyes at the thought of his brother lying in a hospital bed. 'Did I do right, Twink?'

'Yeah, Frank, you did fine.' I reach over and put my hand on his arm. I can feel him trembling.

'What are we going to do?' he asks.

'The first thing we're going to do... is not kill him.' Frank looks as though I've just taken away his favourite toy.

'But ... but–'

'But nothing.'

The man on the floor begins to come around, groaning and moaning.

'Why can't I kill him?'

'Because if you do, he wouldn't be able to carry a message back with him, now would he?'

Chapter 10

Pietersen pushed the button mounted at the side of the glass doors. Malice had both hands stuffed in his pockets, staring at the ground.

'This place gives me the creeps,' he said, shuddering his shoulders. Pietersen cupped her hands and peered through the glass.

Inside the building was another set of doors that opened up onto a small reception desk and a soft-seated area. Vases of flowers adorned the cupboards and shelves. Women wearing light blue tunics and dark blue trousers bustled along the corridor.

Pietersen raised her hand to attract their attention. Nothing.

'Maybe we've come at a busy time,' she said, failing once more to get someone to open the doors.

'I get the feeling it's busy all the time.'

Pietersen pulled her phone and hit redial. The phone at the other end rang out.

'She's not there.' She jammed it back into her jacket pocket and pressed the bell again.

A woman appeared sporting short blonde hair with her glasses perched on top of her head. She tapped a code into the consul and the inner door unlocked. She did the same with the outer door.

'Sorry about that,' she said. 'When the alarm goes off it's all hands to the pump. I'm Senior Staff Nurse Lorraine Taylor, I spoke with you on the phone,' Malice and Pietersen took turns to introduce themselves. 'Please come in.'

All three filed into reception. The smell of the flowers did nothing to mask the stink of bleach.

'Thank you for seeing us at short notice,' said Malice, signing the visitor's book.

'That's okay,' Taylor said, pushing her hair back behind her ears.

'How often does the alarm go off?' asked Pietersen as there was another sharp blast on the siren.

'Most of the time,' Taylor raised her eyes. 'You said you wanted to speak with Wendy Horton.'

'Don't you need to …' Pietersen cocked her head in the direction of the whooping sound.

'That's a different alarm. We're fine.'

'What can you tell us about her?' asked Pietersen.

Taylor ushered them to take a seat. 'Wendy came to us about eight years ago under Section 3 of the Mental Health Act. Her husband had disappeared two years earlier and her mental health had dramatically declined. She'd attempted suicide on four occasions and was eventually sectioned.'

'Section 3?' asked Malice, distracted by the procession of nurses.

'That allows us to revisit her case and if necessary maintain her treatment if we deem she is still a risk to herself and, or, others. Wendy doesn't have any family and isn't able to look after herself.'

'What medication is she on?' Pietersen took out her notebook and pen.

'A range of drugs including Lithium and anti-depressants. She is prone to uncontrolled mood-swings and rages. She's one of our more acute patients.'

'What's her diagnosis?' Malice finally tore his eyes away.

'Where do I start?' Taylor leaned forward, placing both elbows on the armrests. 'Wendy is bi-polar. She suffers with schizophrenia and has psychotic episodes. She's a danger to herself and on occasions a danger to others.'

'And this all kicked off when her husband went missing?' Pietersen jotted notes in her book.

'It's never that straightforward. She had a history of suffering from poor mental health before that happened and was under the treatment of her GP. When John went missing it tipped her over the edge.'

'Does she talk about it?' asked Malice.

'No, she doesn't.'

'Is it still okay for us to see her?' Pietersen asked her eyes squinting.

'You can. Though, as I told you over the phone, my primary responsibility is for her safety and well-being. She's in a good place at the moment. If she becomes distressed I will have to ask you to leave.'

'That's fine. We understand,' said Malice.

'She'll be in her room, let's go.'

All three got up and trooped down a wide hallway with rooms leading off on both sides. Malice glanced in through any open doors as they walked by to see people sitting in chairs or lying in bed. Some were reading, some were sleeping while others were staring into space.

They stopped at an open door and Taylor rapped on the doorframe.

'Wendy, there are some people here to see you. They are from the police and would like to talk to you. Remember I spoke to you about them earlier?'

Wendy Horton was sitting with her back to the door, facing out of the bay window. A single bed was against one wall with a sink in the corner plus a wardrobe. Light flooded in through the big window.

Her hands were dancing across the black and white keys of an electronic organ. On her head she wore a pair of headphones which were plugged into one end of the keyboard. She was dressed in jeans and a baggy T-shirt.

Taylor reached over and touched Horton on the shoulder. She stopped playing, tugged the headphones off and turned in her chair. Her face cracked into a broad smile.

'Wendy, these are the people I spoke to you about,' Taylor repeated. 'They are from the police and want to ask you a few questions. You said that would be alright. Do you remember?'

'Mmmmm… mmmm… mmmm,' Horton swayed her head from side to side, humming the song she'd been playing. 'Yes, I remember.'

'Is it okay if we ask you a few questions, Wendy?' Pietersen took the lead and sat on the bed. Malice remained standing.

'Of course. Mmmm… mmmm… mmmm.' Horton continued to sway back and forth.

'I'll be outside if you want me,' Taylor bustled out the door, leaving it open.

'Wendy, we'd like to ask you a couple of questions about your husband,' Pietersen said.

'Mmmm... mmmm.... mmmm. Do you like music?' she replied.

'Yes, I do.'

'What sort? I like playing the big band songs.'

'I like Glen Miller,' said Pietersen.

'So do I,' Horton shrieked, raising her hands in the air. 'Which is your favourite?'

Pietersen cast her eyes to the ceiling. 'Umm, it would have to be *In the Mood.*'

'Oh my God, that's amazing,' Horton unplugged the lead and started to play. It was a little clunky and had the sound quality of a 1920's picture house organ, but it was a fair rendition of the big band classic. 'I love this one.' She banged away at the keys and hummed along. Then she stopped and stared out the window.

Pietersen looked at Malice who shrugged his shoulders.

'We'd like to ask you about your husband, Wendy. Can you tell us about John?' she said.

'I loved him.' Horton clasped her hands together in her lap and gazed into the middle-distance. 'My mother said he was no good and I shouldn't have anything to do with him. But I could see the best in John. But then over time I knew there was a problem. I knew.'

'What problem, Wendy?' Pietersen asked.

'Dooby – do – bedooby – dooby – dooby – dodo,' Horton continued to sing In the Mood.

'Wendy, you said there was a problem?'

'Dooby – do – bedooby – dooby – dooby – dodo.'

'Wendy, you said there was a problem with John.' Pietersen leaned forwards and touched Horton on the arm. The singing stopped. She turned to face her.

'Yes, there was a problem. I knew it. I could feel it. My mother didn't like him but it wasn't because of that. She didn't know about that.'

'What didn't she know about?'

'My other favourite is *Pennsylvania 6-5000*. Da – da – da, da – da – da, da – da, da – da – da– da.' Horton clicked her fingers in time with the music.

'Wendy.' Pietersen placed her hand on Horton's shoulder. 'Can you tell us about the time when John went missing?'

'Oh, yes, that's right. John went missing. He went away and never came back.'

'Why did he go away?'

'Because he had to, but I knew all along there was a problem.'

'What problem?' Pietersen still had her hand on Horton's shoulder trying to keep her engaged.

'Yes, there was.' Horton nodded.

'What was it, Wendy? Is that the reason John went missing?'

'Yes, that's right he went missing.' Horton began wringing her hands. Her eyes darting about the room. 'He went away and left me.'

'Why, Wendy? Why did he leave you?'

'There was a problem. I knew there was a problem but he wouldn't tell me.'

'What, Wendy? What wouldn't he tell you?'

'And then he went away and never came back.' Tears welled against her bottom eyelids. Rubbing her hands together like she was washing off mud.

'Why did John go away, Wendy? Was it something bad?'

'My mother never liked him. She said he was a wrong 'un.' Horton grabbed the headphones, snapped them onto her head and began bashing at the keyboard. Pietersen glanced up at Malice, who shook his head.

'Let's go,' he mouthed.

'Thank you, Wendy.' Pietersen rose from the bed.

Horton stopped playing and yanked off the headphones. She turned sharply in her chair and grabbed Pietersen's hand.

'He raped her,' Horton said, wiping her eyes with her sleeve. 'I knew there was something wrong. He raped her.'

'Raped who?' asked Pietersen, returning to the edge of the bed.

'The woman.'

'What woman?'

'The woman he raped. I knew there was something wrong, but he wouldn't tell me. And all the time my mother kept saying 'That man's no good, no good.''

'Did John rape someone?' asked Pietersen.

'Yes, he did. How do you know?' Horton let go of Pietersen's hand and scrunched her face up.

'Who was it, Wendy?'

'How do you know?' Horton blurted out, flinging her hands into the air.

'You just told me.'

'Did I?'

'Who did John rape?'

'And there was a baby. A fucking baby.'

Pietersen glanced across at Malice, whose eyes couldn't get much wider.

'John raped a woman and she had a baby?' Pietersen asked, trying to unravel what was being said.

'We couldn't have babies.' Horton put both hands on top of her head and began rocking back and forth. 'Why could we not have a baby?'

'Wendy, listen to me this is important. Who was raped?'

'I told my mum the problem must be with him. We couldn't have a baby because of him.'

'Wendy, listen to me–'

'Then he rapes someone and there's a baby.' Horton jumped from her chair and hurried into the corner, beating her knuckles against the sides of her head. 'Aggghhh, a fucking baby.'

Taylor burst into the room.

'Wendy, Wendy, sit down,' Taylor said, trying to grasp her flailing arms. Horton spun around and hit her in the chest.

'There was a baby,' she shrieked. Globules of spit flying from her mouth. 'How did you know?' She shook an angry finger.

Pietersen jumped to her feet to avoid the airborne saliva.

'I didn't know. You told me.'

'Wendy, let's stop this.' Taylor lunged at Horton. But she shouldered her to one side and leapt at Pietersen, who seized her hands to dodge the wielding fists. The two fell back onto the bed.

Malice went to step in but Taylor held her hand up and yelled at him.

'Pull the cord! The red cord,' she ordered.

A piercing screech filled the room. Seconds later two nurses hurried in.

Horton was snarling like an extra from *The Walking Dead.* Her snapping jaws inches away from Pietersen's face. The nurses man-handled both of them off the bed and onto the floor.

Pietersen tore herself away and darted for the door.

'Shit,' said Malice. 'Where did that come from? Are you okay?'

'Yeah, she didn't get me,' Pietersen said, wiping spit from her cheek.

Horton was screaming all manner of abuse as the nurses restrained her.

'Let's get out of here,' Malice said. 'Told you this place gave me the creeps.'

'Yeah, well now it gives me the creeps as well.'

Chapter 11

Frank and I are sitting in the car watching the clock on the dashboard. He's cracking his knuckles. It's getting on my nerves. The green digits change to 7.59 p.m.

'We're not here to kill anyone,' I place my hand on top of his for him to stop.

'Got it,' he replies, cracking them once more.

'We're not here to hurt anyone, either.'

'Not even a little bit?'

'Frank, we've been over this.' There's more than an edge of frustration in my voice.

'Okay, okay.'

'Let me do the talking and you… you… you stand there and look menacing.'

'So, I can hurt them.' He turns and gives me a wink.

'No Frank, that's not the same thing.'

'I'm joking.'

I flash him a sideways glance. I don't think for one minute he is. The time ticks over to eight o'clock.

'Time to go,' I say, flicking the door handle.

We step from the car and Frank pops open the boot. He dips inside and comes out with a package.

'I won't let anyone hurt you,' he says, slamming the lid shut.

'I know you won't, Frank.'

We cross the road and push on the door to the betting shop. Despite the sign reading Closed, it opens. The shop is empty. The counters that run around the walls have been wiped clean, along with the tables and pin boards. The place is in semi-darkness, lit only by the streetlights outside.

Frank goes first.

He reaches the door at the back marked Staff Only and nudges it open with his foot. It opens onto a passageway with a small office to one side. At the end is another door which opens as we approach. A thick-set guy with a bald head is silhouetted in the doorway. I watch Frank square his shoulders and ball his fists — I touch his arm. Stay calm.

The bald man steps to one side and holds the door open for us to walk in. The room beyond isn't designed to house five big men and a small to medium sized woman. A man with long lank hair is sitting on the edge of the desk, wearing biker gear and four days of stubble on his chin. He's flanked either side by two more bikers, one sitting in an armchair and the other leaning against the wall sporting a red bandana. I step from behind Frank as the big guy lets the door close behind us. A single naked lightbulb hangs from the centre of the ceiling spilling pale yellow light around the room through a thick layer of smoke.

'Fucking hell, It's the President of the Women's Institute,' the seated one says. He cracks a smile, exposing rotten teeth.

'I hope you've brought tea and cake with you, love,' says the one with a bandana.

Frank takes half a step. I grab his sleeve.

'Didn't your mother ever take you to the dentist,' I laugh at the man in the armchair.

'Your smile looks like bird shit on tombstones.'

He bristles.

The one perched on the table puts his hands out, palms down.

'Easy now,' he says. He's obviously the organ grinder.

'Do you always conduct business with the cast from *Sons of Anarchy* in tow?' I say, staring at each of them in turn.

'Shall we say that's the banter over with?' the boss-man says, poking a toothpick in his mouth.

'Not on my account,' I reply. 'I like banter. Especially when my opponents are so... how shall we say... mentally challenged.'

The man in the armchair springs to his feet. Frank curls a smile and steps forward. I grab a handful of his jacket and tug him back.

'Sit down.' The boss-man barks and shoots the man a stare. He slides his arse off the table. 'Looks like you've got an attack dog on a lead there.'

'His bite is way worse than his bark,' I reply. Frank grins.

'What should I call you?'

'How about Madam President?' I say.

'Okay, you can call me Jax Teller,' he says, referencing the *Netflix* programme. 'So, Madam President, you sent back one of my boys.'

'I did.'

'He's in a bad way.'

'Good. So is mine.'

'Yeah, that kind of balances things out I suppose.'

'It does,' I nod my head.

'Only it doesn't,' he shakes his. 'This is not a balanced conversation. This is the way it works: we want to do business on your patch; you currently occupy said patch; and you need to leave. There is nothing balanced about that.'

'That's true.'

'We've done our homework on your firm. We have the muscle and you need to take your toys and go play somewhere else.'

'You do have the muscle,' I say, casting my eyes around the room. 'But you've not done your homework.'

'Why do you say that?'

'Because you have a problem.'

He looks at me like I've just told him I could beat the shit out of all four of them.

'We have a problem?' He throws his head back and laughs. 'Look lady, I'm not sure you quite understand. This is me asking you nicely to fuck off or more of you are going to be eating lunch through a straw.'

'And this is me telling you nicely that you've overlooked something.'

'What?'

'You have the muscle but we have the product.'

'Haha!' The Boss-man belly laughs. 'Do you think you're dealing with amateurs? Do you think we don't have product?' He rakes his eyes around the room and the others crack a laugh.

I take half a step forward.

'I'm sure you do but you don't have our product. We have stuff that will blow your half-arsed shit out of the water and that's what our customer base is used to. You start peddling them sub-standard gear and they ain't gonna buy it.'

'Customer base?' he chortles. 'It's not fucking *Dragon's Den*.'

'That's obvious, given that the average I.Q. in the room jumped twenty points when we walked in.'

'The customer base will buy our gear if it's the only show in town.'

'Get real. They'll buy it from somewhere else. You forget we've been doing this since you lot rode about on mopeds in short trousers. Our network and contacts are all around you, it would be like fighting ghosts.'

'We weren't fighting ghosts when we gave your guy a good hiding.' He wags his finger in my direction.

'No, you weren't, but then we weren't ready either. I agree you have the muscle to shove us out the way but you don't have the wherewithal to maintain the demand. Are the cogs turning now, Jax Teller? You'd have a ton of gear to shift and no takers.'

He taps his foot on the floor and runs his hand through his greasy hair.

'How do I know you're not lying?' he asks.

'You don't, however…' I flash a look at Frank who flips his jacket up at the back. All four men react. 'Take it easy, I got a little something for you to try.' I reach behind and pull a package wrapped in a towel from the waistband of Frank's jeans.

'A present?' he says, his eyebrows raised.

'Here.' I toss it over to him. He catches it and unfolds the towel to reveal a plastic bag tightly wound with floor tape. 'Don't take my word for it.'

'Phew, is this what I think it is?' he says, weighing it in his hands. 'Do you normally carry this much around with you?'

'Sometimes it's necessary.'

'You should be more careful, there are some unsavoury characters about.' He tosses the bag over to the one with a bandana.

'Got to be half a kilo.' Bandana man throws it to the bloke in the chair, who catches it and weighs it in his hands.

'Test it,' Boss-man says. The man nearest the door disappears and comes back with a kit.

He snaps the top off the vial, withdraws the insert and lays it on the table. Then he takes his knife, slits the bag and spoons a small quantity of white powder on the edge of the blade. He tips it into the test tube, replaces the insert and gives it a shake. Next he turns on the torch on his phone and holds the tube against a small colour metric chart. The sample turns from pale yellow to dark orange. He tilts the tube from side to side.

'That's as far as it's gonna go,' he says, handing the tube to the Boss-man.

'That's high,' he says, whistling.

'My customers aren't going to want to eat burgers when they've been used to fillet steak. I want to make a deal,' I say.

'A deal? Fuck me, lady, you're full of surprises.'

'If you put us out of business I guarantee you won't shift an ounce of your product. But equally I'm not looking to go to war either, I don't want any more of my boys winding up in the hospital. So, how about you tax us.'

'Tax you?' he says.

'Yeah, we carry on as usual and you get fifteen percent. We can recoup the shortfall by making a few adjustments. You get a regular income, risk free.'

'That sounds interesting,' he says, running his hands through his hair again.

'You leave us alone and–'

'There's one small problem.'

'What's that?'

'You're not in a position to make deals.'

'But I've got–'

'Listen, Madam President, if there is a deal to be done I'm the one to make it and I don't like your numbers.'

'It's fifteen percent.'

He clucks his tongue against the roof of his mouth and settled back against the desk.

'You might want to go back to the drawing board with those adjustments because the figure is thirty percent.' He points a finger gun at me and fires his thumb.

'I can't do that.'

'You need to find a way while your people still have working kneecaps. And that's got to be worth thirty percent of anyone's money.'

'Twenty-two,' I say with all the authority I can muster.

'Lady, you need to wake up. This is like when the red-letter gas bill falls onto your doormat. It's not a negotiation, it's a final demand. Thirty-five is the right answer.'

'You said thirty!' I choke on the words.

'You said no to thirty, now it's thirty-five.'

'I'll need to make some calls.'

'I thought you would.'

I look at the floor.

'I… umm…' I can't seem to get my words out. They dry in the back of my throat.

'It's time to say bye for now, Madam President. It's been a pleasure.' He shoves himself away from the desk. 'You got three days, and the figure is thirty-five. Or I'll put every one of your crew in traction and take my chances with my own gear. Oh, and I consider this to be a down payment. You know, like a non-refundable deposit.' He holds up the package of heroin, tosses it in the air and catches it.

'You can't take that.' My voice sounds frail.

'Say goodnight, Madam President.' The four men crowd in on us. Frank steps forward and the one with the bandana meets him chest to chest.

'Leave it, Frank.' I take his arm.

'Yeah, leave it, Frank,' sneers the one with his face inches from Frank's. 'Time to go.'

I pull Frank away and we slope back down the corridor and into the shop with two of them marching behind us. I can hear them whispering and sniggering.

'Watch the door doesn't hit you on the arse on the way out,' one of them calls out.

We walk back to the car in silence. I pull a phone from my pocket and send a text.

'You drive,' I say as Frank piles behind the wheel. 'Pull around the corner and stop.'

I snap the back off the phone and slide out the battery. Then I open my window and throw both over a hedge.

We both sit there, saying nothing.

After what feels like an age, an un-marked white van cruises by. Closely followed by another. Their lights are off.

'Wind down your window,' I say to Frank. He does as he's told and a cool breeze washes through the car. The vans disappear around the corner.

We listen — nothing.

A few minutes later, I hear what I'd been waiting for.

A loud bang followed by a cacophony of voices all bellowing the same thing.

'Police! Stay where you are!'

Chapter 12

I wait for the last of the guys to take his seat. Coffees in hand, ten troubled faces are fixed on me. The usual scent of old books and candles is doing nothing to lighten my mood. An hour earlier I'd been squeezing Clem's hand, wishing he'd wake up.

When I arrived on the ward, the nurse had flipped her cheery expression to one of sombre concern. A well-practised tic.

'There's no change,' she'd said as she pushed open the door. Clem was wired and tubed up as before, a new dressing was wound around his head and his face seemed less puffy.

'No change at all?' I could hardly hide the disappointment.

'He's stable,' she'd replied, in the matter-of-fact tone medical staff always employ when there's nothing to report.

I spent the next forty minutes at his bedside. His hand in mine. Then went back to my car knowing that 'stable' was as good as it was going to get.

'Good evening, everyone.' I stand at the front and open the session. The flickering flames dance across the walls. All we need is a cauldron and three witches and the scene would be complete. 'I wanted to get you together to keep you in the picture.'

Operating a drug running business is no different to operating any other business. Employees perform better when they are engaged in the company and feel informed. I suppose this is our equivalent of a team briefing – *Narcos* style.

'Everybody listen up,' Frank chips in. He has to feel he's got an input.

'There are a few points I want to cover,' I continue. 'Many of you will know Clem is in hospital. I've just left him and he's in a critical condition, but stable. Which at this stage is the best we can hope for and while it's only natural you will want to visit him, you can't. Because of his stab wound, the police are taking an added interest and it's better if you're not around.'

'Is that clear?' Frank pipes up again, eyeing each person in turn.

'Yes, Frank,' the faces nod in agreement. Frank snorts his approval.

'A rival gang hit us and in the process Clem was injured. The chances are they've gone away but I want you to be extra vigilant.'

'Be vigilant,' Frank booms, though it's touch and go that he knows what that means.

'Thank you, Frank,' I frown at him. 'If you see any unusual activity, get the hell out of there and return to the house. Contact me or Frank and we'll take it from there. Okay?'

'Yes, Twinkle,' they say in unison.

'Let's go around the room, starting with you, Edmund…'

Each of the team give an update on how their patch has performed this week — reporting on new customers, existing business, any changes in product mix and when the last man had given his feedback I switch topic.

'How's the house?' I ask.

'It's fine,' replies Edmund who is the elder of the group. 'Shopping?' he calls out. Two men put their hands up. 'Cooking?' Two different men hold their hands up. 'Washing and cleaning?' Another two. 'The place is looking good, Twink, and the boys are looking after themselves.'

The household rota is an essential part of the OutReach programme where disadvantaged young men are brought into the fold to be taught responsibility and respect. Oh, and are indoctrinated into the church. Or that's the official line. The unofficial line is if we ever get raided, the house mustn't look like a drug den. Teaching the boys to look after the place is all part of the game. Plus if they take care of the house they are more likely to take care of themselves and stay. A high turnover in personnel is not good in our line of work.

'Has anyone fancied tasting the product?' I laser each face in turn. It's the same question I ask every week. A general rumbling of 'no' goes around the room. 'Has anyone been tempted?'

'Yeah, tempted,' Frank reinforces the same comment every time. It's a weekly ritual.

'No, Twinkle.'

I scan their faces and can tell a liar a mile off. All is well.

'Okay, unless anyone has any questions, we can wrap up this part of the meeting.'

A young man named Brian puts his hand up. 'Twinkle, where's Joseph?'

'We had to let him go. He wanted to take his career in a different direction,' I say, cocking my head on one side to ramp-up the sympathy.

'Will he be coming back?'

'No. I reckon he's gone for good.' Brian nods his head, satisfied with the answer. They've seen other people chose a different career path in the past and never come back. It comes with the territory. 'Right, in a few minutes we will have a guest speaker.'

'Do we have to stay, Twink?' asks one of the new boys.

'You do, and you need to be interested in what he has to say. Is that clear?'

'Is that clear?' Frank mimics.

'Okay.' The lad settles back in his chair. Message received.

There is a knock on the door and a tall man with a military bearing enters the room.

'I hope I'm not interrupting anything?' he says in clipped tones.

'No, Alex, we were just wrapping up. Please come and join us.' I get to my feet and Frank goes to fetch another chair. 'Everyone... I want you to meet Alex Beresford. A good friend of mine and an active member of the church.'

'Good evening.' Beresford crosses the floor and takes a seat next to Frank. 'I'm delighted to be able to meet you all at last. I've heard so much about the good work being done here.'

'They all work hard, Alex, and are a credit to OutReach.'

'Indeed, they are.' He's positively beaming.

'Now, while Alex has joined us this evening wearing jeans and a shirt, he doesn't always wear that gear, do you, Alex?' I say.

'No, I don't.'

'Why don't you formally introduce yourself?' I give him the floor.

'I'm Assistant Chief Constable Alex Beresford. I want to talk to you this evening about the importance of close community relations between young people like yourselves and the police. Let me start by asking a question: What do you think when you see a couple of police officers walking down the street..?'

I've known Beresford since he was a Chief Super in the murder squad. That's when he moved house and joined the church. It's unusual for a force to promote to the rank of ACC from within but he had such a good network of contacts in the community that they didn't want to lose him. He's a good copper and his heart is in the right place. Fortunately for me he believes what I tell him.

I tune out and think about Clem as Alex waxes lyrical about stop and search and the pitfalls of profiling. I've heard it all before.

Then I'm caught off guard when I tune in to hear him say '...I'm parched. Does everyone fancy a refill?'

He gets to his feet and wanders over to the coffee urn and picks up a plastic cup. The rest of them mill around. He brings a second coffee over to me and presses it into my hand.

'The other evening went well,' he says, taking a sip.

'Good. There was a last-minute change of location.' I turn away from the group, keeping my voice low.

'Not a problem.'

'How …?'

'There wasn't as much heroin as expected but we bagged ourselves some nasty characters. Their prints were all over the merchandise.'

'That's good.'

'Thank you.' Beresford raises his plastic cup in my direction, I 'chink' it with mine.

'If I hear anything, there's only one place I'm going to go.'

'I appreciate it.'

'You're welcome.'

'You do the most amazing job here, Twinkle,' he says, looking around the room.

'I don't think of it that way.'

'I know and that makes it all the more remarkable.'

'There's nothing remarkable about it.'

'You have Dennis to contend with and you do all this… these young men are a credit to you.'

He continues to babble on and I tune out again. In all the excitement I'd forgotten about Dennis, I've had to leave him on his own until Rebecca shows up.

Oh well I'm sure he won't mind, at least he's upright.

'And to top it all…'

He's still bloody going.

'You've helped take three dangerous criminals off the street.'

Three?

Chapter 13

Malice turned the key in the lock and clouted the toe of his boot into the bottom corner of the door. The door juddered open as it unstuck itself from the frame. He'd long since stopped telling himself he'd fix it, when it was much easier to simply give it the boot.

He looked down at the letters scattered on the mat; a bill and two pieces of junk mail. He kicked them to the side to join the others.

'Alexa, turn the lights on,' he called out to his new toy.

'Lights isn't responding. Please check its network connection and power supply.'

For fuck's sake.

He hung his jacket on a hook and strolled through to the kitchen, switching on lights as he went. When he reached the fridge, he took out a lasagne and glanced at the best before date — *close enough* — and stuck it in the microwave. Then he wandered into the lounge and opened the lid of his laptop.

A charitable person would describe the style of furnishings in his flat as minimalist. A less charitable person would say he had just enough home comforts to satisfy a homeless person. A two-seater sofa was parked against one wall while a matching armchair, coffee table and TV sat in a line. That was it. No ornaments, no pictures, no frills, apart from a globed paper lampshade that hung from the ceiling and which had been there since before they were popular.

'Let's get a better look at you, Bradley Craven,' he muttered. 'Why the hell are you here?'

There was a loud rap at the front door.

Malice shut the screen, went out into the hallway and jerked it open.

'Hayley' he said, raising his eyebrows. 'This is a s–'

'Can I come in?' she pushed past him. Hayley had only visited his flat on three occasions since they pulled the plug on their relationship. Once when she came around demanding her keys back, a forceful request he was only too happy to comply with while keeping one in his pocket just in case. And the two other occasions were to conduct stand-up rows.

Malice watched her stomp down the hall into the lounge. It looked like, unless she'd found out about the other key, he was in for a further dose of the latter.

There was a time when they had been happily married. Five years they had stayed together before the cracks in their relationship became chasms and the disagreements became all-out war. The biggest point of contention was Hayley wanted kids and Malice didn't — and there's not a great deal of compromise available to resolve that one.

Then one day Hayley announced she was pregnant. She swore it wasn't a trap, she pleaded with him that it was an accident. But it signalled a sharp decline. By the time Amy arrived, their relationship was dead in the water. That was seven years ago.

'You can't keep doing this,' she blurted out. Perching herself on the edge of the sofa while crossing her legs and folding her arms.

'Erm, okay, doing what?' Malice recognised the signs and prepared himself for the onslaught.

'You know.'

'I might do, but it would help if you told me.'

'I don't believe you–'

The microwave went ding. Saved by the bell.

'Do you mind if I…' Malice disappeared and returned holding a steaming plastic tray cradled in a towel with a fork sticking out of the top. He flopped down in the armchair. 'Sorry, you were saying.'

'Eating well, I see,' she huffed.

'I was working late.'

'You're always working late.'

'Do you want some?' Malice held out a fork full of steaming mess.

'No, Mally. I don't want some.'

'Ugggg,' Malice struggled to get his words out when the molten food hit his mouth. 'Who's looking after Amy?' He flapped his hand in front of his mouth.

'Jill has her for an hour.'

'Jill?'

'She's the mother of her best friend. God! You know nothing.' Hayley's right foot began pumping up and down in sympathy with her anger.

'I was only asking,' he said.

'Anyway, you have to stop doing this.'

'You said that once. Stop what?'

'You really don't know? Well, let me take you back a bit: first you come around the house acting all weird and tell us we have to go to my sister's place for a few days while you sort things out. Then we come back and you say all is rosy in the garden again and then start acting like Father-bloody-Christmas.'

Malice chewed his dinner and considered her assessment. He had to admit it was a pretty accurate description of the time when he'd sent his family away so he could kill Lubos Vasco and his crew and relieve them of their hard-earned cash.

Fair enough.

'I said I would sort it,' he said, risking another forkful.

'Only it's not bloody Christmas is it? And it's not Amy's birthday either. But I've got a brand-new kid's bike in my kitchen, because… because… shit… I don't know why.' Hayley jumped up and started prowling around the room, hands on hips.

'Amy said she needed a new one.'

'She might do, though I don't know what's wrong with her old one, but that's not the point.'

'No?'

'The point is she can't go through life thinking she's living in a bloody Disney film where all she has to do is wish for something and then abraca-fucking-dabra, it appears out of nowhere.'

'The old one was a bit ropey.'

'Jesus Christ, Mally, you don't get it do you?' She resumed her position on the edge of the sofa, her foot bouncing up and down.

'Amy needed a new bike. I got her a new bike. I can't see the problem.'

'She asked me if she could have one and do you know what I said?'

Malice waved his fork in the air considering the question.

'You probably said–'

'No, I said no! I told her she had to wait. Then you come along and the next thing I know she's wheeling the damned thing into the house. Do you have any idea how that makes me look?'

'Mean?'

'Agghh! For fuck's sake.' Hayley jumped to her feet again and punched at the air. 'It makes me out to be the bad mummy again. Like it did with the trainers and the straighteners and hoodie… the list goes on and on.'

'My intention was not to make you look–'

'No Mally, it's never your fucking *intention* to do anything. Like the time Al Capone kicked our front door in and trashed our house. It was never your intention for that to happen either.'

'He wasn't Al Capone. He just owned a pizza parlour.'

'Or the time when I'm sitting in my sister's kitchen listening to the kids play in the garden worried sick that I won't have a fucking house left standing when I get back. You never meant to do any of that.'

'It worked out fine.'

'Really? Which part of — they found the charred remains of five dead bodies — sounds fine to you?'

Malice munched the last remnants from the tray, wondering whether or not to pull his ex-wife up on her inaccuracy. Strictly speaking there were the charred remains of four dead people and a fifth man who didn't burn because he'd been kept in a freezer.

'We're okay now.' He decided against it and instead opted for what he thought was the safer option. Then immediately wished he hadn't.

'No, Mally. We are not okay!' she screeched. 'You have to stop buying stuff for Amy. I'm fed up of you being bloody Santa Claus while I'm the wicked witch.'

'Okay, okay, I get it.' He discarded the empty carton onto the table.

'I gotta go.' The exasperation in her voice was a foot thick.

'Okay. It's been nice to see you.'

'Piss off, Mally. I'll let myself out.' Hayley flounced from the lounge and slammed the front door. Malice chewed on his bottom lip, then gazed across the room at an unopened box on the window ledge containing a brand-new kid's smart watch.

Maybe not just yet.

Chapter 14

Malice arrived at work a troubled man. The mugshot of Bradley Craven had kept him awake for most of the night, along with his other dilemma — *what to do with that bloody watch?*

Eventually he'd drifted off to sleep having decided he had two courses of action: get up at stupid-o'clock, drive to the station and do a thorough trawl on Craven. Then take the watch back to the shop. The receipt said he had thirty days in which to return it and he decided that was probably not enough time for Hayley to calm down. Given her performance last night, by the time she did, the damned thing would no longer be the latest model. The watch had to go.

Malice had checked himself over in the mirror before leaving his flat and even the addition of another new shirt didn't hide the fact he looked like shit. He buzzed down his window and held his pass against the console raising an eyebrow when the gate opened.

'Bloody hell, Mally. Did you shit the bed?' A disembodied voice cracked through the loudspeaker.

'Funny guy,' Malice shouted out the window. 'Glad to see you fixed your barrier, at last.'

'It's your card that needs fixing.'

'There's all sorts about you that need fixing.'

'Bugger off.'

Malice stuck his right arm out the window and raised his middle finger. The rotund chap in the control room chuckled as he saw Malice on the CCTV monitor drive through the gates.

He parked his car, crossed the concourse into the building and ran up the stairs to the third floor to find the office lights burning bright. Pietersen was standing at the evidence board, staring at a newly arranged collage of photographs. The clock on the wall said 5.46 a.m.

So much for having a thorough trawl.

'Bloody hell, you look rough,' Malice said, shuffling out of his jacket.

'Thanks for that,' she replied, smoothing back her hair and looking herself up and down. 'I couldn't sleep. What's your excuse?' She waggled a finger in his direction and pulled a face.

'I couldn't sleep either.' He glanced down and tried to flatten the horizontal creases in his shirt.

'That incident at the hospital really got to me. I didn't know what to do for the best. I could have defended myself but I didn't want to hurt her.'

'Yeah, it was pretty scary. How long have you been here?' Malice counted the cluster of coffee cups that were sitting on the desk.

'Couple of hours.'

'What's all this?' He trekked over to the board.

'I've been going through the missing persons files for Horton and Maxwell and found some interesting stuff.

Initially the cases were investigated as separate disappearances. Then when it emerged both men came from the same town, they conducted a joint investigation.'

'What did they find?'

Pietersen went to her desk and retrieved a wad of papers from the stack. She flipped through until she found what she was looking for. Then she handed it to Malice.

'That's the interesting part. There's absolutely nothing to connect the two men,' she declared.

'Nothing at all?'

'Nope, not a thing. Not social media, nor emails, phone records, common acquaintances. Nothing. They all drew a blank.'

'I don't believe that,' Malice said, scanning the densely packed text.

'No, and I don't think the original investigating officers believed it either. But the evidence isn't there. Horton was vice-principal at a local sixth-form college and moved in academic circles. He sat on several development boards and was pretty high up from what I can gather; while Maxwell, on the other hand, was a service engineer for a water delivery company.'

Malice tossed the wad of papers on the desk, then walked over to the board and tapped each photograph in turn.

'Makes no sense. Two men from the same town check into hotels three miles apart on the same day for the same length of time, and both go missing after failing to settle their bill – that's too many coincidences. I don't buy it.'

'Makes no sense to me either. The original investigation threw up a big fat zero.'

'What else?' Malice asked, still tapping his finger on the board.

Pietersen sat at her desk and referred to her laptop.

'A death certificate was issued for John Horton to allow Wendy to claim on his life insurance.' She read the information on the screen. 'Then she sold the family home to pay for the hospital fees and when she was discharged she moved into some kind of sheltered accommodation. As far as I can tell she barely lived there. His suitcase and belongings were recovered from the hotel room and are gathering dust in an evidence store, somewhere.'

'Did he leave behind anything of interest at the hotel?'

'The forensics team took photographs of the items and it all looks straight-forward. Nothing jumps out as being odd.'

'That's not helpful. What about Maxwell?' Malice clasped both hands behind his head and began pacing about the room.

Pietersen brought more information up on her screen.

'He has no next of kin. So his estate is bona vicantia which means–'

'The estate passes to the Crown,' Malice chimed.

'That's right. But the Maxwell case is still open and a death certificate has never been issued. His house and bank accounts are still there.'

'After all this time?'

'Yup. The other interesting thing is the contents of his bag at the hotel.'

'What about it?'

'Witness statements from neighbours and work colleagues all paint a similar picture of Timothy Maxwell.

He's a quiet guy who lives on his own, keeps himself very much to himself, doesn't have a partner and doesn't do much socialising. Yet when they went through his stuff left at the hotel they found condoms.'

She spun the laptop around for Malice to see the collage of pictures. He hunched over the desktop and clicked through them one at a time.

'Maybe he was in the boy scouts? You never know when you might get lucky.'

'I think Timothy Maxwell was expecting to get very lucky. It was a box of twenty-four — and six were missing.'

'He had been a busy boy. But it doesn't automatically mean he'd burned through them while he was away.'

'The box was found in a bag from Boots chemist along with the receipt. He'd bought them on 17th of June.'

'The day before he arrived.'

'He had been a busy boy. I don't get that much action in three months let alone three days,' she said.

'Try a year.'

'Really?'

'It's complicated.' Malice shook his head and straightened up. 'I think we should take a ride out to his house.'

'Good idea. Before we go, I've got a little pressie for you.'

'For me?'

'Yup.' she reached under her desk and brought out a carrier bag. 'Something that might help you get laid more often.'

'Now I am interested.'

Pietersen handed over the bag.

'You might need a lesson or two,' she said, muffling a laugh behind her hand.

Malice delved inside and brought out a box.

'An iron!' he said holding it in the air.

'Who knows. It might help.'

'Cheeky bastard.'

An hour and half drive, and a McDonald's breakfast later, Pietersen drew the car into the kerb opposite No. 43, Almond Close.

'That doesn't strike you as a property that's been empty for ten years,' said Malice, looking across at the semi-detached home of Timothy Maxwell. The front garden was neat and tidy with the grass freshly mowed and the borders decorated with flowering pots and shrubs.

'There's a car in the drive. I wonder who's at home?'

They got out and walked up to the house. Pietersen rapped her knuckles on the front door.

'Check this out.' Malice pointed to the woodwork which had been recently painted.

'Can I help you?' A man in his early sixties wearing baggy jeans, trainers and a checked shirt came out of the house next door. He marched over to the fence separating the two properties and gripped the top with both hands.

'Hi, I'm Detective Sergeant Malice and this is DC Pietersen. Is this house owned by Timothy Maxwell?'

'If you're the police you would know that.' The man puffed his chest out. Malice and Pietersen took out their warrant cards. He read each one. 'Haven't seen you lot around here in… gotta be nine years.'

'Are you Thomas Hartwell?' Pietersen asked.

'That's right.'

'I was reading your statements this morning.'

'Yeah, I spoke to the police on three occasions.'

'Do you know whose car is on the drive?' asked Malice.

'It's mine.'

Malice stared at Hartwell and the penny dropped.

'You take care of the place,' he said.

'I do. I look after the garden and make sure the house isn't going to fall down. We don't want Tim's home to look vacant or it might be a magnet for squatters and the such.'

'That's been quite an undertaking,' said Malice, eyeing up at the house.

'Since I retired it helps to keep me busy and besides, the alternative doesn't bear thinking about. I did it to start with because I wanted Tim to know I'd been looking after the place until he returned. But now I do it out of necessity.'

'What was Tim like?' Pietersen asked.

'I can't add more than I said all those years ago.' Hartwell released his grip on the fence and struck a thoughtful pose; one hand in his pocket, the other stroking his chin. 'He was a good neighbour, a quiet chap who kept the house in good order. He always had time to stop and have a chat and he helped me clear the drive when it snowed one year.'

'What about friends or a partner?' Malice said.

Hartwell shook his head.

'We never saw any comings or goings. As far as I know he didn't have a girlfriend or anything like that. From what I could see, the nearest thing he had to a social life was the church — the whole family were devout

Christians. We were very sad when he went missing. Has there been any new developments? Is that why you're here?'

'Tim's disappearance came up in relation to another case that's under investigation. We are just being thorough,' Pietersen said. She played with her phone and brought an image up on the screen. 'Do you recognise this person? His name is John Horton. He might have visited Tim at the house?'

Hartwell took the phone and stared at the picture. Then he shook his head and handed it back. 'It was a long time ago but I'm pretty sure I've never seen or heard of him.'

'Thank you,' said Pietersen, pursing her lips.

Malice went up to the front window, cupped his hands to the glass and peered in.

'What are you doing?' asked Hartwell.

'Taking a look,' replied Malice.

'At what?'

'The inside.'

'Don't stare through the window like that.' Hartwell wagged his finger and strode up the garden.

'Why not?' Malice asked.

'If you want to look inside, I have a key.'

Chapter 15

One by one, the lads slope out of the house to take care of business. I gather up the plates, empty the crumbs into the waste bin and go back for the mugs. Tea and toast in the morning is a mandatory ritual.

'You'll make bad decisions if you're thinking of your stomach,' Clem would preach to them. 'And we can do without bad decisions.'

As is the case with many of his nuggets of home-grown wisdom, he was dead right. If we were going to carry off the charade, our boys had to be clean, well turned out and healthy. If they didn't eat their breakfast in the morning... they had Frank to deal with.

I sit at the kitchen table, staring down into my cup.

'We might have a problem,' I say to Frank as he fills the sink with water and squeezes in a glug of washing up liquid.

'Oh, what's that?' He rolls up his sleeves and plunges his hands into the hot water.

'You know the four guys from last night?'

'Yeah.'

'One of them got away.'

'Shit,' he spins around, his hands covered in suds. 'Which one?'

'I don't know.'

'I said you should have let me take care of them.' He punches at nothing, sending soap bubbles across the room. I run my finger through the globules of white that have landed on the table.

'I couldn't risk that.' I look up. Frank is not a happy bunny.

'After what they did to Clem, they should all be in wooden caskets.'

'There's more than one way to solve a problem.'

'Only it isn't solved, is it?'

'A temporary hitch, nothing more.'

'What are we going to do about it?'

'When you had that guy strung up in the barn, what did he tell you?'

The tension eases from his shoulders. Frank has difficulty when it comes to doing more than one thing at once — he can't be angry *and* think at the same time.

'Not much, he wasn't very chatty. He said his name was Jez Miller and they operated out of a town called Winfield. That was it. Oh, and he said I was a dead man.'

'I need you to track him down. The chances are with the beating you gave him, he's likely in a hospital somewhere. Probably in the Winfield area.'

'What shall I do when I find him? Finish the job?' He holds up a massive clenched fist.

'No, I want him to get a message to whoever is left in charge and tell him I want to talk.'

Frank turns to face the sink and piles the plates into the water.

'Didn't we do enough talking yesterday?' he mumbles.

'We did. But we need to do some more. With Clem out of action we can hardly afford a war with another crew. I need to convince them we had nothing to do with the raid.'

'I'm not sure that's the right move, Twink. They won't listen. Let me find this Miller guy and take the lot of them out. Finish the job.'

'Frank, that's not the way to sort this.'

'Your way left a loose end that we are now trying to tidy up.'

He's got a point.

'Which is unfortunate, but we need to be smart about this. I'm going to see Clem this morning… keep me posted.'

Frank stops what he's doing and dries his hands. He spins around and throws the towel onto the floor; the veins in his neck are standing proud.

'Then I'd better get in my fucking car and start being smart.' He growls at me, before stomping out down the hall. I hear the front door slam shut.

That could have gone better.

I finish washing up and head off to the hospital.

Twenty minutes later I'm holding Clem's hand and watching the green line blip up and down on the screen. Either they've run out of the bloody stuff or I'm becoming immune to the smell of hand sanitiser. The swelling on the side of his face has subsided but the bruises on his arms have turned an angry purple. The fat wad of dressing protecting the wound in his stomach is visible under the thin blanket. His eyes are closed. He looks like he's sleeping.

When I arrived at the side-ward the nurse gave me the same earnest report as yesterday: 'He's stable. There's no change'. My heart sank. I was hoping for more positive news.

The exchange with Frank is playing on my mind. I should have chosen my words better. For a man with a violent streak a mile wide, he is surprisingly thin-skinned. He's particularly sensitive to anything that reminds him that he's not as sharp as his older brother. Looks like I didn't so much as touch on that raw nerve, as jump up and down on it with both feet.

Clem's hand feels cool in mine, his skin dry and flaky. I can see the word 'Twinkle' tattooed on his bicep under his short-sleeved hospital gown. If I was wearing a T-shirt you would see 'Clem' tattooed on mine. We got them done to cement our business partnership one Saturday afternoon when we were pissed. I remember we fell out of the pub into the tattoo parlour and when we were done we fell into bed.

I'd mentioned to him that I liked to mark significant events in my life by getting inked and this was just such an event. That evening when he held me in his arms, he traced his fingers across the pictures etched onto my body — each one with a story to tell. He reached the strawberry tattooed below my belly-button.

'What's this one?' he'd asked. 'Don't tell me... you owned a fruit and veg stall?'

'Not exactly, I'd replied, sniggering. Over the next hour I unburdened myself with the most painful part of my life.

The third rape was my fiancé at the time. He'd presented me with a gift-wrapped silver necklace and earring set on my twenty-first birthday and considered it ample payment to stick his cock in me. I didn't agree, but he did it anyway. Despite his tears and apologies, we split up and four weeks later I peed on a stick: the blue line informing me I was pregnant.

I was still reeling from the shock when I bumped into him in a pub and told him about the baby. He went into a complete meltdown and demanded I take a paternity test. I refused and called him a twat. He said I was a slapper. Then he yelled in my face, saying how did he know the kid was his? Now, I would agree, the most sensible thing to do would have been to walk away and give him chance to absorb the news. But I glassed him instead. When I was in custody, no one was interested in the rape, all they were concerned with was the ten stitches in his face. I was charged and it went to trial. I might have made matters worse by screaming at him across the courtroom, 'It's a pity it wasn't fucking one hundred and ten'. Or words to that effect.

The day the guilty verdict was announced the bastard did a disappearing act, wanting to get as far away from me and the unwanted child as possible. I lost the baby while I was on bail awaiting sentencing. The doctor said something about 'trauma induced miscarriage'. All I knew was it constituted mitigating circumstances and I got off with a suspended sentence. I'd found a book in the library that took you through a week-by-week breakdown of the various stages of pregnancy and on the day I miscarried the foetus was the size of a strawberry. The tattoo is a fitting tribute. Clem loves my strawberry the most.

I run my fingers across Clem's tattoo and become aware of someone standing in the doorway. I look up to see a man whose mother never took him to the dentist.

Chapter 16

I freeze. He's grinning at me with his tombstone teeth and swaying from side to side. His hair is greased flat to his head and his eyes are crazed-red. He looks as if a lorry load of coke has already been up his nose.

'Fuck me, two for the price of one,' he rasps and staggers inside, closing the door behind him. 'If it isn't the president of the Women's Institute.'

He stumbles forwards and steadies himself with both hands on the bed. I squeeze Clem's hand and try not to react.

'You have been greedy boys,' I say. 'Don't tell me, you've used it up already? Told you it was good shit.'

'You bitch,' he sneers. The stink of hard liquor wafts across to me.

'That's no way to get a new working relationship off on the right foot?' I edge my chair away from the bed.

'You set us up,' he leans forwards and slurs.

'What are you talking about? Do you like the new shit or not?'

'You played us.' Dribble falls from his mouth and lands on the covers. He pushes himself upright and adjusts his footing.

'Have you been at the merchandise? I have no idea what you're on about.'

'Yes, you do. You conniving fuck.' He lumbers around to my side of the bed using the handrail for support. I bounce from the chair and look around for something to defend myself — there's nothing to hand.

'I have no idea what you're talking about.' I back away until I'm up against the wall. 'Go get your boss, he might be a thieving shit but at least he could talk sensibly.'

'He's not around,' he snarls and lurches at me. 'You… you… screwed us.'

'Where is he? Look, what's this about?' I try to duck to one side but he blocks my path.

'The filth showed up and carted him and my brothers away.'

'The police… showed up… when?'

'After you left.'

I hold my hands in the air in a sign of surrender.

'I know nothing about that.'

'You're lying.' He steps forwards and bumps his chest into me, sending me back into the wall.

'I'm not. I swear. Do you think I tipped them off?' My eyes dart to the window. There's no one there.

'How the hell else would they know to turn up?'

'Don't be stupid. You stole half a kilo from me and you think I set you up?'

'That's right.'

'Give your head a wobble, will you. The police showing up had nothing to do with me. Think about it — do I look like I have a fucking crystal ball?'

'Eh?' He steps back, his head on one side.

'Or do you believe I had some sort of a premonition that you would rob us of our gear? How would I know you were going to do that?'

'Well ...'

I can see the cogs turning.

'Have a word with yourself. You're telling me that I purposefully brought fifty grands worth of heroin to a meeting, knowing full well you were going to steal it from me. Does that sound a smart move to you?'

I sidestep him and make a dash for the door, but he puts out his arm and shoves me back.

'You tipped them off.'

'Oh, so now not only do I bring a pack of heroin knowing you were going to take it, now I'm supposed to have the cops on call to conduct a raid whenever I feel like it. Listen to yourself. You're talking rubbish.'

'There's no other explanation.'

'Here's one... you idiots were tailed to the meeting because you're clumsy fuckwits.'

I spit the words in his face. He backs away.

'That didn't happen.'

'Oh no, *that* didn't happen... but me doing a Mystic Meg is fine; knowing you were going to steal my gear and calling the police — that's a far more sensible option.'

'Mystic Meg?' He screws his face up.

I sigh. A deep, heavy sigh.

'You took the decision to steal the package, I didn't give it to you. If you hadn't have done that the cops would have shown up and done what? Arrested the four of you for loitering in a public place dressed like wankers?'

'You set us up,' he growls through gritted teeth.

'If you're the only one left, your business is fucked.'

'You got a smart mouth,' he shoves me in the chest.

'Smarter that yours, that's for sure.'

He slaps me across the face, sending me spinning to the far wall. It stings like a bastard.

'It's good you're here 'cos you can say goodbye to your boyfriend.'

I flash a glance at Clements.

'You're going to kill him? What the hell for… revenge? I did not set you up, I promise.'

'I *am* going to kill him, but only after I kill you first.'

He lunges for me and grabs my arm. I twist my body but his other arm is tight around my chest. Then he clamps his hand over my mouth to stifle my scream. I try to bite him. I can't breathe.

He yanks me off my feet and we crash to the floor. In an instant he's sitting astride me with his hands gripped around my throat. Bearing down with all his weight. Choking the air from my lungs. His contorted face towering above me.

I try to gouge his eyes but my flailing arms aren't long enough, all I can do is claw at his neck. My legs are kicking wildly, trying to buck him off but he's too heavy. Too strong. My vision begins to fog as blood and oxygen are shut off from my brain.

A thick black arm winds itself around his neck. His head snaps back and he's heaved off me. I can hear gargling and choking. But it's not coming from me. I roll onto my side, both hands around my neck. The rasp of air burns my throat. Large boots thump into my side as the man writhes around on his back, his feet kicking out at thin air.

Frank has his forearm locked in place, legs wound tight around the guy's waist. The man's eyes are bursting from his face and his tongue is protruding from his mouth. His hands flail around, tugging at Frank's clothing, trying to tear at his face. Frank holds him in place and squeezes the life out of him.

The man's feet hit the floor and begin to twitch. His body spasms. Hands falling away.

Franks throws the guy off him, onto his side. A trickle of blood is running down his face where a finger nail has scored a groove on his cheek. He scampers across the floor.

'Are you okay Twinkle?' he says, kneeling beside me.

'Yeah,' I croak, 'I'm fine.' I rub my neck. Frank grabs a handful of the guy's collar, heaves him across the floor and rolls him under the bed.

'We got to–'

'I got this,' Frank says, jumping to his feet and disappearing out of the room. A couple of minutes later he returns pushing a wheelchair. 'Find a blanket.'

I open and close cupboard doors until I find a blue throw. Frank slides the guy from under the bed, puts his arms under his armpits and heaves him into the chair. I cover him with the blanket. His head lolling forward.

'Let's get him out of here,' I say. 'Where's your car?'

'In the main car park.'

I open the door and Frank wheels the chair behind me. The guy with the rotten teeth looks as if he's asleep if you don't stare at him for too long. However if you allow your eyes to linger, he looks like he's dead.

The lift arrives and a couple appear from nowhere to join us. Frank turns to face the wall.

'Ground floor?' I ask.

'Please.'

I press the button and the doors close. I smile at the woman and stand in front of the wheelchair blocking their view. Frank has his hand on the man's shoulder, holding him upright. It's the longest fucking lift ride in history. The doors open and the couple leave first, thankfully none the wiser.

We emerge at the front of the hospital and Frank turns sharp left. The car park is close and in no time he's manhandling the guy into the back and snapping the seat belt in place. He pops open the boot and folds away the chair. We both sit in the front and close the doors.

'Shit, I thought I was a goner.' My voice sounds alien as it comes out of my mouth.

'I won't let anyone hurt you. What was he doing there?' Frank dabs the back of his hand to his eye. It comes away streaked with blood. I rummage in my pocket to find a tissue.

'He'd come to kill Clem as revenge for us setting him up.'

'He must have been thrilled to bump into you.' Frank holds the hankie to his face.

'Good job you came along when you did. What are you doing here?'

'I got half-way to Winfield and turned back.'

'Why.'

'I was having second thoughts about what you said.'

'Oh, why was that?'

'I had a better idea and wanted to run it past you first.' He examines the blood absorbed in the material.

'I'm glad you did,' I put my hand on his shoulder. 'I'm sorry about what I said this morning, it was a poor choice of words.'

'You have to like me now, I saved your life.' He turns his head and gives me one of his 'Happy Frank' grins.

'Friends again?' I say.

'Yup, friends.'

'What was your idea?'

'I thought that rather than finding Miller and having a chat, we should kill the fuckers.'

'Maybe on the face of it, you were right.' I ruffle the back of his hair. 'I still want you to go find him and I'll join you later.'

'What for?'

I flip down the sun visor and open the mirror. The marks on my neck are coming up a treat.

'There's a gap in the market that's opened up in Winfield,' I say, touching them with the tips of my fingers.

'Are we going to buy a house?'

'Nope, you're going to find us a cuckoo's nest.'

Chapter 17

Thomas Hartwell opened the back door onto a galley-style kitchen with cupboards running down one wall and a cooker, sink and washing machine against the other. A mug and a bowl were sitting on the draining board. The accumulation of dust had turned the white glaze a grubby yellow.

'It's a while since I've been in here,' he said. 'Watch where you put your feet, there are trays of rat poison in every room.'

Malice pointed to the neatly stacked unopened mail, sitting on the worktop.

'You did this?' he asked.

'I did at the beginning. Then when the utilities people cut off the supplies due to the bills not being paid, I stopped. After a while it was only junk mail and takeaway menus being stuffed through the letter box, so I boarded it over.'

Pietersen mooched through the hallway and into the lounge. It was obvious the windows hadn't been opened in years.

'It's like it's been frozen in time,' she mused to herself.

'Pretty much,' replied Hartwell. 'The police went through the house from top to bottom. Not sure what they were looking for, but they put everything back where they found it.'

Malice joined her in the living room and scanned around. A copy of the *Radio Times* lay across the arm of the sofa and a newspaper was lying on the floor next to the armchair. Malice took a pen from his pocket and opened the paper. It was dated 17 June, 2009.

'Did Tim live here on his own?' he asked.

'Yes, he kept the house after his parents died,' replied Hartwell, running his finger along the window sill and then blowing off the dust.

'Was he close to them?' asked Pietersen.

'It hit him hard when George and Daisy passed away. I remember loads of folk from the church came to visit to make sure he was okay... but I don't think he ever got over it. You'd like to believe in those circumstances your faith would be a comfort, but I think in Tim's case it only served as a painful reminder.'

'Do you remember the day he left?' said Malice.

'I do. That's how I have the key. He asked me to look after his cat while he was away, feed it and such like.'

'Where's the cat now?' Pietersen asked.

'We had it for a few years then it died. Look, I have things to do, are you okay if I leave you here?'

'Yes, that would be fine,' Malice said. 'We just want to look around.'

'Lock up and drop the key off when you leave.' Hartwell shuffled down the hallway and out the door.

'He's looked after the place for *ten years*.' Malice let out a low whistle.

'That's some commitment,' Pietersen replied as she padded around the room snapping away, taking photographs on her phone. 'I wish he lived next door to me.'

'There's something not right.' Malice shook his head.

'What is it?'

'I don't know. Can't put my finger on it.'

Malice took the stairs two at a time up to a landing where three bedrooms and a bathroom branched off. He went into the bathroom. A towel was hanging from a rail and the toothbrush holder was empty. He popped open the cupboard under the sink to find cleaning products, soap and toilet rolls.

Then he went into the main bedroom where Pietersen was already opening and closing drawers. She straightened up when she slid open the bedside drawer, passport in one hand and a box of condoms in the other. 'He didn't take this with him and these are the same brand as the ones found in the hotel room.'

'Is it a box of twenty-four?'

'Yup and almost empty.'

'For someone who seemed to live a vanilla lifestyle he sure as hell got his rocks off often enough.'

Malice opened the double doors of a built-in wardrobe. Rows of shirts, trousers and jackets hung on hangers from a rail. He looked up to see spare bedding, pillows and a box. He pulled the box down, lay it on the bed and lifted the lid. His fingers worked quickly sifting through the contents. There were old photographs, a school tie, postcards, a few football programs and two orders of service for funeral ceremonies.

'His mum and dad,' Malice said, taking them from the box and turning them over in his hands. 'They both died in their mid-fifties.'

'That's young,' Pietersen called from the other room.

Malice rummaged around some more and felt something solid. He removed a three-inch by three-inch square block with Polaroid written on the front.

'Bloody hell, I've not seen one of these in a long while,' he said, peeling back the Velcro flap and taking out the camera.

'What is it?'

'An old Polaroid 2070. This was quality kit twenty years ago and could set you back the thick end of a hundred-quid. It's a miniature digital camera with a zoom lens. They were all the rage and allowed you to download pictures to your computer.'

Pietersen appeared in the doorway.

'Let me see.' Malice handed it over and she opened the rubber flap to reveal the USB port before furrowing her brow.

'What is it?' he asked.

'There's a desktop computer in the other room and Maxwell owned a laptop. I read a digital forensic report saying there were no pictures found on any of the devices.'

'That's odd. This thing had an 8MB flash-memory which could store between eight to one hundred photos depending on the resolution. You had to keep downloading the photos because it got full. And it shot video clips, which blew people away at the time. You could buy memory extensions to increase the capacity. I remember my mate's dad had one and he raved about it–'

'How can you remember shit like that, but not your wife's birthday?'

'Ex-wife... and that probably says it all.'

Pietersen pushed the 'on' button, nothing happened. She flipped open a compartment — no batteries. Then she handed it back to Malice who slid it back in the case.

His phone went off in his pocket.

'Hi, Candice,' he answered as he got up from the bed to wander off. Pietersen continued to poke around, marvelling at her partner's capacity for retaining useless information.

The minutes ticked by and Malice hadn't returned. Pietersen made her way onto the landing, followed the sound of his voice and found him sitting on a chair in one of the spare bedrooms. She pushed open the door and mouthed to him, 'Well?'

'I have to dash, Candice, thanks for that. I'll be in touch,' Malice said, disconnecting the call.

'What did she say?'

'She called to say the dental records came up with a match. The body we found is that of John Horton.'

'All that time to tell you that?' Pietersen said, tilting her head. 'Maybe you'll be using that iron sooner than you thought.'

Chapter 18

Pietersen came into the office carrying two coffees; one outstretched towards Malice.

'If you need to see Waite, my advice is *don't*,' she said, handing it over before slumping into her chair and twirling the seat from side to side.

'Oh,' Malice looked up. 'Trouble at mill.'

'Could say that.' She beckoned for Malice to lean in closer. 'You know how she always likes to think of herself as top-dog?' she said under her breath.

'And some.' Malice flicked a glance at the door while he rolled his hand back and forth over his desk.

'Well, that accolade for this week definitely goes to the Drug Squad.'

'How come?'

'I was ear-wigging by the coffee machine so the details are a little sketchy… but apparently they got a tip off from either a member of the public, or an informer, about a drugs cache.'

'Jammy bastards.'

'They staked out one location only to be told the drop had changed. Then raided the place and recovered a half-kilo of H and bagged themselves three blokes wanted for dealing. Their finger prints were all over the drugs package. I think they're still celebrating.'

'Waite isn't going to like that one bit.' He sat back, shaking his head

'Exactly. By the way … what are you doing?' she asked. Malice lifted his hand from the desk to reveal four AAA batteries. She shrugged her shoulders. 'Where did you get those?'

'I nicked them from the remote controls in the conference room. But the more important question you should have asked, Detective Constable, is 'why do you need those?''

'Okay, smart arse. Why do you–'

'To which I would have replied… 'for this baby.'' Malice opened his top drawer and brought out the Polaroid camera from the Maxwell house.

'You nicked it.'

'Borrowed it. I can always take it back.'

'Found anything interesting?'

'Not yet. You know I said there was something not right with the house?'

'Yeah.'

'It finally dawned on me; it was too tidy. Let's face it, apart from a newspaper, a magazine, a mug and a plate, there was not a thing out of place. Maxwell was a single bloke, living on his own — does that seem right to you?'

'You got a point.' Pietersen got out her phone and began flicking through the photos she'd taken at the house. 'Let's be fair, the majority of blokes I know struggle to keep their sock drawer in order. His house looks like the cleaning fairy has just done her rounds.'

'Yeah, alright. Rein in the prejudice.'

'It's true. Maybe he had a clean-up before going away.'

'Who does that?' Malice popped open the compartment and slid the batteries inside.

'My mum's friend cleans her house from top to bottom before she goes away on holiday.'

'What for?'

'In case the plane crashes.'

Malice looked up from the camera. 'Why would she ...?'

'Then when people come into her house to mourn her they won't think she was a messy cow.'

'Thanks for that insight. Also, did you notice, there were no pictures or photographs anywhere in the house. Not one.'

'What are you driving at?'

'Why have this?' He held up the camera.

'Have you got it to work?'

'No.' Malice snapped the lid shut. 'It won't start up.'

'You'll have to give it to imaging.'

'And wait three weeks to get it back... I'd rather play around with it first.'

'Where did you find it?'

'That's the other thing,' Malice said, pushing at the 'on' button again. The one and a quarter inch LCD screen remained stubbornly blank. 'I found it in a memory box on the shelf in his wardrobe.' He flipped off the lid and fiddled with the batteries.

'It must have sentimental value. Perhaps it belonged to his mum and dad.'

Malice squeezed the lid down on the battery compartment and the green LED next to the viewfinder flashed into life.

'Bloody hell, it's working,' he said, maintaining pressure on the lid.

'What have you got?' Pietersen joined him on his side of the desk and squinted at the tiny screen. After a few seconds it lit up with the word 'Polaroid' in blue and purple lettering.

'Shit, that's small,' she said. 'State of the art you said?'

'It was in the day.' Malice moved his finger to the top and pressed the buttons marked 'Next' and 'Prev'. A grainy colour photograph came onto the screen.

'Is that...?' she peered at the image.

'Horton and Maxwell together in a bar.' He indexed to the next frame. 'And another, this time on a beach.' The screen went blank. 'Bollocks, I must have lost the contact.'

'So, they did know each other,' she said, slapping her hand down on the desk.

The camera started working again, Malice turned the screen to face Pietersen. The picture showed Maxwell and Horton with their arms around each other smiling into the lens.

'How would you characterise that shot?' he asked.

'If I didn't know any different, I'd say... romantic?'

'Hmm... I got a feeling they were more than just friends.'

'Okay, let's see what we have.' Pietersen grabbed a marker pen and marched up to the board. 'Maxwell and Horton stayed in hotels a couple of miles apart in the same town on the same nights. They both go AWOL and leave behind unpaid bills. Horton ends up being murdered and his body is dumped in a shallow grave. Maxwell is still missing and yet the two of them have no common connections whatsoever.'

'We know Maxwell was sexually active despite there being no talk of a girlfriend,' said Malice.

'What about a boyfriend?'

'Perhaps they were in a relationship.'

'Could be. Horton was married so they would have every reason to keep it under wraps.'

'Another theory could be that Maxwell murdered Horton?' Malice tapped his pen on the desk.

'That's a possibility and could explain why he disappeared afterwards.'

'But it was one hell of a disappearing act if that was the case — not a trace in ten years.'

'Why stop using the camera and put it away for safe keeping?'

'That's easy — mobile phones. They knock this into a cocked hat,' Malice said, pointing at the Polaroid.

'Of course. Wait a minute… phones?' Pietersen plucked a photograph from the board and took it to her desk. She clicked away with her mouse then sat back in her seat. 'It's so bloody obvious, it's painful.'

'Oh,' said Malice, putting the camera back in the drawer and sidling over to her desk.

'When they went through Maxwell's stuff at the hotel room they found this,' Pietersen said, holding up the photograph. 'He'd printed out the hotel confirmation for his booking. In the space marked *Contact Details* he'd given a mobile number which is different to the one we have on record. The reason we've been unable to finds any emails, calls or social media contact between the two of them is because they had two phones.'

'If we pull the call records for that number, we'll identify the other.'

'That does throw up another possibility into the mix; that Maxwell was murdered as well. Supposing…'

Malice wasn't listening as Pietersen laid out her theory. He was staring out the window across the car park at the Blue Mondeo parked outside the station gates.

Sometime later Malice was sitting in the conference room nursing an A4 sized piece of paper on the desk in front of him. Pietersen piled into the room and he turned it face down.

'Mally, where the hell have you been?' she asked. 'And what are you doing in here?'

'I needed to take care of something,' he said, staring down at the paper.

'There's me waxing lyrical about what could have happened to Maxwell and Horton and you walk off without saying a word.'

'I'm sorry.'

'Are you not interested in what I have to say?' She slapped her hands against her legs and turned away.

'No, it's not that.'

'What is it then? Are you bored with the case?'

'It's not that either.'

She leaned over with both hands on the edge of the desk.

'Then you'd better start talking to me because from where I'm standing this is the biggest case we've had on our plate and you're not at the party.'

'Sit down,' he said.

'We are supposed to be working on this together, and–'

'Sit down!' Pietersen took a seat. 'You know when we were in the courtroom waiting for the verdict on Elsa Kaplan...'

'Yes.'

'And you said to me 'No more secrets'.'

'I remember.'

'Well, I think I have a problem. I'm not sure if it's connected to Lubos Vasco or it could be linked to a whole host of other people, but I need to tell you something.'

'Go on.'

Malice turned the paper over to show the face of a man sitting in a blue Mondeo. He'd spent the last forty minutes on the phone to the company who ran building security. Malice knew that if he'd dashed from the station to confront the man he'd have taken off. The best course of action was to get security to train the CCTV camera mounted on the front of the building at the car, zoom in and take a snap.

He spun the picture around and presented it in front of Pietersen.

'This guy has been following me. The first time I clocked him he drew his thumb across his neck.' Malice mimicked the action. 'I don't know what he wants, but I've seen him now on three occasions. His name is–'

'Brad Craven,' she interrupted.

Malice jumped back in his seat.

'How the hell do you know that?' he blurted out.

'Christ! You two are keen.' Waite rushed into the room, Malice and Pietersen flashed glances at each other. 'Don't tell me you've forgotten we have a team brief this morning?'

'Erm, no, ma'am,' they both lied.

'Kelly and I needed a quiet place to chat things through,' said Malice, trying to keep the tension from his voice.

'How lovely.' Waite unpacked her files and began fiddling with the lead to set up her laptop. 'When we finish with the briefing I want you two in my office because I need to know where we're up to with the unidentified body. I've got a meeting with the Dep and he's bound to ask.'

Malice folded the sheet of paper into four and stuffed it in his pocket. While Waite was on her hands and knees, swearing at the IT equipment, he leaned forward and whispered to Pietersen.

'How the hell do you know Craven?' he hissed in her ear.

She looked around before whispering back.

'He's not after you. He's after me.'

Chapter 19

I skip up the stone steps of the Medieval building and pass through the vaulted arch. The heavy metal ring turns in my hand and the big oak door swings open. I step inside. The sound of my heels echoes against the walls. I check the silk scarf is in place around my neck. Before I left the house, my dressing table mirror confirmed what I'd feared — the bruises were coming up nicely.

Malissa waves to me from behind the counter in the coffee shop and a bevy of volunteers mop and dust their way along the benches and pews. I see Ketchup coming from the vestry. I take a deep breath.

'Twinkle twinkle, little star,' he crows at the top of his voice.

My uncle's rhyme goes off in my head:
Twinkle, twinkle little lies,
How I see them in your eyes...

Ketchup bounds up to me like a kid who's eaten too many Smarties; his arms waving in the air, swatting away invisible flies.

I swear one of these days...

He flings his arms around me and hugs the breath from my body. I shrug him off. He's wrapped in the sickly odour of cheap soap and hair wax.

'I wonder if I could have a word?' I ask, looking sheepish.

'Why stop at one when you could have three, or four, or five…'

Twat.

'Can we have a chat?' I ask again.

'Of course, step into my office.' He links his arm through mine and waltzes me off in the direction of the altar. 'We have a christening this afternoon and I want to make sure everything is ready.'

'It won't take long.'

'What can I do you for?' he strikes a pantomime pose as if delivering his best punch line.

'I'm worried.' I look away.

'Oh, about what?'

'After the talk with ACC Beresford, one of the new boys asked if he could see me in private.'

'I must say, I thought the talk went really well. He's a pillar of this church, and he never ceases to praise the work you do with those young men.'

'That's kind, he's a tremendous support.'

'Yes, and I wish we had more like him. I was only saying to Mavis, you know her, the woman who sits on the council—'

For fuck's sake stop talking!

'Please…' I put my hand on his arm. 'The new boy told me of a group of young men just like him who are being targeted by drug gangs.'

'That's terrible. But it's the way society is going these days,' he says, topping up the font and folding freshly laundered linen.

'They're being sucked into that way of life. I feel dreadful that we can't help. I didn't sleep last night, thinking of them. I don't know what to do.' I turn away from him and let my head drop. I feel my eyes tearing up.

'You can't take the world's troubles on your shoulders.'

'That's true but this feels really close to home. I feel like we should help.'

I turn to face him and wipe away tears with my sleeve.

'Don't upset yourself.' He takes my arm and leads me to the nearest pew. 'I can see it's had an effect on you. Come and sit down.' We slide along the wooden bench and I fold my hands in my lap, staring down at the floor. His knees are pressed tight against mine.

'It's the thought of boys, like ours, with nowhere to turn. No one to talk to. Being preyed upon by gangs and dealers.'

'That's the trouble with you, Twinkle, you want to help everyone.' He puts a comforting arm around my shoulders and gives me a squeeze.

'I don't know what to do?' I dab my eyes with the back of my hand.

'Come on now, don't cry. Where do these boys live?'

'Winfield, I think.'

He casts his eyes to the heavens and scratches the back of his head. The silence seems to go on forever.

Come on, come on... Fuck me he's slow on the uptake today.

'What if we look at extending the OutReach programme?' he says.

Bingo!

'How do you mean?' I turn my gaze to meet his.

'I've been thinking about this for a while. The work we do here goes down a storm at the joint council of parishes and… if I'm honest …' he leans in to whisper in my ear. 'I think everyone is a tad jealous of what we've achieved here.'

I shift my position and his arm falls away.

'How would that work?' I ask, my voice breaking.

'I know Reverend Bertram who's the vicar at St. Juniper's church. How about I give him a call and you could go along to talk to him? It would be good for us to be seen to be spreading our best practice to other communities.'

I pull away and give him my best 'that's an amazing suggestion' look.

'That's a wonderful idea. Would you do that?'

'Of course, we can't have you worrying, now can we?' He moves in for another hug. I get up and walk back to the font. He follows me.

'Thank you, I needed to tell someone. That's a huge weight off my mind. I didn't know what to do.'

'You can always come to me, Twinkle. You know that.'

'But you're such a busy man.'

'Never too busy for you. I'll make the call straight away,' he scuttles to his office.

As easy as taking candy from a baby.

An hour later and the glass doors in front of me swoosh open like I've uttered the magic word. I stroll into the reception area, head straight for the shop selling flowers and pick out a lovely bouquet of yellow blooms. I hand ten pounds to the woman clad in a red pinafore and smiling her head off. At ten pounds a pop, I'm not bloody surprised.

I make a bee-line for the ladies' toilets. The place is empty. I rest the flowers in the wash basin and rummage in my bag for my make-up. To help my performance this morning I decided to give my usual routine a miss. I study my reflection in the mirror – I look an absolute fright. A dab of foundation, scrape of lipstick and mascara and I'm feeling human again.

The lift is crammed with visitors and they jostle with pointy elbows to get out at their chosen floor. I want level seven, which seems to take an eternity. Eventually I exit onto a wide corridor and check the signs — ward 7D is to the right. A couple of minutes later and I'm counting the rooms as I pass them on my left-hand side. One… two.

The ward has six beds. Three of which are occupied with sleeping patients while a woman dressed in a green tunic administers to a man in the corner bed. Frank is sitting on a plastic chair, facing the door looking very pleased with himself. He's popping grapes into his mouth from a brown paper bag. The man lying in the bed next to him is sporting a broken arm, a swollen face and a thick wad of bandages wound around his chest. He looks much less happy. In fact, he looks fucking terrified.

'Jez,' I walk up to him. His eyes get wider with every step I make. 'When I heard the news I came straight over. How are you? I can't believe what happened.'

The woman in the green tunic glances over as I place the flowers at the foot of the bed.

'I'll get you a vase, love,' she calls over.

'That would be nice,' I fake a smile. Above the bed is a square whiteboard. Scribbled on it in block capitals is the name Jeremy Miller. In brackets below is written the name Jez.

Miller's head flips from side to side like a wind-up toy. From me to Frank and back again, as I take the seat on the other side of the bed and grasp his hand. Receiving his second unwanted visitor of the day is draining his colour even further.

'Who the fuck are you?' He yanks his hand away.

'Now, now, Jez, that's not nice. You owe me.'

'Owe you what?'

'I'm the one who stopped him from killing you and sent you off with a message to arrange a meeting with your top guys.'

'You set us up,' he sneers through gritted teeth.

'Whether I did, or whether I didn't is irrelevant now.'

'It won't be when Tonka gets hold of you.' He sits upright and winces. Frank puts his hand on Miller's chest and eases him back down.

'Is he the one with the rotten teeth?' I ask, settling back in my chair.

'Erm, I suppose so.'

'Then it's irrelevant,' I say, with a wave of my hand. 'I have bad news for you, Jez. You're unemployed.'

'What are you on about?' he says.

'None of the brothers are around anymore and as of this morning your firm went out of business — which leaves you without a job.'

'That's bullshit,' he says, trying to sit up again, but Frank holds him down. 'I spoke to Tonka earlier today. He's gonna fucking sort you pair for good.'

'You might have done but he's not in a position to sort anything right now.'

'Bollocks!' He slaps Frank's hand away, reaches over to the night stand and picks up his mobile phone. 'He's gonna kick your arses when he finds out you're here.' He pushes a couple of buttons. There's a low buzzing sound.

Frank fishes a phone from his pocket and pops another grape into his gob.

'Thought it might have some useful numbers on it,' Frank says, laying the mobile on the bed.

Miller looks at the phone, then at his, then back to the phone. His jaw drops open.

'I'm afraid you're out of a job, Jez,' I take his hand again. 'But it's not all doom and gloom.'

'What the... where is..?' he jabbers.

'With you boys out of the way it allows us to make a move. And while we know what we're doing, we lack local knowledge, and that's where you come in. I'd like to offer you a job, working for us.'

'Shit, man.' Miller stares at his phone and gives it a shake, as if that was going to make everything better.

'Before you answer...' I lean forwards, placing my elbows on the bed. 'It's only fair to let you know that if you say 'no', Frank here will ignore what I told him the other day and finish what he started.'

Frank grins.

'Fancy a grape, Jez?' he says.

'Erm, what? I don't know,' Miller blubs.

'It's a one-time offer. Take it or leave it,' I whisper, as Frank dangles the mobile back and forth between his fingers.

'Looks like I don't have a choice.' Miller grunts.

'Smart lad. I knew I was right to keep you alive.' I pat him on his plaster cast, get up and begin to draw the curtains around the bed. 'Get dressed.'

'Why, where are we going?' he asks.

'I need you to take us to one of your customers who either owns or rents their own property. Someone who would appreciate getting their gear for free.'

'How am I going to do that?' He raises his busted arm in protest.

'You're discharging yourself. Come on, chop, chop.'

Frank slides a large hand behind Miller's back.

'Time to go, mate.' He helps him to sit up.

'By the way, are you religious, Jez?' I ask, pulling the last curtain into place.

'Umm, no.'

'You will be.'

Just bagged my second piece of candy of the day.

Chapter 20

The team brief had ground to a mind-numbing halt. There's only so many Power Point slides a person can stomach at one sitting and this had gone way over the top.

By the time Malice and Pietersen had reached Waite's office she already had someone in the hot-seat. She saw them loitering in the doorway, got up from behind her desk and closed the door.

'His name is Bradley Craven. He's ex-CID,' Pietersen whispered, turning her back to the other people walking down the hallway.

'That's right.' Malice hissed as he squared up to her. 'How do you know him?'

'When I was in anti-corruption he was implicated in a case we were investigating. I was working undercover because we suspected him and two other coppers were on the take.'

'What were they doing?'

'To start with, it was illegal imports of tobacco and alcohol, then they branched out into counterfeit clothing.

Craven was the most senior member of the group. We ran the operation for five months during which time I gathered a stack of evidence. These guys were rotten to the core and in over their heads. We were confident of a result.'

'What happened?' Malice turned to face the wall and began tapping the toe of his shoe against the base of the plasterboard.

'When we pulled them in, all hell broke loose.'

'In what way?'

'Craven was golfing buddies with the Deputy Chief Constable who stuck his size nines in wherever he could. The other two had get-outs for everything we threw at them. What was, on the surface, a slam-dunk case was sliding away from us, but we had an ace up our sleeve.

'Oh?' Malice stopped kicking the wall and turned to face Pietersen.

'We followed the money chain and posed as punters, buying hooky goods using marked notes. When we took them in for questioning we executed warrants to search their homes. Sure enough, the notes showed up — game over.'

A group of people spilled out of the conference room, filling the corridor with excited chatter. Malice grabbed Pietersen by the arm and pulled her into a side office.

'So why is he following you around? Shouldn't he be banged up?' he said.

'When the case came to court, it collapsed.'

'Why was that?'

'Why do you think?'

'They got to the witnesses.'

'Exactly. Three failed to show up and two changed their testimony on the day.'

'What a fuck up.' Malice turned and dug his hands deep in his pockets.

'It was a disaster.' Pietersen shifted to the side to face him. 'Craven took early retirement and the other two were re-instated.'

'I still don't get it…'

'They claimed the notes found in their possession had been planted.'

'Not that old chestnut,' Malice huffed.

'Craven is here to give me the gypsy's warning.'

'What do you think he'll do?'

'I don't know but he's a nasty piece of work.'

'Shit, Kelly. Why didn't you say something?' Malice was letting his exasperation show.

'I clocked him but convinced myself I was seeing things, you know, the product of galloping paranoia.'

'This isn't paranoia.' Malice pulled the crumpled piece of paper from his pocket and unfolded it. He waved it in her face. 'This is real. We need to say something to Waite. I know she's got a reputation for being an awkward bastard but she looks after her team. She needs to hear this.'

'I don't think that's a good idea.' Pietersen shook her head and turned away.

'She'll be fine.'

'No, I don't mean that.'

'Then who should we take it to? Your ex-boss in anti-corruption?'

'No, not him either.'

'I don't get it.' He walked around in small circles, looking up at the ceiling. 'We can't just pretend this isn't happening. He's cruising around out there!'

They heard Waite's door open and an ashen face hurried past. Malice stuffed the photograph in his pocket and marched out. He paced around in the hallway not wanting to go in. His head was a mess.

What the fuck is she playing at?

'In here, you two,' Waite yelled. Pietersen got there first and took a seat. Malice finally joined her and closed the door. Waite didn't look up. 'What do I need to tell the Dep?'

Malice cleared his throat and tried to click his brain into gear.

'The body we dug up has been identified as John Horton,' Pietersen said, jumping in, filling the awkward silence. 'Who went missing in June 2009. He was killed by a blow to the back of his head. We are still awaiting the full post-mortem report. We interviewed his wife who unfortunately has been in hospital having been sectioned shortly after he went missing. Her testimony was... let's say... unreliable.'

'That's an understatement,' Malice added.

Pietersen continued. 'The second needle we found in the haystack is a man called Tim Maxwell. There is evidence to support that both men knew each other and we're exploring the possibility that they could have been in a secret relationship.'

'What were they doing here?' asked Waite, scribbling in her day book.

'Don't know,' said Malice. His head still running riot with the man in the blue Mondeo.

'If they wanted to keep things under wraps that would explain booking into separate hotels,' said Waite.

'Yeah, that fits,' Pietersen said.

'What are the next steps?' Waite asked, looking up and pushing her glasses to the end of her nose.

'We need to follow up on the case file information regarding—' Malice was finally in the game.

'I got a theory, ma'am,' Pietersen interrupted. Malice choked back his words and gave her a sideways look.

'Go on,' Waite said, putting down her pen.

'We could explore the possibility that Maxwell killed Horton. Maybe over an argument, or in a fit of jealousy and then did a disappearing act. But to slip off the radar completely for ten years? That takes some planning and execution. On the day they checked into their respective hotels they had arrived in separate cars and the vehicles were reclaimed by the police weeks later. It doesn't stack up. I think it's more plausible to say that Maxwell was killed at the same time as Horton. I think we should be looking for a second body.'

'Really?' Waite adopted her 'unimpressed' face. The prospect of a second historical case landing in her lap was not what she wanted to hear. 'And where do you think we should start looking?'

'The same place we found Horton,' Pietersen replied. 'If someone murdered them at the same time, why haul one of the bodies to a different location to dispose of them? You'd do it once — why take double the risk?'

'What are you suggesting?' asked Waite. The same question was rattling around in Malice's head.

'Sweep the location with a cadaver dog. If there's a second body buried, the dog will find it in minutes.'

Waite slapped her book closed and clicked her pen.

'Well, let's hope you're wrong.' She got up and tucked the book under her arm. 'I have what I need. As these are cold cases I'm not proposing we push for any more resources. You can handle it. Keep me posted.' She skirted around the desk and out the door.

Malice took a seat next to Pietersen.

'When were you going to let me in on your theory,' he said, shifting in his chair.

'If you'd been listening rather than pissing about taking pictures of people in cars, then—'

'I thought Craven was after me.'

'Yeah, well, he's not.'

'Looks like I've done you a favour.'

'How come?'

Malice took out the folded photograph.

'This is clear evidence. At least now you can do something about it,' he said.

'I can handle it.'

'You need to talk to someone. You need to alert a senior officer that this guy is stalking you.'

'I can't.'

'Why the hell not?'

'Their claim that the evidence was planted is a problem.' She stared at the back wall and her head dropped.

'Come on, Kelly think this through. What you need to do is–'

'It's a problem!' She spun in her seat and grabbed him by the shoulders. 'It's a problem… because I planted it.'

Chapter 21

Malice and Pietersen were gazing out of the windscreen at the expanse of wasteland leading to the derelict factory. She was tapping her fingers along the top of the steering wheel while his right leg danced up and down. Not a single word has passed between them in the last forty minutes; each of them occupied with weighing up the gravity of the situation.

Malice put his hand on his leg to stop it jigging.

'How did you plant the evidence?' He broke the silence.

'Craven had two accomplices, James Bailey and William Maddocks. The three of them were getting back handers every two weeks. It was always the same MO every time, brown envelopes stuffed with notes, handed over in car parks and pubs. We had a ton of photos showing the bungs being handed over. The team staked out one of the vendors and purchased eight thousand pounds worth of hooky cigarettes, using marked notes and known serial numbers. By our reckoning that was a large enough amount of money that some of it would trickle down to

Craven and Co. The day we served the warrants to search their houses we also raided the shop where we uncovered a load more illegal cigarettes, along with the money. When I found the cash, I realised it was all there. It was even in the same bloody packaging — untouched.'

'The full eight grand?'

'Yeah, none of it had filtered through.'

'So, you creamed some off the top.'

'Yup.'

Malice's leg began to bounce up and down again. Pietersen's fingers continued to dance across the steering wheel.

'Then what?' he said.

'I went to the houses of the three officers and planted the notes.'

'How much?'

'Maybe a grand in each.'

'How do they know it was you?'

'Because their 'friends' told them I'd visited all the locations on the day. They put two and two together and came up with four.'

'Fucking hell, Kelly. What were you thinking?'

'They were bent, Mally.' She gripped the steering wheel, her knuckles turned white.

'I wanted to make sure they went down.'

'Except they didn't.'

'No the case collapsed.'

'And you were left with your arse hanging out in the wind.'

'Pretty much.'

'What do you think Craven has in mind?'

'I don't know but the man has a track record of busting heads.'

'Do you want me to…'

She spun in her seat to confront him.

'No,' she barked. 'I *don't* want you involved.'

'He's seen me with you on three occasions, so I think ...'

'Leave it Mally. I'll sort it out.'

A CSI van pulled into view and Catherine Anders jumped out.

'They're here.' Malice pointed out the window. 'Let's go. We'll continue our little chat at another time.'

'No, we won't.'

She got out of the car and slammed the door. Malice scowled at her over the roof of the vehicle. She ignored him and walked off.

A police car with Dog Unit written on the side pulled up next to the CSI vehicle.

'DS Malice and DC Pietersen,' he called out when they were in earshot.

'Chrissie Jacobs from the K-9 unit. Come on, there's a good boy.' She raised the tailgate and a chocolate coloured Labrador jumped out. 'His name is Remy.' The dog came up and sniffed at Malice and Pietersen, then went back to his handler.

'Glad you were able to come at short notice,' Pietersen said, resisting the temptation to fuss over the dog.

'What have we got?' Jacobs asked, as Remy scampered around her feet.

'We discovered a body here yesterday that had been buried for ten years. We suspect there might be another,' Malice said.

'Okay, that's pretty straightforward. Do you want to lead the way?' Jacobs took a tennis ball from her pocket and Remy went potty. 'C'mon boy,' she said.

'Are we gonna play catch?' Malice asked.

'Something like that,' replied Jacobs, putting Remy on a lead.

The four of them trudged across to the factory, heading for the roller shutter door at the back of the building.

'How does this work?' asked Malice.

'For Remy, it's all about the ball. It's his favourite game. He sniffs out human remains and he gets to play. It will be more difficult because there is already the scent of a deceased person but we can work around that.'

Anders was already there, standing at the yellow tape still stretched across the opening.

'Hi,' she called out before handing a clipboard to Pietersen along with sets of overshoes. 'Fill in the log.'

They completed the admin and then Jacobs bent down to Remy and snapped the release on the lead. 'Go find Harry.' The dog bounded across the overgrown land to the perimeter fence, sniffing the ground and wagging his tail.

'Go find Harry?' Malice said.

'It's his trigger phrase, telling him the game has started. We often have to work where members of the general public are within ear-shot. It's better than saying 'Go find the dead guy.''

Remy bolted towards the hole in the ground under the corrugated, tin-sheeting structure. He sat down and barked three times.

'That's where we found the body,' Pietersen said.

Jacobs ran after Remy, took out the ball and tossed it in the air. The dog leaped up and caught it. Malice and Pietersen watched the two of them play with the ball. It was difficult to tell which one of them was having the most fun. Then Jacobs put the ball in her pocket and bent forward. 'Find more Harry,' she said and Remy went running off again sniffing at the ground.

Two minutes later he barked three times.

'Shit,' said Malice marching towards the bike shed. Remy was sitting at a spot three yards away from the first grave.

'He's found something,' said Jacobs, producing the ball once more. Remy broke his stance and started jumping around, Jacobs moved away, taking the dog with her.

'Let's make a start,' said Anders to the two CSI men who were standing by. They knelt down and began scraping away the top-soil with hand tools.

'We may as well get a coffee,' said Malice. 'This could take a while and we got things to discuss.'

Pietersen shook her head.

'Think I'll stay here.' She held her ground.

'Suit yourself.' Malice sloped off in the direction of the factory, hands dug deep in his pockets.

'Mally! Hold up.' Pietersen called after him. 'You might want to come and see this.'

'Bloody hell, that was fast,' he said, returning to the spot where the dog had barked. The men in white boiler-suits were scratching away at the soil.

'Take a look,' Anders said.

Poking through the dirt was the toe of a shoe. They removed the soil and lifted it out. The leather had degraded and the laces had been reduced to strands. They continued to pick away at the earth.

Gradually a decomposed human foot revealed itself. Pietersen gave Malice a sideways glance.

'Waite's not going to be happy,' she said, taking a deep breath.

Chapter 22

The wooden clad spire comes into view. The church looks smaller than the stone monstrosity I'm used to and has the impression of being newly renovated. Perhaps their fundraising amounts to more than a poxy café and the occasional jumble sale. Ketchup was as good as his word and Bertram is expecting me. He also said something about a cake and coffee morning; God forbid — excuse the pun.

I park my car and walk the short distance to the gravelled entrance. The oak doors are open and I can already hear high-pitched chatter coming from inside. I steel myself for the pain that's about to engulf me.

The central aisle stretches up to the altar which is framed at the back by six massive stained-glass windows. Two banks of pews line either side, with walkways running along the walls.

A gaggle of people are standing off to one side, drinking tea and coffee. They're flanked by two trestle tables, groaning under the weight of home-made goodies.

The majority of the gathering are women and as I approach the shrill tones set my hearing on edge.

A middle-aged man wearing black trousers, a jumper and a tie, looks up and smiles. He trots over and shakes my hand.

'You must be Twinkle,' he beams, pumping my arm.

'That's right. You must be Reverend Bertram.'

'I am. Does the shirt and tie give it away?'

'Just a little.'

'Welcome to St. Juniper's.' He beams. 'We are not as grand as what you're used to, but we're an intimate and friendly bunch.'

'I'm really pleased you could see me at such short notice.' I wrestle my hand from his grasp. He's almost as clammy as Ketchup.

'It's my pleasure. I've heard so much about you and the OutReach programme. The work you do is incredible.'

'That's very kind, the grapevine must be working overtime.'

'Nothing to do with the grapevine. Peter Collins doesn't shut up about it.'

'He is a great supporter of the project. If it weren't for him these young men would be in a bad place.'

He places his hand in the small of my back and walks me up the central aisle. I try to walk faster to break contact with his palm, but he speeds up with me.

'Come over and meet a few people,' he says. 'I've been telling them you were going to pay us a visit.'

'I'd rather not, if that's okay. Can we talk in private?'

'Are you sure? They'll be so disappointed.'

I couldn't give a fuck.

I stop and place my hand on his forearm.

'Maybe next time,' I say in my most sympathetic tone. 'What I have to say is of a sensitive nature and I would feel awkward... well... you know.'

I feel his hand fall away.

'Certainly... come with me.' He veers off to a door on the right. It opens up onto a good-sized room with arched windows and dark wooden beams. 'This doubles as our Sunday school and bible study classroom.'

I glance around to see tables and chairs dotted about. The walls are lined with shelving, rammed full of books.

'This is a nice space,' I say.

'Yes, we get a lot of use out of it.'

'What did Reverend Collins tell you when he called?'

'He said you were considering extending the OutReach Programme and wondered if we'd be interested.'

I sidle over and take a seat.

'There's a little more to it than that,' I reply, putting on my most earnest expression and folding my hands into each other on top of the table.

'Oh?' he says, joining me and leaning forward on his elbows. 'I'm all ears.'

'One of our group is a young man named Sherbet. He took me to one side the other night and told me about a lad he knows called Jez who comes from Winfield.'

Bertram shakes his head. 'Can't say I've heard the name before.'

'Sherbet told me that Jez and his circle of friends are being targeted by gangs, putting pressure on them to join.'

'What for?'

'They're into drugs and are threatening these young men that if they don't do as they say they'll beat them up or hurt their families.'

'That's awful.' He recoils back from the table.

'The same thing happened with us before we set up OutReach. Our boys were being threatened and bullied, that's when we stepped in.'

'How many of them are involved?'

'Sherbet didn't know.'

'Can't they go to the police?'

'They won't. They don't trust the police, unless we help them they're stuck.'

'How real is the threat?'

'Sherbet contacted me to say that Jez has already been beaten up for trying to stand up to this gang. They put him in hospital. Some of his friends are already being sucked in.'

'My goodness, that's terrible.' Bertram gets up from his chair and paces about the room.

'And I'm sorry to say, but it's happening on your patch.'

'We should do all we can to support these young men.'

'That's what I was hoping you'd say.'

He scurries back to where I'm sitting and leans across with both hands on the table.

'How can we help?' he says.

'I want to set up OutReach in your church. We could use this room for meetings. It's perfect?'

'Of course.'

'Our aim is to teach these young men respect. Teach them about taking responsibility and providing them the support to enable them to say no.'

'But how can you stand up to a gang?'

'I don't. Frank does.'

'Who's Frank?'

'He's my business partner, I'd like you to meet him. He'll work with me to set up what we need and help the guys seek safety in the refuge of the church.'

'We don't have much money to fund this.'

'Don't worry. All we need is coffee, tea, a room and your good grace and we'll do the rest.'

'I'd like to be there when you find these young men.' He stands up straight like he's on parade. I shake my head.

You must be joking, mate.

'Sorry Father but that's not a good idea. They need to see people who look like them in the first instance. They already have a mistrust for authority, so it's best if we leave it to Frank and a few of the boys. They'll soon get them onside.'

He goes on another walkabout around the room, rubbing his hands together like he's bagged a win on the horses. He looks like a well-dressed Fagin.

'This… is an exciting project,' he crows.

'It will be. Just think in the months to come you'll be able to sing the praises of your own OutReach programme in the joint parish meetings.'

'That would be amazing.'

We chat some more and I shake his hand to leave. We'd said all there was to say fifteen minutes ago but I can't fucking shut him up.

'So, expect a visit from Frank,' I cut him off mid-sentence and head out the door. 'He might bring Jez and a couple of guys with him.'

'How will I recognise him?'

'You know the big guy out of *Game of Thrones*?'

'Yes.'

'He's a black version of him. You'll know Frank when you see him.'

I leave Bertram rubbing his hands together at the prospect of giving Ketchup a run for his money at the next meeting and walk back to my car, happy that all the plates are now spinning. I just need to move fast to stop any of them crashing to the floor.

I think about Bertram with his creepy disposition and clammy hands.

My third piece of candy of the day.

Chapter 23

Malice and Pietersen weren't speaking to each other as they pecked away at their respective keyboards. The air between them crackled. It's not that they didn't have anything to talk about — on the contrary there was shit loads — it's just that Malice only had one topic of conversation. The very thing Pietersen didn't want to hear.

The last remaining copper in the office scooped his jacket off the back of the chair and bolted for the door.

'Good night,' he said, finishing work for the day.

'See you in the morning,' Malice held up his hand as the man beetled off.

The room fell silent.

'Don't,' Pietersen said, not bothering to look up.

'Don't what?' Malice kept his head down.

'Bang on about Craven.'

'I wasn't going to.'

'Yes, you were.'

'I wasn't going to say… that you need to let me help sort this out.'

'Fuck me, here we go again.' She threw herself back in her seat and flung her arms in the air.

'I wasn't going to say it because according to you, doing nothing is the right answer.' By the end of the sentence Malice was shouting. 'Doing nothing will make Craven drive back home. Doing nothing–'

'I said I don't need your help.' It was her turn to yell. 'I'll sort it in my own time. In my own way.'

Malice got up from behind his desk and inched over to Pietersen. She buried her head in her keyboard and refused to look up.

'All I'm saying is…' His voice had returned to its usual volume. 'If Craven is half as bad as you say, he's not going to simply get bored and piss off. He's here for a reason. He's a dangerous man. You're in deep shit.'

She broke away from her desk.

'So far all he's done is drive around with his dick in his hand staring out the side window of his car. It's hardly heavy stuff now is it?'

'You're in danger.'

'Since when did you jump to that monumental conclusion?'

'Since you told me you fucking did it!' Malice turned away and scraped his fingers through his hair.

'Yeah, well, I told you I was never cut out for anti-corruption.'

Malice spun around, pulled a chair up to Pietersen's desk and plonked himself next to her.

'There's a massive difference between you turning a blind eye to what I did and planting bloody evidence. Can't you see that?' He was trying to play nicely.

'Maybe there is …'

'At least take this guy seriously. He's not here for the benefit of his health.'

She looked at him and cracked a smile.

'You're like my bloody dad,' she said.

'Why? Is he always right as well?'

'No, he gets on my tits as well. Can we please talk about something else?'

'Like what?'

'Like the fact that we dug up the remains of a second body today with a hole in the side of his skull big enough to stick your thumb inside. We have a double murder to solve.'

'Yeah, that is a lot to talk about. Tell me you'll take Craven seriously?'

'Will you then get off my back?'

'Promise.'

'Okay, okay, I'll take him seriously.'

'Good.' Malice dragged the chair back to where he found it and returned to his desk. 'Now can we move on, please?'

'You're an annoying twat.' She shook a clenched fist at him.

'Thank you for that. At the moment, I don't remember marrying you, but it doesn't half feel like it.'

'God forbid.'

'Okay, back to business. We should get a hit on the dental records tomorrow, but I think it's safe to assume that the body is that of Maxwell.'

'The big question for us to answer is what were they both doing here?' she asked.

'Don't know.'

'I've read the case records about Maxwell and they all say the same thing – he was a quiet man who kept himself to himself.'

'If he was in a relationship with Horton then I get why they would want to keep it hush-hush because John was married. But why keep his own sexuality a secret? It was 2009 after all.'

'I think there's a straightforward explanation to that — the church. Many of the witness statements came from people who attended the same ministry. Even Hartwell told us Maxwell was big into religion. Being gay and being in the church don't mix well.'

'It could have been a homophobic motivated killing,' Malice offered.

'Maybe someone saw them together and took offense.'

'I know that's a possibility but my gut feel says 'no'.'

'And what does your gut feel tell you?'

'That we're missing something.'

'We're missing a ton of shit,' she said.

'No I mean, there's something we've overlooked.'

'Like what?'

Malice marched over to the board which was fast running out of space. He touched each photograph hoping they would give him inspiration.

'I don't bloody know. But I think this was not a spur of the moment killing. Someone set out to do them harm.'

Pietersen rifled through a mound of paperwork and came out with a buff coloured file. She flipped open the cover.

'It says here that Maxwell was done for speeding in 2005 and other than that, he's got a clean sheet. Horton is also clean apart from that altercation he had in the pub in 2003.'

'Have you found out anything more about that?'

'The records are sketchy.' She fanned the papers out on the desk. 'Apparently, he had an argument with a woman and she glassed him, causing him to have ten stitches in his face. The case went to court and she got a suspended sentence.'

'What was the argument about?'

'It doesn't mention it here. These are the summary notes, but it does say that the woman in question was Horton's girlfriend at the time.'

'Fuck me. He doesn't have a lot of success with women, no wonder he's—'

'Mally, that's not nice.'

'Just saying. First a woman glasses him, then he marries Wendy who—'

'Mally! Pack it in.'

'Okay, okay. Is it worth following up?'

'It was twenty-six years ago, but it's the only thing we have to go on.'

'Who's the woman?'

'Hang on.' Pietersen typed away, accessing the records. 'Now that's interesting.'

'What?'

'Her name is Brenda Copeland and she lives twelve miles away from where we're sitting.'

'What's interesting is, she lives eight miles from where the bodies were buried. Definitely worth a visit.' Malice picked up his jacket. Pietersen did the same and they walked out of the office together.

'Am I really like your dad?' he asked.
'No, you're bloody worse.'
'How come?'
'You're here, he's not.'
Normal service had been resumed.

Pietersen pushed her key in the lock and nudged open the door to her flat. She dumped her bag in the hallway and walked through to the kitchen carrying a plastic bag containing two cartons of oriental loveliness.

She broke out a bowl and a fork and went into the lounge. Then she peeled away the lids and the aroma of sweet and sour pork and egg fried rice filled the room. She switched on the TV to watch the ten o'clock news — it had been a long shift. The first forkful didn't touch the sides as she gobbled it down. The second one followed in quick succession, obviously arguing the toss with Malice all day was hungry business.

She was annoyed with herself because she knew deep down he had a point. The problem was the know-it-all way he was behaving — just like her bloody father! The man who'd convinced her that following a career in fine art was a waste of her talents and her career path lay in doing a law conversion course. When she had enrolled he was delighted, though, he was much less impressed when ten weeks later she jacked it in and joined the police.

Malice's heart was in the right place but she vowed all those years ago that she would never put herself in that position again. She wasn't a damsel in distress waiting for a man to rescue her. She got herself into this mess and would damned well get herself out of it.

Her phone pinged. It was a text from Malice.

Sorry if I went too far today, I just wanted to help.

There was a staccato rapping on the door.

'Very funny …' she muttered under her breath. 'Turning up with a 'sorry I was a knob' bottle of Chardonnay is one thing, but if he thinks he's sharing my Chinese, he's got another thing coming.'

She drifted down the hall, still clutching her fork and opened the front door.

'Hello, Kelly.' It was Bradley Craven.

Chapter 24

Pietersen slammed her weight behind the door but Craven was too fast, too strong. His left boot crunched into the bottom holding it firm. He shouldered his way in, shoving her down the hallway. She stumbled against the wall.

Craven banged the door shut and stepped past her into the lounge where he scanned the room. He picked up her phone from the table and slipped it into his pocket.

Pietersen leapt to her feet and flew at him, her arms outstretched. He sidestepped and held his hands aloft.

'Wow! I'm here to talk, that's all,' he yelled.

She spun around and was about to charge again. 'Get out of my flat!'

'That's no way to welcome an ex-colleague. I want to talk. If I was here to do you harm I wouldn't have said 'Hello'.'

Pietersen held her ground.

'Get out,' she snarled through gritted teeth.

'I'm gonna sit here.' Craven motioned to the sofa. 'Stop going all *Rambo* on me and put that bloody fork down. Cos if you're thinking of stabbing me with it, you and I are going to have a rumble and I'll end up with your blood all over my new shirt. My wife will do her nut. She bought this for me. Now... calm the fuck down.'

He flopped down on the sofa and ran his hand along the cool leather. He mouthed the word 'Nice.'

'What do you want?' she asked, edging her way towards the kitchen.

'That's better. I want to chat, that's all.'

'About what?'

'Jimmy and Will send their best regards.'

'Piss off, Brad.' Pietersen was eyeing him with her back to the wall, still holding on to the fork.

'There you go again. That's not polite, Kelly.'

'I'll ask you one more time. What do you want?'

'I came to put you in the picture, because things have moved on since you stitched us up.'

'I did not plant that money.'

'Sure you did, Kelly.'

'Were my fingerprints found on any of the notes?'

'No but then you were part of the team who raided the shop. So, you'd be wearing gloves. And you were wearing gloves when you planted the cash in my house, and in Will's house and in Jimmy's gaff.'

'I was the UC person on the ground. I had a roaming brief across the operation.'

'That's true, but you *roamed* into my place with a pocket full of marked notes and hid them under my sink.'

'That's bollocks.'

'No, I tell you what's bollocks — I would never hide anything under the sink. You're not married, are you?'

'What the hell has that got to do with anything,' she shrugged.

'I wouldn't hide money under the sink because that's where my missus keeps her cleaning gear, and she is a devil for keeping the house spick and span. Like a show home, it is. So, I would never have hidden the roll of notes there because my wife could have found them and fucking spent it.'

'She sounds like a smart woman.'

'Oh, she's smart alright. She already has a stack of brand-new shoes hidden at the back of the wardrobe which she thinks I don't know about. She's simply waiting for the right moment to bring them out with the words 'this old pair' and afterwards she'll tell the women down the gym what an idiot of a husband she's married to. And they'll all have a bloody good laugh at my expense.'

'Have you come here for marriage guidance?'

'No. I'm trying to make the point. I notice things. And I know I didn't bring that cash into my house and if I did, I wouldn't hide it under the sink.'

'You're a lying bastard.' She took half a step to the side.

'Why would I do that? Do you have the place bugged? Are you recording our conversation?' He shook his head. 'I didn't think so. What would be the point of me telling porkies?'

'You can't help yourself.'

'I tell you what I can't help... I can't help thinking that you thought the case was in danger of collapsing so you gave it a little nudge in the right direction. Your prints weren't found on the notes and neither was mine, nor Will's, nor Jimmy's. You planted that money — you know it and I know it.'

'Get out, Brad. I don't know why the hell you're here.'

She bolted into the kitchen and seized the chef's knife from the block. Then she darted back in the lounge brandishing it in the air.

'Oh, for fuck's sake. Put it down,' Craven said, stifling a laugh.

'You come at me again and I swear to God I'll slit you wide open.'

'You've been watching too many films.'

'Try me,' she growled.

'Don't be so dramatic.' He stroked his chin and plumped up one of her cushions which was laying on the sofa. 'Sorry, all this talk about my missus and her shoes, I clean forgot. I came to tell you that we've not decided what we're going to do with you.' He leaned forwards, picked up the carton of sweet and sour, delved his fingers into the food and put a pork ball into his mouth. 'Man, that is lovely,' he said speaking with his mouth full. He pulled another out. 'Did you get this from the takeaway on the corner? No, wait, of course you did I watched you buy it.'

'You were always a bent copper.' She shifted her weight from one foot to another, ready to dart in either direction should the situation turn bad.

'Takes one to know one. Anyway I got sidetracked.' He put the carton back on the table. 'Oh, yes, we haven't decided what to do with you. Now me, I've always been a bit of a hot-head and I want to string you up by your tits and batter you with a pickaxe handle, while Jimmy wants to take a more-subtle approach and ensure your new team mates know all about what you did. You know what coppers are like if they think they can't trust you. And Will — you know what Will's like — can't make a decision so long as he's got a hole in his arse. He prefers a bit of mix and match, bit of battering, bit of bubbling. And between the three of us we are in a right muddle as to what to do. So, I thought it was only right to bring you up to speed with our thoughts.'

'Fuck off, Craven.' She flipped the blade in the direction of the door.

'On the other hand, we could torch your car or wreck your flat. The options are endless. We sit in the pub wracking our brains trying to work out what's best to do. Or, from what I've seen, we could beat the living daylights out of your black boyfriend who you seem to enjoy spending so much time with. You make a lovely couple.'

'Leave him out of this,' Pietersen sneered.

'We might, we might not. As I say it's driving us bananas. There are so many fun things to do.'

'You've said your piece, now fuck off.'

Craven jumped up from the sofa. Pietersen thrust the knife out front. He let out a laugh then leaned over and plucked another pork ball from the carton.

'These are top-bollock,' he said, shoving it into his mouth and sucking on his fingers as he walked into the hall. He reached into his pocket and brought out her phone, then held it up for her to take. His sticky fingers leaving a smudge on the screen. She didn't move. He let it slip through his fingers onto the floor. It landed with a clatter.

'Don't come here again,' Pietersen hissed.

'Can't promise that. What I can promise is you might see me around for the next few days. Me and the guys chat about you all the time and when we decide what to do you'll be the first to know. I promise.'

Craven opened the front door.

'If I see you again, I'll—' she waved the blade at him.

'Yeah, whatever. By the way, I'd pass on the rest of that takeaway if I was you. I took a piss in the pub across the road before I got here and forgot to wash my hands.'

Chapter 25

Malice was standing in his kitchen, his head racing with the revelations of the day. He opened the fridge and twisted the cap off the bottle, guzzling it down to the label. Then he meandered into the lounge and switched on the TV.

'Alexa, turn the lights on,' he called out. The blue ring spun around on the device.

'I'm not sure what went wrong,' came the synthetic response.

For fu…

'I should call you Samantha Waite, not Alexa,' he said to his disobedient new purchase. 'She doesn't fucking listen either.'

'Sorry, I don't know that one,' the device replied.

'No, I bet you don't.'

There was a loud rap on the front door. Malice opened up to find Hayley standing outside.

On second thoughts, I could call her…

He snapped out of his musings. Two visits in quick succession was a clear signal that all was not well.

'Can I come in?' she said. The look on her face confirmed his fears.

He ran through his latest list of transgressions in his head: he'd turned up a day early to pick up Amy and had arrived late for her birthday tea, and of course there was the damned bike. Which, to be honest, was an issue he still couldn't fathom. He'd received the customary bollocking for each offence, so in that regard everything was in order.

Hayley brushed past not waiting for an answer… it would appear things were anything but in order.

'Umm, yeah,' Malice said following her into the lounge. She picked up the remote and switched off the TV.

'How's your day been?' she asked, folding her arms across her chest.

'Busy.'

'I've been ringing you.'

'Oh, yes… sorry, we've been full-on today. Why don't you sit down?' He mentally kicked himself for not returning her calls or listening to the voicemails. He dropped onto the sofa and motioned for her to join him.

'I'm fine. For what I have to say, I'll stand.' She tapped the toe of her right foot on the carpet. 'Three times I tried to get hold of you and you didn't ring back once.'

'As I said we've been—'

'I got called into school today.'

'Is Amy okay?'

'Oh, you're interested now.'

'What was the problem?'

'It's that bloody bike.'

Malice glanced across to where the smart watch was sitting on the window sill. He crossed the room and pulled the curtains shut.

'Look, about the bike, I said I was sorry—' He held his hands out.

'Some lad stole it,' Hayley interrupted.

'Shit. How did that happen?'

'She took it to school as part of cycling proficiency week and he nicked it.'

'Who the hell did that?' he said, perching himself on the arm of the settee.

'His name is Tristram Hester, apparently he's a right handful. He comes from a family of Travellers and has only been in the school a couple of months. Amy initially reported that the bike had simply gone missing. Then when one of the teachers investigated, it turned out she was riding it in the school yard and this lad told her to get off and walked the damned thing out of the front gates, brazen as you like.'

'Why didn't she say that in the first place?'

'He's got a reputation for being a bit of a bully.' The toe of her shoe was now tapping away like mad.

'What did the school say?' Malice took a well-needed swig from the bottle.

'They've washed their hands of it. When I challenged them, they said that it wasn't clear the theft took place on school property.'

'What does Amy say?'

'She says it most certainly did.' Hayley relented and slumped down into the armchair. She rubbed her hand against the material and held it up to her face, then wrinkled her nose.

'Is she alright?' Malice asked, cradling what was left of his beer.

'She's upset, as you can imagine. And now she doesn't want to go back to school because she's afraid of what this lad will do. He's older than her and has a track record of doing whatever he wants, the teachers can't control him.' Hayley couldn't get her words out fast enough.

'We should report it to the police, get a crime number.' Malice went to get his phone. Hayley stopped him by snatching it off the table.

'That's the very thing Amy doesn't want to happen. She's afraid that will make matters worse.'

'Stuff that, the boy needs to be taught a lesson.'

'That's your answer to everything, isn't it? Let's teach someone a lesson.'

'It's the right thing to do. He can't go around stealing people's belongings and think he can get away with it. Plus, the school has to shoulder their responsibility—'

'Yes, thanks for stating the bloody obvious! If you'd been there you could have made that point yourself, instead of leaving it to me to juggle everything. The Head was adamant, it was not the school's problem.'

'What does this boy want with a girl's bike?'

'Amy says he's got a younger sister, who's just as bad as him. She thinks he nicked it for her.'

'The school can't simply walk away from this.' Malice got to his feet and motioned for her to hand over the phone. She ignored him.

'I reckon they're running scared confronting this boy and upsetting this family. If you hadn't have bought her that bloody bike…' She put her head in her hands.

'Hang on, this isn't my fault.' Malice pointed his own finger at his chest.

'Looks like it from where I'm standing and as usual I'm the one left picking up the pieces.'

'Come on, Hayley, that's not fair.'

'I'll tell you what's not fair. Making me look like a terrible mother when I tell Amy she can't have a new bike; having to explain to the school why I'm the only parent who's turned up when they called and then to have you spout the bloody obvious, like I hadn't thought of it.'

'The best thing to do is report it to the police, this kid might have a history of theft and—'

'Why don't you listen, Amy is shit-scared of this getting out of hand. She has to go to school and face these children every day and the last thing she needs is having to spend her time looking over her shoulder.'

'Then what do you want me to do?'

'How about fucking being there when we need you?' Hayley jumped to her feet.

'I told you, I was up to my eyes in it today.'

'Yeah, and I was up to my eyes placating our daughter, fighting with the school and all the while trying to ensure all the wheels don't fall off.'

'I'm sorry.'

'I don't know why I came here.' She slapped her hands to her sides and stormed into the hallway. Malice followed.

'Then why did you?' he asked.

'Do you know what Mally? I don't fucking know. Maybe I had this crazy notion that sharing parental responsibilities with you would make life easier.'

'I'll sort it out.'

'By doing your usual and making the situation a whole heap worse?'

'I get it that Amy doesn't want to make a fuss but the school–'

'The school... nothing. They don't want to know.'

'I'll think of something.'

'Yeah, whatever.' She tossed the mobile in his direction and he caught it. 'Pick up the damned phone the next time I call. Try that for starters.'

Hayley let herself out slamming the door behind her.

'I'll sort it,' Malice mumbled to himself. Not having the first idea how.

Chapter 26

Pietersen jumped when the 6 a.m. news blared from her radio, shattering her train of thought. The headline announcement was of a terrorist attack somewhere in Europe but the details of the incident passed her by. She wasn't listening. Her head was a mess.

Before retiring to bed she'd convinced herself that she would put the visit from Craven behind her and wake the next morning cool, calm and collected. Then she'd then spent the next seven hours whipping herself up into a sleep deprived frenzy.

Fucking Craven.

She bounded out of bed and into the shower. She knew what the visit was all about. It was designed to destabilise her, get her off balance, cloud her thinking. And for all her resolve to not let that happen, it was a battle she was losing.

She finished showering, got dressed, downed a cup of strong coffee and dashed off to work. This was not going to rattle her.

She was going to sort it out.

Malice flicked the stalk on the steering column to clear the morning drizzle from the windscreen. He was also struggling to keep his mind focussed.

That bloody bike.

After the visit from Hayley, he'd drained his fridge of beer while racking his brains trying to figure out what to do. The problem was his course of action should have been clear — drive to wherever this Hester boy lived and take the bike back. But if Hayley was right then Amy was in the firing line and he couldn't risk putting his daughter in that position.

He cleared the windscreen again of drizzle, then stepped on the accelerator. He'd received a call, less than an hour ago that had catapulted him out of bed and into the shower. Bradley Craven's car had been spotted parked in a Premier Inn car park on the outskirts of town. His late-night calls to his friends in traffic had come up trumps.

In many ways Craven, and the damned bike, posed the same type of problem.

Because both dilemmas should have been ended in seconds; both confronted and wrongs put right. But the reason he didn't confront Craven and break his arms and legs was because of another woman in his life. Kelly Pietersen.

She'd made her views clear. She'd been as concise as she could be: 'Back off, I'll sort it.'

He swung the car into a vacant parking slot and the wipers made another pass, bringing the blue Mondeo into view. Malice killed the engine and stepped out into the fine mist. The woman on reception, Florence, looked startled at the sight of an early morning guest. She was engrossed in the contents of her phone while sitting behind a forest of Perspex covered advertisements showing the latest deals. He flashed his warrant card and her eyes widened.

'Morning,' he said.

'Morning,' she straightened herself in her seat and hid her phone. Her voice betrayed a French accent.

'There's a vehicle in your car park that may have been involved in an incident,' Malice reeled off the make and registration number. 'Can you tell me how long the guest is planning to stay with you?'

'Umm... sure. If you give me a minute.' Florence leapt into action and tapped away at her keyboard. 'What kind of incident?'

'I'm not at liberty to say.' He looked around. The big glossy sign on the wall which showcased the delights of the breakfast being served next door made his stomach rumble.

'It belongs to—'

'I know who owns the vehicle. Can you tell me how long he's booked in for?'

'Till the end of the week, but he can check out at any time before then. If he gives us enough notice he won't have to pay for the remaining days.'

'Thank you.' Malice went to leave.

'He's in room 514,' she over-declared.

'I would appreciate it if you didn't mention my visit to Mr Craven,' he tapped the side of his nose and winked.

'Of course. In my job you have to be discreet.'

'I can believe that. Have a good day.'

Malice returned to his car when every muscle in his body wanted to charge down the door to room 514 and stamp his boot on Craven's neck. But he knew that wasn't the answer. If what Pietersen said was true, then he would only come back with his friends and Malice would have a war on his hands — and he didn't want another one so shortly after the last. Anyway, if it turned into a bloodbath and Craven didn't kill him — Hayley would.

He needed a strategy whereby the bent bastard wouldn't want to come within fifty miles of this place.

Malice shoved the key in the ignition and the engine roared again. He powered his way onto the ring road heading for the station. Then changed his mind. The tyres screeched as he spun a U-turn in the road and headed for the school.

Unusually for him, Malice had chosen to use the correct protocol. He'd stopped off at a greasy-spoon Café to resolve the issue of his empty stomach before making two phone calls. One to Pietersen saying he was going to be in late and the other was to arrange an urgent meeting with the Head, John Carlton.

When he'd arrived at the school, the secretary had ushered him into Carlton's office where he could wait until the Head had finished doing his rounds. Which meant he had time on his hands to think through his approach. He needed to get this right. The last thing he wanted was another ear-bashing from Hayley.

Unfortunately, all he could think about was the prize-giving evening when the two had first met. Carlton had been all slashed back hair and chiseled jawline, wearing a sharp suit. A real young go-getter who was no doubt a hit with the female members of staff and the yummy-mummies.

Malice was jolted from his thoughts when Carlton strolled in the room. The two men shook hands and the same thought burst into Malice's head as the evening of the prize giving.

What a dick.

'Please take a seat. I believe you want to see me about Amy?' Carlton said.

'More specifically I wanted to talk to you about the theft of her bicycle.'

'Ah, yes, a most unfortunate incident.' Carlton settled into his oversized chair behind his oversized desk. He was safer there.

'Only if you consider being the victim of a crime as… unfortunate.'

'As I said to your wife, the incident took place away from the school. So, it isn't something we would take further.'

'But it took place in the school yard when Tristram Hester told Amy to get off her bike and waltzed it out the front gates.'

'We've spoken to Tristram and he denies taking the bike. He said he saw another person take it from Amy on the road outside the gates. It's his word against hers and we have to be sensitive to the circumstances.'

'What circumstances?' asked Malice, already feeling this was a bad idea. 'I don't understand why—'

The phone rang.

'I'm sorry, do you mind?' Carlton didn't wait for a reply and lifted the receiver.

'Sure. Go ahead.' Malice said anyway. He gazed around the office at the dark wood cabinets crammed full of books and trinkets. The photographs and certificates adorning the walls all had a common theme — they were all about John Carlton. They either crowed about his academic excellence or shouted about his achievements.

Even in the pictures depicting him with the children, he was front and centre, soaking up the limelight. There was a whiteboard secured to the wall behind the desk. It was in pristine condition and looked like it had just been taken out of the shrink-wrap.

Malice snapped himself back to the matter in hand when he heard the phone go down.

'Sorry about that,' Carlton said. 'As I was saying; Tristram comes from a troubled background and the other children see him as an easy target. The fact that he's been in trouble before encourages others to single him out and blame him when things go wrong.'

'Are you telling me Amy's lying?'

'No, no, Mr Malice. I would never suggest that. All I'm saying is that in this case we have two conflicting accounts and have to be sensitive to both parties.'

'And you're being sensitive towards Amy by discounting her version of events in preference to a lad with a history of causing trouble.'

'I would not characterise it as that.' Carlton placed both hands flat on the desk and pushed himself back in his chair.

'Then how would you characterise it, Mr Carlton?' Malice leaned forward.

'We have a duty of care to all pupils in our school and have to be seen to be even-handed with situations such as this.'

'How is it even-handed when my daughter gets her bike stolen on school premises and you chose to not to believe her?'

'Things are seldom that black and white.'

'They are in this case.'

'I appreciate you want to take your daughters side, but I have to remain impartial.'

'By impartial do you mean running scared?'

'I don't understand.'

'From what I've heard, this lad has a reputation for causing trouble and you're not getting to grips with him. Are you afraid of the backlash from the family?'

'I'm not afraid of anything, Mr Malice. And I will not engage in a conversation about the conduct of another child.'

'This is going around in circles. I want a meeting with this Hester boy and the Chair of governors.'

'That won't be possible. I've briefed the Chair on the salient points so she is fully aware and happy for me to deal with it. Plus, it would be wholly inappropriate for you to challenge another pupil in the school.'

'But I'm not happy for you to deal with it. I want a sit-down with the Hester family to thrash this out.'

'That won't happen Mr Malice. It's not for the school to play the role of negotiator between sets of parents who happen to disagree with each other.'

'I don't believe this.'

'Sorry, Mr Malice, but it isn't a matter where we can get involved. If you are still unhappy may I suggest you go to the police and report the theft. You are a police officer, I believe?'

'Amy is scared that if we escalate this Tristram Hester will make her life a misery. He's a bully, you must know that, right?'

'I cannot comment on pupils in our school. May I suggest–'

'No you may not, Mr Carlton, it's pretty clear where you stand on the subject,' Malice got up, straightened his jacket and put his hand on the door handle.

'I'm sorry, I couldn't have been of more help,' Carlton stood up and offered his hand. Malice left him hanging. 'I hope this discussion hasn't coloured your view of me or the school.'

'Not at all, it's only served to reinforce my opinion,' Malice opened the door.

'I'm pleased that's the case.'

'You're a dick.'

Chapter 27

I lie in bed staring up at the ceiling. The house is quiet and the sun is dappling the walls with flecks of orange as it breaks through the curtains. It's going to be another busy day without my lover around to help take the strain. I miss Clem and I'm worried his condition is not improving. The words 'stable' and 'no change' are beginning to grate on me.

I glance at my phone to see the message from Frank that came through in the early hours.

Found a bird's nest. Settling in nicely.

I run through my to-do list in my head. My peace is shattered by the sound of Dennis coughing and grunting, he's calling for the hawk-faced piece of shit to help. I know he can't be asking for me because he's learned I don't show.

I get up, throw some clothes on and clean my teeth, anything else I need to do can wait. I go downstairs, fasten the scarf around my neck and head out the door; leaving the guttural sounds of my mill-stone of a husband behind me.

The drive to Winfield passes quickly due to the roads being clear of the morning commuter traffic. The McDonald's coffee hits the spot and gives me a well-needed caffeine boost. The block of flats is straight ahead and I park my car against the railings beneath a sign that reads Claremont Towers. A heady community of five skyrise buildings which probably looked dodgy when they first went up in the seventies.

Flat No. 628 is situated in the third block from the right on the sixth floor. The lift is out of action so I slog my way up the concrete staircase that separates two of the towers. Each of the stairwells are occupied by a person sleeping on cardboard and shrouded in blankets.

I come to level six and trek around the exterior of the building. From the outside it looks like the flats fall into two categories; ones that look like the occupants take pride in their homes while the others prefer to live in a shit-tip. Thankfully No. 628 appears to belong in the former category.

I knock on the glass panel in the door and Frank opens up.

How wrong can I be?

The whiff of stale cigarette smoke and fast food hits the back of my throat as I step across the threshold. He's rubbing his eyes and looks like I've woken him up.

'Morning, Frank,' I give him a hug. He needs a shower.

'Morning, Twink, come in.'

I pick my way down the passageway trying to avoid the burger wrappers and beer cans. A bedroom and a bathroom are off to my left and the living room is at the end. The lounge is a fair-sized room with a dining table and four chairs crammed into one corner and a dark-brown three-piece suite that looks like it's just been reclaimed from a skip. An oversized TV hangs flat on the far wall and there's a small kitchen leading off to one side. I have no idea what colour the carpet is because I can't see it buried beneath the clothes and debris strewn about.

On a low coffee table there are tin foil wraps, lighters and a spoon, plus an array of small silver canisters that once contained Hippy Crack. Jez is curled up on the sofa, fully clothed and fast asleep.

'Okay, Frank, talk me through what we have.' We both choose to remain standing.

'The place belongs to a bloke called Precious. He rents it off the council and has been here about four years. He used to live with his girlfriend but she buggered off, sending him off the rails.'

'Is this him?' I point to a second man crumpled in the chair. His jogging bottoms have slid down to reveal more than I want to see of his tatty underwear.

'No, don't know who he is. He showed up last night. I could have got rid of him but didn't want to draw attention to ourselves.'

'Where's Precious?' I ask, looking around.

'In the bedroom.'

'What did he say to the deal?'

'He was like a dog with two dicks when he realised he'd be getting his shit for free. I'm not really sure if anything else sunk in after that.'

'The cover is good, but the place is not. If the coppers pay this flat a visit it screams drug-den. I want you to get Sherbet and a couple of the lads over here to clean this place from top to bottom and get rid of any drug paraphernalia you find. Tell them to go easy, there may be hidden needles. If Precious wants to shoot-up he can't do it here. This is for supply and distribution only — that understood?'

'Sure thing, Twink.'

'And the place is off-limits to his mates. They need to find another place to crash.'

'I can fix that.' Frank smacks his hand against the side of the armchair and the man doesn't stir.

'How was Jez last night?' I ask, peering into the kitchen. A mound of foil takeaway containers covers the worktops and the sink is filled with dirty plates and cups. Plastic bags and bottles litter the floor. I look away, feeling nauseous.

'He kinda flips between being really excited about what he calls his 'new beginning' and looking like he's about to piss his pants and do a runner.'

'Is he a user?'

'I think so. Though he didn't do any gear last night. He knows his stuff though…'

Frank walks over to the TV stand and comes back with several A4 sized sheets of paper on which are street maps of the surrounding area. 'We did this at the library. He's marked the trading hot-spots. There's a lot to go at.'

'Nice one. Find out more about Precious to make sure we don't get a problem further down the line. Is there anything else you need from me?'

'Nope. I know what to do.'

'I spoke to the vicar in charge of the local church and we are all systems go. His name is Bertram and he presides over St. Juniper's church. I said you would pop along and introduce yourself.' I hand Frank a Post-It note with the details. 'I need to confirm the arrangements with

Collins when I see him this morning but I'm not expecting any issues.'

'Okay.' Frank takes the note, scrunches it up and puts it in his pocket.

'You've done good Frank.' I hold my arms outstretched and he bear hugs me. I feel my feet lifting off the floor. 'Call me later today.'

'How's Clem?'

'There's no change, I'm afraid. When we get set up here you and me will go visit him one evening.'

'I'd like that.'

'Talk later.' I reach onto my tip-toes and kiss him on the cheek. His stubble irritates my skin. 'Oh, and one more thing. Don't eat or drink anything that comes out of that kitchen. I don't want you winding up in hospital as well.'

I arrive at the church to find the front doors wide open. Looks like Ketchup has had an early start as well. Despite him being a complete waste of space, I always find it best to keep him on-side, however much it sticks in my craw. And no doubt, I will choke on my words again this morning.

I want to tell him about my conversation with Bertram and ask his permission to 'borrow' a few of the boys in order to get their OutReach programme off the ground. I don't have to ask him, I'm simply playing the game. With my business head I realise it's a move that will leave us stretched until we back-fill with fresh talent at their end, but it's worth it in the long run.

I walk up the steps and elbow open the inner door. I can see Ketchup in the coffee shop with a couple of people. His head flicks up and he waves at me. I wave back. There's no point talking to him when he has company. I need him on his own.

He beckons me over.

What now?

I walk past the line of pews to join them.

'Twinkle, I'm glad you've shown up. These people have come to see you,' Ketchup says. 'You must excuse me I have to dash.'

He gives his apologies and hurries away.

The man and woman both reach into their pockets.

'Hi, are you Brenda Copeland?'

Chapter 28

The guy takes out his warrant card and the woman standing next to him does the same. I read the information on the cards. Then I look up. It's more difficult to read their faces.

What the fuck is this about?

'DS Malice and Detective Constable Pietersen,' she announces. 'Do you mind if we ask you a few questions? We called at your house and a woman told us we might find you here.'

It takes a few seconds for my head to click into gear.

'Ah, that will be Rebecca,' I eventually recover. 'She cares for my husband when I'm not there. She's a godsend, I don't know where I'd be without her. How can I help? Please take a seat.'

My head is running amok. I motion at the tables and chairs in the café.

This must be about Clem.

'I'm afraid I can't offer you a hot drink because we've not opened up,' I say, trying to control the thumping in my chest.

Maybe they've picked up Frank? No that's stupid, I've only just left him.

'That's no problem, Brenda. We won't take up much of your time,' the guy says, squeezing his large frame into one of the chairs. His partner takes a seat opposite and opens her notebook.

Perhaps that fucking Jez has run to the nearest cop-shop...

'What is this about?' I ask.

'Do you know a man by the name of John Horton?' she asks.

Bloody hell...

'My word, that's a name from the past.' I look at each of them in turn. They're giving nothing away. 'If it's the same guy, then, yes I knew him. Got to be over twenty years ago.'

'Were you in a relationship with him?' he asks.

'Yes, you could call it that.' The banging in my chest is getting worse. I gulp down a wave of panic. 'We were going out together and we split up in 1991, maybe '92. It was a long time ago.'

Where the fuck is this going?

'Did you know he went missing ten years ago?' she asks, writing in her book.

'No, I didn't.

'You had an argument with him in a pub which turned physical. Can you tell us what happened?'

'I remember now. It was 1993, John and I used to go to a pub in town. It played all the best music of the time — Whitney Houston, UB 40 — they were great songs.

We'd been going steady for a while but I had my suspicions he was playing around. I remember I confronted him about it and we had a massive argument.'

I run my fingers through my hair and tuck it behind my ears. It gives me something to do with my hands.

That's better. I'm getting into my stride.

'You thought he was seeing someone else behind your back?' she says.

I was hoping she'd hook herself into that one.

'Yeah, you know how it is. Anyway, I challenged him and it all kicked off.'

'What took place that evening?' he says, it must be his turn to join in. I avoid making eye contact.

'We'd been drinking in the pub and were having a row. Now, either he slipped from his bar stool or he lunged at me, I couldn't tell. But next thing I know he'd shoved me off my stool and we both fell on the floor.'

'The police records say you assaulted him with a broken glass,' he adds.

'I had a pint in my hand and it must have shattered against the bar when we fell. He landed on top of me and the glass went into his face. I would never have done that on purpose, I'm not that type of person.'

'So, you're telling us it was an accident?' He's persistent.

'Yes, like I told the police at the time but they wouldn't listen. The case went to court and I was convicted and given a suspended sentence. I suppose that's on my record?'

'It is, but we wanted to hear it from you.'

'That was twenty-six years ago?' I say in my best incredulous voice.

'When was the last time you saw John?' she says.

'In court, that day.'
'You never saw him again?'
'Nope. Can you tell me what this is about?' I ask.
I need to know more ...
'Did John ever mention a man by the name of Tim Maxwell?' he replies, his eyes boring into my face.
Oh, fuck ...
'No never heard of him.' I reply, clasping my hands in my lap to stop them fidgeting.
'You say John disappeared ten years ago, what happened to him?'
'That's what we're trying to determine,' she says.
'And you think that because him and me had an argument twenty-six years ago, I might have had something to do with it?'
'We need to follow up every lead, Brenda.'
'Doesn't sound like you've got much to go on if you're talking to me.'
'We have to rule everything out.' The woman closes her notebook and glances across at her partner. There's a pause in the conversation.
'Well, I'm sorry I can't be of more help.' I get up from the table, eager to bring this to an end. 'I've not seen or heard from John since then. I guess he was embarrassed because he knew things didn't happen the way he said.'
'How do you mean?' She's not taking the hint.
'He told a pack of lies to the police and then repeated them in court. There was no going back after that.'
'You split up.'
'Yeah, or more to the point, he went AWOL. I still had some of his stuff for ages, you know — CDs, DVDs, things like that. I was expecting him to get in touch to pick

them up but he didn't. In the end I sold them in a car-boot sale.'

She puts her pen in her top pocket. He's staring at me, chewing his bottom lip.

'Thank you for your time,' she says, standing up. Her partner gets to his feet, still biting his lip.

'If there is anything else, please come and find me. I'm only too happy to help,' I say.

I follow them to the door and watch them walk to their car.

Shit...

Chapter 29

The dilemma of what to do about Craven was still occupying Malice's thoughts as he pulled into the car park outside the church. When they had arrived back at the office, him and Pietersen had agreed to divvy-up their growing to-do list. She'd been keen to follow up with the mortuary and dig around for more information, while Malice had a burning desire to poke around at the church, to see if he could find out more about Copeland. There was just something about her that didn't ring true.

'We've only just left there.' Pietersen had challenged him when he said he wanted to go back.

'I know, but I got a feeling. I can't put my finger on it,' he'd replied.

Normally such a response would have elicited peals of derision and protest, but not today. Pietersen appeared pre-occupied and distant and all he got in return was an 'Oh, okay'.

His stomach rumbled. The effect of the greasy-spoon had worn off and it was past lunchtime.

Malice skipped up the steps leading up to the front doors. The vicar was chatting to a group of people who were on their way out.

'Oh, hi,' he said when he clapped eyes on Malice. 'Sorry I had to run off earlier. I had a meeting with a young couple wanting to talk about a christening.'

'I didn't get a chance to introduce myself properly. I'm DS Malice.'

'Peter Collins. I'm the vicar here.' He came over and offered his hand. 'I'm afraid if you've come to see Twinkle she left shortly after you.'

'Twinkle?'

'Brenda. Everyone knows her as Twinkle.'

'As in …?'

'Twinkle, twinkle little star, yes that's right. And she is a star, I can tell you.'

'Is she a key member of your congregation?' Malice said.

'That's an understatement.' He began walking down the central aisle and motioned for Malice to join him. 'That woman is a marvel. You should ask your Assistant Chief Constable, Alex Beresford — he knows all about her and the fabulous work she does here.'

'I didn't know he was a church member.'

'Oh yes, he's been coming here years. He works closely with Twinkle on the OutReach programme. They take vulnerable young men under their wing and steer them away from drugs and gangs. The results are excellent.'

'I never knew.' Malice shrugged his shoulders.

'Well, you learn something every day.'

'Is the programme run out of here?'

'We host the meetings and help organise events. Twinkle has turned her mum's old house into a hostel where these young men have a safe place to stay and turn themselves around. It's a selfless act of pure kindness.'

'Have you been here long?'

Collins stopped and struck one of his theatrical thinking poses. Malice squinted as he was left waiting for a response. It wasn't a tough question.

'A little over six years.' He waved his finger in the air. 'My predecessor was George Ailing who retired from the ministry.'

'Have you ever heard Twinkle talk about men called John Horton or Timothy Maxwell?'

'No never. Can you tell me what this is about?' Collins went to walk on but Malice stayed put.

'We're following up a lead on a case. It's early days and we thought Twinkle might have known these men.'

'If I'm honest, DS Malice, I feel a little uncomfortable answering questions when Twinkle isn't here.'

'That's fine, I don't wish to make you feel awkward in any way. It's purely routine, that's all. Do you mind if I look around?'

'Not at all. If you want access to any of the locked rooms marked Private please come and find me.'

'I will do, thank you.' Malice watched Collins scuttle away and sauntered over to the café where he found a woman standing behind the counter stacking cups and saucers. A home-made sticker on her top read Malissa. 'Americano, black, please,' he said.

'Certainly,' she replied. 'I saw you here earlier speaking with Twinkle. I hope every thing's okay?'

'Everything's fine.'

'Only I was worried it was something to do with Dennis, what with him being so ill and all. I mean he's been so poorly for such a long time you have to worry that it's just a matter of time. How she does her charity work and runs OutReach with all that going on at home is beyond me — I'd be a wreck if it was me.'

'Have you known her long?' said Malice.

'More years than I care to remember,' she said, placing a warmed cup under the dispenser. 'She is nothing short of a saint that woman.'

'Did you know her before Dennis fell ill?' Malice pulled his wallet from his back pocket and fanned his thumb through the notes and receipts.

'To be honest, I can't remember when that was. It's been such a long time.' She scooped a saucer from the pile and placed the finished drink in front of Malice. 'That's one pound eighty please.'

'Must be the cheapest coffee is town.'

'And the best.'

'Keep the change,' he said, passing over a five-pound note.

'Thank you.'

'Put it to a good cause.'

'We always do.'

A man turned up next to Malice, pushing a brightly-coloured canvass shopping bag on wheels. Malissa moved along to serve him, leaving Malice with his coffee and his thoughts.

He heard the sound of chatter as a man and woman walked in to the church carrying their shopping and turned to see them make their way up to a bank of tea lights, sitting in rows on a black metal stand. The man picked a taper from a bowl, lit the end of it and transferred the flame to the wick on one of the candles. Then he handed it to his wife who lit a second.

The man opened a large book which was lying on a table next to the display. He picked up a pen and wrote a message. Malice sipped his coffee and watched the couple cross themselves, pick up their bags and leave. He wandered over, still clutching his drink. In the book the man had scrawled:

Jessy and Paul, always in our thoughts.

Malice picked it up and turned it over to reveal the front cover. Written on it was: 2019. He gulped down what was left of his coffee and hurried off to find Collins who was talking to a woman with a trolley laden with freshly cut flowers.

'Mr Collins, do you have a moment?' Malice asked.

'Of course,' he touched the woman on the arm to excuse himself and walked over. 'How can I help?'

'The book at the front of the church next to the candles …'

'The remembrance book, what of it?'

'Do you keep past copies?'

'We do indeed. It is an important record for us and contains private and solemn messages from people thinking of loved ones who have passed over.'

'Can I see where they're kept?' Malice asked, the coffee gurgled in his empty stomach.

'Follow me. We archive them in the reading room. Not sure how far they go back but it's quite a way.' They trooped across the aisle and entered a room stacked to the ceiling with books. 'They're kept here, all in date order.

Some years we have two books other years just the one. Help yourself.'

Malice thanked him and began running his finger along the spines of the hard-backed books. He found the one he wanted. Three minutes later he was back in his car and on the phone to Pietersen.

'Hey, Mally,' she picked up straightaway.

'How's your morning been?'

'Good. I've identified the second mobile phone and both were registered to Maxwell, which would support our theory. And the preliminary findings from forensics suggests that Maxwell and Horton were killed with the same murder weapon.'

'That's good work. What else?'

'The transcripts and interview notes from the assault investigation are incomplete. Apparently, the force moved to a bright shiny new headquarters in 2013 and managed to lose most of the paperwork in the process. They keep telling me it's there, but they can't find it. From what I've read, the account of the altercation in the pub is very different to the one Copeland gave us when we saw her in the church. She and John Horton did end up on the floor but only after she'd smashed the glass and shoved it in his face.'

'So, she was lying?'

'Yup. What have you found?'

'Much the same — she's lying.'

'Oh?'

'You know I said we were missing something?'

'Yes.'

'I need you to follow up on an urgent item.'

'Okay, I can do that. But tell me, what have we been missing?

'Wendy Horton.'

Chapter 30

Slate chippings crunched under the tyres as Malice turned into the driveway. In front of him was a thatched cottage that looked as though it had just fallen off the front of a chocolate box. The scent from the roses framing the front porch met him as he knocked once on the door. It opened before he could knock a second time.

'Hello, are you George Ailing?' Malice said to the short balding man wearing spectacles and a checked shirt.

'You must be DS Malice; great name for a copper. Please come in.'

Malice went inside and found himself in a large lounge with a low ceiling and dark wooden beams running the full length of the house. A Welsh dresser took pride of place against one wall, brimming with decorative plates. Pallet knife oil paintings adorned the walls, depicting scenes of rolling landscapes and angry skies.

'Thank you,' Malice said. 'Nice place.'

'One of the advantages of spending fifteen years working in the city before going into the church. Oh, and mind your head, these houses weren't built for people your height.'

'City to ministry, that's quite a career move.'

'Let's just say, I fancied a change. Please take a seat, you have us intrigued.'

Malice sunk into a large armchair and Ailing sat opposite.

'Hello,' a shrill voice sounded from another room. 'I've put the kettle on. Do you take coffee, Mr Malice?'

'Umm… yes that would be good, thanks,' Malice replied.

'You said on the phone you had some questions regarding my time in the church,' asked Ailing.

'You were there in 2009?'

'I was, I spent eight years altogether. It was a lovely place and we enjoyed ourselves.'

'When did you leave?'

'In 2013. By then I had one foot in the church and the other firmly planted in my allotment and it was a job to work out where I'd rather spend my time. I'd had a good run and it was time for me to go. The church needs a modernising agenda with fresh ideas and innovative thinking. It's a young person's game these days. It came down to the pull of the church versus the pull of my vegetables and I'm a firm believer everything and everyone has a sell by date, and I'd reached mine.'

'Sounds like you fancied another change?'

'Ha, yes… something like that. I'm seventy-two, and while it might take me a little longer to get about the garden, up here…' he tapped the side of his head. 'I'm still sharp as a tack and twenty-one years of age.'

'That's a lie, George Ailing.' A small woman with a shock of white hair bustled into the room carrying a tray of mugs and a plate of biscuits. Her glasses were buried in her frizzy locks. 'You've never matured past fourteen. And as for being sharp as a tack you spend half the day drifting about the house looking for your glasses — which are normally perched on top of your head.'

'And this is my lovely wife, Cheryl,' Ailing said. 'We've been married forty-five years though there are times when it feels a lot longer.'

Cheryl put the tray on a low table and handed Malice a coffee.

'Please, help yourself,' she said, waving her hand at the tray and taking a seat next to her husband. 'Have you taken your tablets?'

'No, I thought they looked better in the box, so I left them there.' George reached for a chocolate biscuit. 'Are you married, Mr Malice?'

'Divorced.'

'Very wise.' He bit the corner off the biscuit. 'Now you see why I have an allotment.'

'It's all very well you saying that—' she protested.

George put his hand on his wife's leg.

'Cheryl, this nice gentleman has come all the way out here to ask us some questions and I'm dying to know what he wants.'

'You bloody forgot the other day.' She sank back into the cushions and nursed her drink on her lap. 'That's all I'm saying.'

'Carry on Mr Malice.'

'What can you tell me about Brenda Copeland?' Malice asked.

They both looked at each other and back to Malice.

'Don't know anyone by that name,' they said in unison.

'She also goes by the name of Twinkle.'

Cheryl made a snorting sound and straightened her shoulders.

'You know I said the church needed folk who are modernisers with fresh ideas?'

George tipped his mug in Malice's direction. 'Well, every church needs a Twinkle. She's a force of nature that woman.'

'Not sure about that,' Cheryl snorted again.

'Did you know her well?' Malice said, reaching for a biscuit.

'I did,' said George. 'She was the driving force behind most of our church initiatives. How she had the energy I have no idea given her husband's condition. Dennis has been bed-bound or in a wheelchair all the time I've known her, the strain on her home life must be enormous.'

'Did you ever see her with these men?' Malice placed his mug back on the tray and fished two printouts from his pocket. He handed them to George, each one showing a mugshot of Horton and Maxwell.

'I don't recognise them.' He held them up for Cheryl to take a look. She tugged her glasses from her hair and slid them onto her nose before pursing her lips and shaking her head.

'We have reason to believe they visited your church on the 19th of June in 2009. They may have visited a number of times. On each occasion they were probably there to see Twinkle.'

'Sorry, I don't recall ever seeing them.' George shook his head.

'I don't remember them either but I do remember the date,' Cheryl piped up. 'Twinkle had that massive bust up with two men in the church. You remember, George. We were due to go on holiday and had to delay it because of the complaints.'

'Oh yeah, was that then?' George said.

'Yes, I remember it like it was yesterday,' she continued. 'The bad language made my hair stand on end. I'm no prude, but using it in church is a bit much. We had to ring the hotel to cancel our booking. You remember, George.'

'You're right.' George eventually caught up. 'I had to smooth things over with the bishop.'

'We drove up there a couple of days later in all that rain,' she added.

'Sorry, can you start again,' Malice said, taking his notebook from his pocket.

Cheryl leaned forward, putting her mug on the tray.

'We were due to go on holiday to Scotland and popped into the church before we set off to check everything was in order. Twinkle was there and all of a sudden she had a blazing row with two men.'

'These two men?' asked Malice, holding up the mugshots again.

'Now, that I can't say,' said Cheryl. 'All I know is there was shouting and swearing and all sorts going on.'

'The men were shouting at Twinkle?' asked Malice.

'Everyone was shouting at everyone and it was Twinkle who was doing the swearing, you've never heard the like of it. I remember she shoved one of them so hard he almost fell over. Screeching she was, at the top of her voice. We had a group of children visiting with their parents from a local school and had so many complaints that the bishop had to get involved.'

'Can you remember what was said?' Malice said.

'No, nothing. All I know is she kicked off big style. In the end two other men she was friendly with stepped in and threw them out of the church.'

'Other two men?'

'Yes, she was friendly with two guys from Botswana, no, Nigeria, no—'

'Malawi,' George intervened. 'The brothers were from Malawi. Can't remember their names but Twinkle was working with them on the OutReach programme... where they supported vulnerable young men in the community.'

'What happened?' asked Malice. He was struggling to keep up and his handwriting was getting worse.

'That was it,' Cheryl said. 'The brothers manhandled the men out the church and there was a bit more shouting in the car park. We didn't see them again.'

'Are you sure of the date?' asked Malice.

'Positive,' she said. 'And why am I so certain of the date, George?'

'Because the 19th of June is your birthday, my loveliness,' he said cocking his head in her direction.

'Well done,' she patted him on the arm. 'We were having a few days away to celebrate.'

'I've taken up enough of your time,' he said, sinking the last of his coffee. 'Thank you.'

'I'll show you out,' Cheryl said, getting to her feet. Malice shook hands with George and made his way outside.

'One more question,' Malice asked when they reached the car. 'Did Twinkle have any children?'

'No. She often said that was one of the saddest things about Dennis' illness. It robbed them of the opportunity to start a family.'

'Thanks again.' Malice shook her hand and opened the car door. He went to sit in, but Cheryl stopped him by putting her hand on his shoulder.

'You need to watch her,' she said.

'Who?'

'That Twinkle. George always wants to see the best in people and to be fair there is a lot of good to see in her. But do you know what it's like when you meet someone and think, you're not all you're cracked up to be?'

'More times than I've had hot dinners.'

'Well, that's what it was like with Twinkle.'

'You don't like her much.'

'It's not that.' She glanced over her shoulder at the house. 'I wouldn't trust her as far as I could throw her.'

Chapter 31

Pietersen had completed the immediate actions on her list and was waiting for Malice to return to the station. He was late and she was fed up with pacing around the office, drinking machine-made coffee. Which also had the downside of allowing her ample time to fixate on Brad Craven.

His message had been clear. This was going to be a long and tortuous process, designed to inflict the maximum personal angst for her and the maximum entertainment for him. He had a reputation for being a tough operator so his words couldn't simply be dismissed as hollow threats. Malice's opinion raged in her head — 'You're in deep shit'.

As she was thinking of him, he rushed in carrying a hard-backed book under his arm and broke her train of thought.

'Hey,' he said, unloading pens and a notebook from his jacket before slinging it over the back of the chair. 'Busy day, or what?'

'Where the hell have you been, Malice?' she asked.

'Chatting to a retired priest.'

'Retired? You need redemption from a practising one.'

'Ha, very funny. What have you got?'

'Okay.' She resumed her circuit of the office. 'Let's start with Horton and Maxwell. They didn't so much meet over a drink in a bar, rather they met over a water fountain in the college where John was the vice-principal.'

'A water fountain?' Malice leaned against his desk and rolled up his sleeves. 'Maxwell was a service engineer for a water delivery company. I contacted the firm and they are still in business. They confirmed that the sixth-form college where John Horton worked was on the delivery schedule for Tim Maxwell. We've been struggling to put the two men together in any social situation and it looks like they met at work.'

'That's good. What did you find out regarding my Wendy Horton hunch?'

'Looks like you were right. There was an allegation of rape. Copeland did accuse Horton of raping her at the time of the assault but it was never followed up, and nothing was done about it. They found the rest of the police interview notes and it would confirm that to be true.'

'And what about the baby?'

'That proved a bit more difficult. The hospital was not very happy disclosing details of Copeland's medical records, saying I needed her consent or a court order which would have taken a few days to organise. I told them that under section 29(3) of the Data Protection Act the information could be disclosed where a serious offence was being conducted, but the red tape was getting too thick.'

'Damn, that's a shame. I'm sure that–'

'Hold on, I'm better than that. I spoke to a registrar. He obviously had Copeland's records in front of him, and when I mentioned the dates there was an inflection in his voice that told me we were on the right track. I got hold of the court transcript and it makes specific reference to her having a miscarriage two weeks before the sentencing hearing.'

'Bloody hell. You hit the jackpot.'

'If Copeland is telling the truth, and Horton did do a runner after the trial verdict, then he might not have known she lost the baby.'

'So…' Malice joined her on her office walkabout. 'It would also follow that when Horton confessed to his wife about what he'd done they would have both been under the false impression that John had a kid out there… somewhere.'

'Exactly. But how Maxwell fits into this puzzle, I'm not sure. We know he was religious, maybe Horton told him about the child and turning up at the church was some kind of act of atonement. Perhaps Horton had asked Maxwell to help him find his estranged child and the first place to start was to find Twinkle?'

They both stopped pacing and Malice sat at his desk. He pulled up a chair and motioned for Pietersen to take a seat. Then he grabbed the remembrance book.

'I spoke to the man who was the church vicar back in 2009 and he had a lot to say about Copeland, but not half as much as his wife had to say. She remembers Copeland having a blazing row with two men on the 19th of June that year.'

'Bloody hell she's got a good memory.'

'Apparently it was her birthday.'

'Was it Horton and Maxwell?'

'I showed her the mugshots and she couldn't confirm it was them.'

'Shit. That would have been too good to be true.'

'But when I was at the church I did find this,' Malice opened the hard-backed book at the marked page. She studied the hand-written message, then looked up from the page and tapped the book with her finger.

'We need to talk to Copeland again,' she said.

'Let's see if we can rattle her.' Malice got up to leave, his phone buzzed in his pocket. He took it out and pulled a face. It was Hayley and after the scorching she gave him last time he clicked the green button.

'Hi, how—' He got no further.

'Did you call the Head a dick?' she yelled down the line. Malice didn't have it on speaker phone but that didn't matter. Pietersen heard it all and raised her eyes before turning away.

'Erm, I might have done.' Malice scurried over to the far side of the room cupping his hand to the mobile as he went.

'What the hell were you thinking?' Hayley was cooking on gas mark twelve.

'He was being unreasonable.'

'I'll have a chat with him, you said; don't worry, you said. I'll sort it out, you said. Now you're the talk of the bloody school gates.'

'I don't see how—'

'You probably didn't notice the woman passing in the corridor when you stormed out of his office. It was Lilly Graham, otherwise known as Foghorn Lil. She heard everything and, knowing her, was probably earwigging outside the office door the entire time you were in there.'

'I was frustrated that—' By now, Malice was hunched over in the corner, trying to turn down the volume on his phone.

'It would get less coverage if you put it on the six-o'clock news. Now it's all the mums are talking about. Why the hell did you call him that?'

'Cos he was being a dick.' Malice hissed into his cupped hands.

'And now everyone knows it. Jill took me to one side and told me. I thought I was getting the side-eye from some of the stuck-up cows when I went to pick up Amy and now I know why.'

'I asked for a meeting with Hester's parents to sort this thing out and he point-blank refused. He as good as called Amy a liar. I wasn't going to stand for that.'

'Brilliant! So long as you feel better about things. But I'm the one who has to put up with the sniggering and being the talk of the playground for God knows how long. All because my ex-husband called the poster boy of the school a fucking 'dick'.'

'Strictly speaking, I didn't call him a fucking dick. I just called him—'

'How do you think that's going to help Amy?' Hayley was now on gas mark thirteen.

'He was bang out of order,' Malice growled.

'He's the Head of the school! Not some tosser you've nicked for possession.'

'Does Amy know?'

'Not sure, but it won't take long.'

'It wasn't as if I was being unreasonable.'

'Is that before or after the Dick comment?'

'It wasn't like that.'

'Thanks for making a bad situation worse.' Hayley disconnected the call.

Malice ambled back to his desk, shuffling past Pietersen.

'Everything okay?' she asked.

'Yeah, bloody marvelous. Come on, let's pay Copeland another visit.' He tugged his jacket from the chair and the arm caught on the back, sending it flying across the floor. 'Fuck it.'

He righted the chair and stomped away.

Pietersen remained seated.

'Mally, before we go there's something I need to tell you.'

Chapter 32

I'm sitting in a windowless interview room at the police station. The bastards turned up at my house and brought me here. Thankfully the car was unmarked; otherwise the neighbours would have had a field day. I've been twiddling my thumbs for the past half an hour. I check the silk scarf is in place around my neck. I can do without the ring of bruises prompting awkward questions. The room has a slight whiff of vomit.

The one called Malice and his South African sidekick come into the room and sit at the opposite side of the table. He's carrying a hard-backed book in one hand and a notepad in the other.

Let's get this party started.

'When I said I was only too happy to help,' I'm off and running. 'I didn't realise it would lead to a full-time job.' I fold my arms and huff at them.

He glares at me.

'Can I remind you, Brenda,' she pipes up. 'You have not been arrested and you are not under caution. You may have a solicitor present if you wish and you are free to leave at any time. We have a few more questions if that's okay?'

'And you had to bring me down here to ask them?' I snap back.

'We thought it might be easier,' she says.

'Easier than sitting on my sofa drinking tea?'

'Are you okay to answer a few questions?' she tries again.

'I suppose so. But if it's about John I'm not sure what else I can tell you?'

'You can start with why you didn't tell us the full story the last time we spoke to you,' he jumps in, leaning forwards with his elbows on the table. All threatening, like.

Nice opener. Let's see what you got copper...

'You were asking questions about John,' I reply, mirroring his pose. It looks like we're about to arm wrestle. 'And that happened a long time ago. So, you'll have to excuse me if a few of the details are a little hazy, but I can assure you I was being straight with you.'

'You told us that the last time you saw John Horton was at the trial. That wasn't true, was it?' she asks.

He leans back and clicks the top of his pen, over and over. He's studying me like I'm some kind of science project. They glance at each other and he gives her a nod. It's obvious she's going to take the lead.

I puff my cheeks out and shake my head.

'To the best of my recollection, it is true,' I say.

'He came to see you at your church and brought another man along with him. His name was Timothy Maxwell.'

'I don't recall that ever happening.'

'You argued with them and two of your friends ejected them from the premises.'

She's getting on my tits.

'This is nonsense.' I shove myself away from the table.

'Maxwell lit two candles in your church on the 19th of June 2009 to commemorate the death of his parents.'

'How the hell do you know that?' I laugh. He opens the hard-backed book, turns it around and slides it in front of me. I stare down at the pages. 'What am I supposed to be looking at?'

'Maxwell wrote a message,' he says, stabbing his finger at the page.

Mum and dad, always in my thoughts forever in my heart.
Tim

'So?' I say pushing the book away.

'If Tim Maxwell was at the church then it is highly likely John was there too,' she continues.

'This proves nothing.' I fling my head back and laugh. 'Did you also check to see how many other *Tims* there were in the book?'

'I did,' he says. 'For June 2009, this was the only entry.'

'Still means nothing.' I bat his reply away with a wave of my hand.

'I think Horton and Maxwell came to your church and you argued with them.'

'What? Even if he did come to the church, I'd not seen him for sixteen years. What the hell would we have to argue about?'

'How about the rape...' he says, eyeballing me.

Fuck!

I take a breath.

'What are you talking about?'

'You accused him of rape when the police interviewed you about the assault in the pub.'

'This is rich. You're interested now after all this time? Cos back then no one wanted to bloody know.'

'Did John rape you?' she asks.

'No.'

'Then why did you accuse him?'

'Isn't that obvious? I wanted to lash out. Remember I told you he'd been cheating on me. Mind you, fat lot of good it did.'

'It was a lie,' she says.

'Yup, it was. I'm not proud of myself.'

'Perhaps you argued about the miscarriage, or did you lie about that as well?' he says.

Holy shit. They have been doing their homework.

It's her turn to lean forwards.

'I believe John Horton raped you,' she chips in. 'You fell pregnant and that's what you fought about when you glassed him in the pub.'

'That's ridiculous. I just told you he didn't rape me,' I say, adjusting the position of my chair.

'It's a matter of record that you were admitted to hospital around the time of the trial, having suffered a miscarriage,' she continues. 'A grievance that big is worth keeping alive for sixteen years. So, I'll ask you again, did you have an altercation with Horton and Maxwell at your church?'

'No. I. Didn't.' I emphasise every word.

This is getting too close for comfort.

'We have a witness who says you had an argument with two men,' he says.

'Did the witness confirm who it was?' I look at each of them in turn. 'No, I didn't think so.'

'Who were the two men who ejected Horton and Maxwell from the church?'

'That's a stupid question. If I didn't have an argument with anyone in the church, then it must also follow that no one was thrown out.'

'The witness said the two men you argued with were escorted from the building. Who escorted them?'

'How the hell should I know? Seems to me you need to go back and talk to your witness again, because they seem to have all the answers.'

'John didn't know you'd had a miscarriage, did he?' she asks.

'I have no idea what John knew. He pissed off and I never saw him again.'

'John thought he had an estranged child and that's what he came to talk to you about.'

'I keep telling you, the last time I saw him was at the trial.'

'John Horton told his wife about the rape and the child. It contributed to her falling ill. We believe he came to you in order to make amends.'

'How do you know that! You said John's been missing for ten years.'

I'm getting well pissed off now. They're not letting this drop.

'She told us.' He delivers the line like it's his ace card.

'You also said she's been sectioned under the Mental Health Act. How reliable do you think her testimony is going to be?' I blurt out.

They both look at each other. Their expressions say it all.

Shit! I just fucked up.

'No, Mrs Copeland,' she says, shaking her head. 'We didn't tell you that.'

'You… must have.'

'No, we didn't.'

'Maybe… I don't know…'

Bollocks.

'How do you know she was sectioned? Did John tell you about his wife when he came to the church to ask about the child? The child he believed he'd fathered when he raped you back in 2009?' he says. 'Only there was no child, was there, Mrs Copeland? But John Horton didn't know that. He didn't know, did he?'

'Why are you asking me these questions after all this time?' My chest begins to tighten. 'You said John went missing, have you found him?'

'Please answer the question, Mrs Copeland,' she says.

'Is he dead? He is, isn't he?' I try to divert them.

'Mrs Copeland, how did you know Wendy Horton had been sectioned?' She presses the point, lasering me with her stare.

It's not working.

'I'm not sure you must have…' My mouth is drying up.

'John came to your church to talk and you had a blazing row. Then two blokes ejected Horton and Maxwell from the premises. Who were those men and what happened next, Mrs Copeland?' His voice is hard and clipped.

Shit. I was not expecting this. What the hell am I supposed to say now?

Chapter 33

I arrive back at the house late. The coppers might be fizzing with ideas and theories regarding what happened to John and Tim, but they've got nothing other than a witness statement, the ravings of a woman in a mental hospital and a scribbled note in a book. That hardly flickers the investigative needle. They're floundering in the dark.

I watched their expressions change when I quizzed them about John. I reckon they've found his body along with Maxwell, and I'm kicking myself for letting the cat out of the bag about Wendy. I was getting flustered which is not like me. It must be the pressures of the past few days taking a toll.

I decided my best course of action was to hit the eject button. So, I burst into tears and terminated the interview. I needed to get out of there. I complained that they were confusing me and putting words into my mouth, which was true, but I wanted to get away and give myself time to think. And there's a lot to think about.

After I left the police station I drove to Winfield where I met Precious. He greeted me like I was Mother Christmas and Frank and the boys had done a cracking job cleaning up the flat. I don't think the full extent of what's happening has sunk in for him yet; he hasn't got past the fact that he's getting his drugs for free. There's always a realisation lag but it will kick in eventually.

We also went to see Reverend Bertram and I introduced him to Frank and Jez. He was horrified at Jez's injuries and wanted to do all manner of things, including involving the police. It took a while to talk him down and persuade him that was not the right way to tackle this. He eventually got a grip and we chatted about setting up a branch of the OutReach programme at the church. He was like a kid in a sweet shop when he could see the amount of kudos that would be coming his way.

I park my car and step out into the night air. The house should be in darkness but it's not. That bitch should be snoozing in the chair in the downstairs bedroom while Dennis coughs and glugs his way through the night. But the living room light is on. She's watching TV when she should be watching him. I'm gonna have words.

I push open the front door to find her standing in the hallway.

'Rebecca, is Dennis alright?' I ask.

'Dennis is fine, he's asleep.'

'Shouldn't you be—'

'I need to talk to you.'

She's shuffling from one foot to another and looks like she's been caught smoking behind the bike shed.

'About what?' I slip my coat off and hang it up on one of the hooks on the wall. 'You look awful. What's wrong?'

'It's a little sensitive,' her hands are clasped in front of her, fingers fidgeting with some imaginary object.

'What is?'

'It's about Dennis.'

'There's nothing sensitive about Dennis.'

'Actually, I disagree.'

'Oh?' I move past her into the sitting room and perch on the edge of a chair to remove my shoes. I'm looking forward to this. 'What do you know that I don't?'

She's standing in the doorway, framed against the hallway light.

'Dennis says you're not very nice to him,' she says, her voice wavering.

'Define 'nice to him', because if he means I don't buy him the latest fashion or take him to Centre Parks, then yes he probably has a point.'

'It's nothing like that.'

'Then what is it?'

'Dennis has been telling me things.'

'That's a joke, love, because he's not had anything coherent to say since 2008.'

'That's not true,' she gives her foot a little stamp on the carpet. 'I'm able to understand what he says.'

'What are you, Google Translate?' I toss my shoes into the corner.

'I don't understand—'

'No but apparently you seem to miraculously understand my husband. A man who's not uttered a distinguishable sentence in years.' I stand in front of her, hands on my hips. She blanches.

'Why would you say that? Dennis tells me you know what he's saying perfectly well.'

'What do you want, Rebecca? I'm tired and I need to go to bed.'

'Dennis says you abuse him when there's no one else in the house,' she blurts out.

'Oh give me a break.' I walk past her into the kitchen and pour myself a glass of water from the tap. She follows me and stands in the centre of the room. 'Come on let's have it. What am I supposed to have done this time?'

'He said you tipped him out of his wheelchair and withheld food from him when he was hungry.'

'Did he also tell you that I string him up by his balls and sell tickets to the neighbours to come and watch.'

'This is serious.'

'Have a word with yourself, will you? I've lived with this for years and periodically he comes out with this claptrap.'

I brush past her and wander back into the lounge. She scurries along behind me.

'I checked him and he had bruises on his elbow and wrist where he fell,' she says.

'Well you of all people should know that the cocktail of medicine he takes causes his skin to mark easier that an over-ripe peach.'

'That's not what I saw.'

'And what did you see, Florence Nightingale? Cos what I see is a man who is resentful of his life and yearns for what should have been. A man who occasionally strikes out at those closest to him. Do you know what Munchausen Syndrome is?'

'Yes, of course.' She nods like a toy dog on the back shelf of a car.

'And so do I, because every now and again he purposefully hurts himself to gain attention and blames me for it. But this time he's managed to suck you into the charade.'

'He says you do it a lot.'

'Come on, Rebecca,' I flop onto the sofa and sip my water. 'Think this through. When do I have the opportunity to do that? In the narrow time window between Zoe leaving and you turning up? That's the time when I'm trying to keep the house in order, doing the washing, feeding myself and getting things sorted out for the following day. Does it seem right to you that the one thing I'd much rather be doing is torturing my husband?'

'I can only go on what he's said.'

She's standing with her feet together and hands clasped in front of her. I hadn't realised my lounge doubled as a Headmaster's study.

'Was that before, after, or during the coughing, gasping and gargling?' I say. 'Cos when he talks to me it's a bloody lottery as to what he's on about. But apparently you have the gift.'

'I understand him fine. Dennis has been very clear telling me what you do to him, I've not gone to the authorities yet. I wanted to talk it through with you first.'

'Rebecca,' I get up and put my arm around her shoulder. She tries to shrink away but I hold her tight. 'I appreciate you talking this through with me. I really do. But please believe me when I say I would never hurt Dennis. I've stuck with him though his illness and who knows how much longer he has left. He does this every now and again to get more attention. I'm sorry he's roped you in and put you in this difficult position.'

'So, you've never tipped him out of his wheelchair?'

I pull a face.

'Of course not, he's spinning you a line.' I take her hand in mine. 'I'm sorry Dennis has put you though this, Rebecca, really I am.'

'I didn't know what to do for the best.' She gazes down at the floor. Her face is red.

'You did the right thing and I appreciate the courtesy. Now if you don't mind I'm going to bed and you've got a job to do.'

'You're not going to get rid of me?'

'Heavens no. Dennis likes you and so do I. You do a good job. Why would I want to replace you with someone else over a silly misunderstanding?'

'I was worried how you'd react.'

I think she's going to cry.

'Like I said, this isn't the first time we've had to deal with Dennis making things up. I was hurt the first time it happened and cried for a week but then I realised what was behind his accusations and he can't help himself. Sometimes you hurt the ones closest to you the most. Is your supervisor Debra Grey?'

I know damned well she is.

'Yes.'

'If it makes you feel any better why don't you talk it through with her. She is an experienced care professional who's seen this type of thing before. Have a chat with her to put your mind at rest.'

'I'm on rest days from tomorrow.'

I know you are ...

'It's obviously given you a nasty shock.'

'Maybe I'll chat to Debra when I get back to work.'

'Can I get to bed now?' I curl my finger under her chin and tilt her face towards mine.

'Yes, sorry, Twinkle I just–'

'You did the right thing now go and keep my husband safe. I sleep better knowing he's in good hands.'

Rebecca squeezes my hand and I flash her a reassuring smile. She lets go and ambles out of the room.

Dennis… you little fucker.

Chapter 34

Malice's problems were beginning to feel like a running sore. No matter what he did to relieve the irritation, the pain kept getting worse. He'd made up his mind that pussyfooting around wasn't getting him anywhere, and he should be doing what he was good at — taking care of business the only way he knew how.

He yanked on the door to the club and was hit by a wall of sound from the sofa-sized speakers hanging off the walls. If it wasn't for the pounding beat and the wail of the vocals, the whole place would have had a tumbleweed moment. Fifty faces turned to stare at the new arrival.

Half-moon booths lined one side of the room and a three-feet high glitzy runway took centre stage down the middle. Three women twirled around silver poles in high heels and not much else, while goggle-eyed men sat on bar stools, trying not to fall off. A cascade of blue and red lights whirled around, illuminating the garish decor and splashing the women with colour as they showed the punters as much as the entertainment licence permitted. Bolton wasn't there.

One man got to his feet, pulled on his jacket and headed for the door. Malice would enjoy looking him in the eye the next time he bumped into him at work.

When it became apparent Malice was on his own, the clientele went back to their glassy-eyed evening. He went to the bar and looked into the CCTV behind the counter. The minutes ticked by. Bolton was never normally this casual when it came to business. The bar man came up and slapped a coaster down on in front of Malice.

'What will you have, fella?' he asked.

'Nothing thanks. I'm waiting for someone.'

'Mr Bolton says he's going to be a few minutes, so it's on the house.'

'A small beer, then. Thanks.' Malice turned his back to the bar and surveyed the club. It had been a while since his last visit and the girls were new, but the men sporting their vacant faces were disappointingly familiar. He heard the sound of a drink being banged down on the bar behind him. He turned to see a pint of lager.

'Mr Bolton said if you asked for a small to give you this.'

'Did he now?'

'Yes, sir. Enjoy.'

Malice raised his glass to the CCTV camera and took a slug. If he was going to be inconvenienced he could think of worse places to wait. He watched the girls go through their acrobatic routines all the while thinking, does your mum know you do this?

He sipped his beer and re-wound the conversation he'd had with Pietersen hours earlier. He'd bought two coffees in a café located a short drive from the station and handed one to her. She'd worn a pinched expression which betrayed the pain she was going through. This is not what she wanted, it was going to be a tough conversation. She'd recounted what had happened the previous night and how Craven had made it clear she was firmly in their sights. Malice had listened without interrupting. Then she said the words he'd hoped she wouldn't say.

'I'm telling you, Mally, because he mentioned you.'

'What exactly did he say?' he'd asked, trying to keep his emotions in check.

'He said that one of his options was to beat the living daylights out of my black boyfriend, who I seem to enjoy spending so much time with. He went on to say we made a lovely couple.'

Malice had cast his eyes to the ceiling and clicked his tongue against the roof of his mouth.

'Now it's my problem as well. We're going to fix it my way,' he'd said, balling his fists.

As much as she'd protested, she knew that events had spiralled out of control and she was in over her head. Malice could no longer stay out of it. He had his family to think about, as well as himself. Eventually she'd nodded and he'd got up from the table, leaving his coffee untouched. He had to make a call.

Malice took a slug of the cold beer and licked his lips. A big guy wearing a leather jacket that bulged where it touched appeared from behind a curtain at the far end of the club like a bad cabaret act. Malice recognised him as one of the firm's heavies. Not that Bolton needed much help in that department. The man approached the bar.

'If you'd like to come with me,' he growled.

Malice took another swig of beer and followed the man across the club and through a side door marked

'Private'. The big guy bounded up a set of stairs and waited at the top. Malice plodded along behind him. He wasn't running anywhere. When the hulk opened a door Malice saw Harvey Bolton sitting in a fat leather chair behind a huge oak desk; dressed in a three-piece suit.

Bolton liked to consider himself an entrepreneur, though the police referred to him as a career criminal with fingers in more pies than the local bakery. Drugs, extortion, prostitution, you name it, Bolton was involved — all under the cover of a legitimate chain of late-night boozers and clubs. He had once been in Malice's pocket. Though if you asked him, he would say it was the other way around.

Malice stood with his arms extended at his sides while the big bloke in the leather jacket patted him down.

'Apologies for the formality,' Bolton said. 'But if half of what I've heard lately is true, you're a dangerous man.'

'I'm no danger to you.'

The big guy ran his hands down Malice's legs to his ankles, and then nodded to his boss.

'I have to say, Mally, this is a welcome surprise,' Bolton said, giving Malice the benefit of his winning smile; a smile that was brought to life by three gold teeth.

'I appreciate you seeing me.'

'It sounded urgent. How long has it been now since we last spoke?'

'A while.'

'Eleven months, three weeks and two days... to be precise,' replied Bolton. 'I've missed our little chats.'

'Yeah, well, things change.'

'They certainly changed for Lobos Vasco. More to the point, my business interests have missed our little chats.'

'That's not what I do any more,' Malice said.

'I respect that. Though I must admit it's much the pity.'

'I need a favour.'

'It'll cost you.'

'What do you want?'

'Don't know yet, depends on how big the favour is.'

Malice approached the desk and placed both hands on the edge. Bolton got to his feet and fingered his cufflinks.

'I need a location big enough to hide three vehicles,' said Malice.

'Not a problem.'

'And... I want to borrow three of your boys.'

Chapter 35

With item number one in place, Malice turned his attention to his second issue. He was tired, but the night was far from over. He had one more call to make before calling it a day and this one could be tricky.

He slowed his car to a crawl as he drove past the entrance to the field. The long, metal, five-bar gate was gaping open with the severed chain draped around the right-hand post. He craned his neck and caught sight of four caravans parked on the grass. His near-side tyres sank into the soft verge as he pulled over and killed the engine.

He stepped out into the cool night air and blew a breath into his clasped hands. This could go one of two ways and he was prepared for both.

He'd done his research. The Hester family had moved about the country, leaving a trail of unhappy neighbours, traumatised schools and out-of-pocket councils in their wake. They did so with a random set of fellow travellers who stayed as long as it took for the local authorities to serve them with a trespass and eviction order. So far, they had been in the area for three months.

The field was awash with domestic litter. Vehicle parts and pallets along with patches of burned grass were dotted around. A motley selection of old cars and flat-bed trucks were parked close by. Malice took a deep breath and strode through the entrance towards the cluster of white vans.

'State your business!' A gruff voice came out of nowhere. Malice looked around and saw a stout man wearing grey overalls appear from around one of the trucks. The poppers down the front of his boiler suit were under increasing amounts of strain as they neared his belly. 'This is private land,' he bellowed.

Maybe, but it's not your private land.

'I'm here to see the Hester family,' Malice replied.

'That don't help much. There are two families here by that name.' The man closed the distance between them. Malice marveled at the man's haircut which looked he'd done it himself using a strimmer.

'Tristram Hester, I'm here to see him.'

'Now what would you be wanting to see him for?'

'It's regarding the school.'

'You'll find him in the one with the yellow curtains.' He pointed a sausage shaped finger in the direction of one of the caravans.

Malice nodded a sterile smile, and then trekked across the grass conscious of the man's gaze boring into his back. He looked around and could see Amy's bike laying on the ground. The flat of his hand rattled the door and a woman answered.

'What?' she barked, a glass of pale-yellow liquid in her hand. The TV was blaring out some gameshow.

'Does Tristram Hester live here?'

'Who wants to know?'

'He's in the same school as—'

'Abel!' she bellowed over the noise of the tele. 'There's a guy here from the school wanting to talk to our Tristram,'

'Oh, for fuck's sake.' A deep voice responded. 'It's the bloody tiebreak as well!' A tall man nudged the woman out of the way and filled the doorway. He was a carbon copy of the bloke Malice had encountered earlier, right down to the boiler suit and strimmer haircut.

'What is it pal? We're busy.'

'Your lad is in the same school as my daughter and—'

'Tristram! Get here yer little bastard. What's he done this time?' he yelled.

A boy around eleven years of age with angular features popped his face around the door.

'What?' Tristram said.

'You go to the same school as my daughter and you took her bike. It's the one over there.'

'Did he now?' Abel stepped out of the van and down the three steps, invading Malice's personal space.

'I want it back,' Malice said, backing away.

The man yanked Tristram from the van by his collar.

'Did you steal that bike?' he pointed to it lying on the grass.

'No. I don't know what he's on about.' Tristram shrugged himself free.

'You did. You took it from my daughter in the school yard,' replied Malice.

'The fuck I did.' Tristram was having none of it.

'I'll take it home with me,' said Malice, walking over to the bike.

'Not so fast there, brother. My boy said he didn't do it, so you can't just take it,' Abel called out.

'That's my daughter's bike. I bought it for her, so I know what it looks like.'

'I'm sure she was dead pleased with that, but unless you had it made for her special like… it's just a bike. How do I know it belonged to your daughter? Did you have it custom made?'

'I'll take it and be on my way,' Malice replied.

'Tabitha, get out here now!' the man tilted his head back and hollered. A small mousy girl with long straggly hair appeared at the top of the steps; a rainbow coloured unicorn horn sticking from the top of her head.

'What now?' she sighed.

'How long have you had that bike?' Abel pointed at the bicycle.

'I don't know, couple of months.'

'Are you sure?'

'Course I'm sure, I should know. Can I go now?' She disappeared back inside before waiting for an answer.

'You see… that might look like your daughter's bike.' Abel's delivery was low and slow. 'But if she's had it that long, then it can't be. Now can it?'

'Mr Hester, I can assure you that's my daughter's bike. Your son stole it from her in school and I've come to take it back, so if you don't mind…' Malice continued walking over to the bike.

'But I do mind.' Abel put his hand inside the door and brought out a shotgun. 'You can't come around here taking people's belongings. That's against the law. Only we don't tend to engage much with the law, we like to settle things our own way.'

Abel levelled the gun at Malice, who stopped. He heard a sound behind him and half-turned to see the thick-set man holding a heavy wrench.

'I hope you have a licence for that and a lockable cabinet,' Malice said eyeing the gun.

'Yeah, and I cover it in tinsel and baubles when it's not in use. I suggest you do one, brother, while you still can. This thing will cut you in half.'

'I've come for the bike,' Malice replied.

'You need to fuck off,' said the fat guy behind him.

The door to the caravan on the left swung open and a woman stood on the top step surveying the scene. 'Mat! You'd better get your arse out here,' she screeched.

'That bike is mine,' said Malice.

'First of all you say it's your daughter's… and now you say it's yours. Make your mind up, brother. I think it's you who's confused. What do you think, Abe?'

'Sounds like it to me, Cain,' the fat guy said, slapping the wrench into the palm of his hand.

'Cain and Abel? Seriously?' Malice replied, holding his ground.

'Yeah well, we're the religious types,' said Cain.

'Does that include thou shalt not steal?' said Malice.

'I tell you what?' said Abel. 'If you like the bike so much, why don't you buy it off us?'

'Now you're having a laugh,' Malice replied.

'Can't see anyone laughing. Can you Cain?'

'Nope.'

'How about you Tristram?'

'I can't see anyone, Dad. Sounds like a good deal to me.'

'How about five-hundred pounds?' said Cain.

'No, that isn't going to happen.' Malice shook his head. 'I'm going to take my bike and leave.'

'I'll tell you what's going to happen. As you've come here to see Tristram, I think it's only fair and fitting that he escorts you off the premises.' Cain handed Tristram the shotgun. 'Show the nice man out son.'

Tristram took the gun and hooked it under his arm, like he's been handling it ever since he could walk.

'Off you go.' he said, flicking the barrel up and walking towards Malice.

Malice snaked his hand out, grabbed the barrel and wrenched it from the boy's grasp. He gripped the gun with two hands, stepped back and sent the stock smashing into Abel's face. Knocking him to the ground.

Cain leapt forward. Malice swung the barrel of the shotgun and caught him on the side of the head, sending him scurrying sideways towards the van.

'Dad!' Tristram screamed as his father staggered around under the weight of the blow. Abel was sparked out. Blood streaming from his shattered nose.

Malice swung the gun around and aimed it at Mat who was now framed in the doorway of the neighboring van, fastening the belt on his jeans. The colour drained from his face.

'Don't,' Malice said. 'Get back inside and close the door. All I want is the bike.'

Mat held his hands up and disappeared inside.

Malice marched over and yanked the bicycle upright by the handlebars. Tristram ran to his father who was crouched over holding the side of his face.

'I'll fucking…' Abel spluttered.

'Yeah, I'm sure you will but you're gonna have to do it without this.' Malice held the shotgun out in front of him. 'Cos this is coming with me.'

'But I need that,' Abel snorted through his fingers.

'Maybe I'll sell it to you. How does five-hundred pounds sound?'

'Bastard.'

'Yup, but now I'm a bastard with a twelve-bore. In fact, I'm a bastard with your twelve-bore. Have you got the money or shall I take this as a sorry gift?'

'You'll regret this.' Abel straightened up and shoved Tristram away. The boy skidded onto his knees.

'Nope, don't think I will. And talking about saying sorry, when you get to school in the morning Tristram the first thing you're going to do is find the Head, Mr Carlton, and tell him you took the bike. You'll tell him you had second thoughts and returned it. Once you've done that you're going to say sorry to my daughter. Is that understood?'

Tristram grunted.

'I can't hear you. I said is that understood?'

'Yeah, understood,' Tristram said and ran into the caravan.

'Oh, and just so we're both on the same page, Mr Hester, if my daughter so much as catches a cold from any member of your family I'll bring the gun back and ram the business end two inches past your front teeth. And if your brother is around I'll do the same to him. I'm assuming there are two cartridges in here?'

'Piss off.'

'Are we clear?'

'Yeah, we're fucking clear.'

Malice wheeled the bike around the prone figure of Abel.

'Nice doing business with you.'

Chapter 36

I watch Rebecca through the living room window as she trots across the road to her car. She was quiet this morning, not her usual can't-shut-the-fuck-up self. But then the poor-love has had a torrid time, wrestling with her conscience. I made her a cup of tea when I got up and once she'd drank it, I sent her home early. I check my watch. Zoe will be here soon to takeover for the day-shift.

Dennis is sitting in his wheelchair dressed and ready for the day. He's pretending to watch the news, when actually he's watching me. I tap a text message into my phone and press send. It pings a response pretty-much immediately.

'You okay, Dennis?' I ask. He mumbles something which, roughly translated, means 'Where's Rebecca gone?' I ignore the question, wander into the kitchen and return with a kettle full of water and a large mug containing instant coffee granules. I plug the kettle into the socket on the wall and it begins to blip and pop.

I kneel down in front of him and look up into his big watery eyes.

'What have you been telling Rebecca?'

'Agggghhh ggrrr ukkk,' he gurgles.

I reach down and pull the slipper off his left foot, then do the same with the right.

'She says that you've been saying nasty things about me. She says that I've been mistreating you.'

'Grruuu agghhh.' Dennis jerks around in his chair.

'She says I've been hurting you. Now why would she think that?'

I tug at the toe of the sock and pull it off his foot.

'Kkkkah bbbbluggg.' Drool is running from the side of his mouth and his eyes are beginning to bulge.

I shuffle across the carpet and put my hand on the kettle.

'Not boiled yet.' I say before removing his other sock. He's trying to kick his legs, but the ankle straps on the foot rests holds them in place. 'She thinks that because you told her.'

His drool is bubbling now.

The noise from the kettle gets louder.

'You told her a pack of lies about me, didn't you?' He's jerking his head from side to side, gasping. 'That's not a nice thing to do, now is it? After everything I've done for you and this is how you repay me — by telling lies. That's not good.' He's blubbing and groaning, sending globs of spit onto his chest. 'It's not good because it puts me in a bad light and I work so hard at being a good person, but you're making that difficult for me.' Steam begins to rise from the spout as the water rumbles to the boil. 'The thing is, Dennis, if you're going to spread lies about me then I may as well hurt you. Goodness knows what she's going to tell the authorities. Then when she does, we will probably get a visit from the police and they'll cart me away… and then where will you be?'

Dennis has one eye on me and the other on the plume of steam rising into the air. The kettle clicks off. I pick it up and pour the boiling water from a height into the oversized mug.

'Accidents do happen, you know? I mean what if I came into the room to watch TV with you, and I happen to be carrying a cup of coffee. And what if my foot catches on the rug forcing me to trip. That would be terrible wouldn't it?' Dennis is flailing around, well as much as he can. 'And what if I dropped the cup and the scalding water went all over your feet? That would be awful, can you imagine how painful that would be? Let's try it out.'

I get up and walk to the doorway to the lounge.

'So, imagine if I came in like this…' I walk to the centre of the room. 'And then I catch my foot on the edge of the carpet…' I stamp my foot down on the floor. 'I fall, spilling the drink all over your exposed feet…'

I lurch forward and land on my knees in front of him. The mug hovering inches above his exposed skin. Dennis' face is glowing red, and saliva is flying through the air. I stop and look up. 'Just imagine, Dennis. It could so easily happen.'

I stand up and take a sip of coffee.

'Think about it, Dennis.'

I hear the sound of a key sliding into the lock. It's Zoe. She's come to do her shift. I'm sitting on the sofa while he gazes out the window. Then I rub my eyes hard with my knuckles.

'In here, Zoe,' I call out. 'Dennis hasn't been feeling good this morning.'

'Oh no, that's a shame.' I can hear her removing her coat and putting her bag onto the floor.

I run into the hallway and launch myself at her, throwing my arms around her neck. My shoulders heave as I begin to sob.

'What is it, Twinkle? What on earth is the matter?' she says.

I sob on her shoulder.

'I can't talk about it. It's too upsetting. I'm so glad you're here.'

'What's wrong?' she asks.

'I need to take care of an urgent appointment.' I pull myself away and wipe the tears from my eyes with a hankie.

'What's happened?'

'I can't say. I need to go.'

'Is it Dennis?'

'Kind of.'

'Do we need to phone for an ambulance?' she fumbling around for her phone. I grab both her arms and pull her close.

'No. It's Rebecca...' I let the last word ring out with a sigh.

'What about her?'

'She... she... I can't say.'

'What is it Twinkle?'

'I've got to go.' I grab my jacket from the hook and hurtle out of the door, running to my car. The engine roars and I race up the street.

That should do it.

I take a tissue from my pocket and blow my nose. After a short drive I park the car and run to the large glass double doors, shoving them open with my shoulder. I speak to the woman on reception and within a couple of minutes I see Carol Tennant walking down the stairs towards me.

I've known Carol for many years and she has been a huge support. She's dressed in a smart fitted trouser suit with her hair pulled back in a ponytail. She takes my hands in hers and I burst into tears.

'What's the matter, Twinkle? I got your text, it sounded urgent. Is it Dennis?' she says.

'He's fine. I didn't know what to do,' I splutter my response. 'Can we go somewhere where we can talk?'

'Of course, let's go in here.' She guides me into a side office and closes the door. I take a seat and dab my face with a tissue. 'It was a shock when I received your message, I feared the worse.'

'I can't believe it,' I blurt out, placing the palms of my hands flat on the table-top. 'I had to talk to someone.'

'You know you can always talk to me, what is this about?' She reaches across the desk and places her hands on mine. 'Talk to me Twinkle.'

'It's Rebecca,' I say, pulling my right hand away and rubbing my face in my sleeve.'

'What about her?'

'I came home last night and…'

'What?'

'I caught her.'

'Doing what?'

'I… I…' My shoulders slump forward and I collapse on the desk, sobbing for all I'm worth. Tennant leaves her chair and comes around to my side to console me. She's rubbing her hands across my back.

'Twinkle, what is it?'

I straighten myself in the chair and clear my throat.

'I came back late last night and let myself into the house. I went through to the downstairs bedroom to find Rebecca with... with... I can't believe it.'

'What, Twinkle? What did you find?'

'She was... interfering with him.'

'What do you mean?'

'I saw Rebecca with her hands under the bedding giving Dennis a... I can't even bring myself to say the words.'

'She was doing what!'

'She had her hands under the duvet and it was obvious what she was doing. The bedding was going up and down and Dennis was lying there all...' I slump forward again with my head on my forearms. My shoulders shake.

'Are you sure?' Tennant shrieks.

'I couldn't believe what I was seeing. She saw me and pulled herself away.'

'What did you do?'

'I don't know. I was so shocked I ran upstairs to my bedroom.'

'What did Rebecca say?'

'Well, she denied it ,of course. But I know what I saw.'

'This is terrible, Twinkle. What we need to do is...'

Carol Tennant proceeds to prattle on for ages, quoting their disciplinary procedure and the steps she would take to conduct an investigation. To tell you the truth, I'm not listening. I can't be arsed what happens to Rebecca. The important thing is no one will believe her when she slings around her accusations about me. They'll see it as the work of a vengeful woman who's been caught out.

Carol is getting emotional. She's telling me how this has never happened before in all her years of managing care provision. I couldn't give a toss. I'm already thinking through my next move. I reckon I've sorted this little problem but there is a massive fly in my ointment which refuses to go away.

I almost feel sorry for Carol. I've ruined her day. She's a lovely woman and generous to a fault. Though she is little misguided. Then most of the people who sit on our church council are exactly the same.

I wish she'd bloody finish. I need to make a call.

Chapter 37

Craven whistled as he walked across the car park with a late-morning Brewers Fayre breakfast in his belly. He unlocked his car and as he flopped into the driver's seat his phone rang. He switched on the ignition and the ring tone came through the speakers on his hands-free.

'Hello Will, my old mucker,' he said, closing the door.

'How's it going? I got Jimmy here and you're on speaker phone.'

'Morning James.'

'Morning Bradley.'

'I told him about your text last night saying you'd paid the bitch a visit,' Will said.

'You should have seen her,' replied Craven with a chuckle. 'Shitting herself she was. I went to her gaff and invited myself inside with the toe of my boot, if you know what I mean. She was huffing and puffing and red in the face. She even pulled a knife on me!'

'Mate, I wish I could have been there to see that. Sounds like you put the squeeze on her good and proper,' said Will.

'She'd brought home a takeaway and I ate some of the sweet and sour with my fingers and then told her I'd not washed my hands after having a piss.'

The sound of raucous laughter filled the car.

'That is fucking quality, mate. Fucking quality,' said Jimmy. 'What did she do?'

'Chucked it in the bin I expect!'

More laughter erupted from the speakers.

'What did you say to her?' asked Will.

'I said that we'd not decided what we were going to do. She denied everything but then she's a lying cow so that's par for the course. I ran through a few of the options: Torch her car, wreck her flat, stuff like that. You should have seen her, she was shaking like a jelly by the time I left.'

'Fuck me, I wish I could take a few days off to join you,' said Jimmy. 'She'd crap her pants if the pair of us showed up. Or even better if the three of us paid her a visit.'

'If we did, she'd collapse on the spot,' Will shouted.

The laughter was so loud it distorted the sound coming through the speakers.

'Stop it. I think I'm gonna piss myself,' yelled Jimmy.

'When you coming back, Brad? asked Will.

'I'm booked in till the end of the week, but I might leave sooner depending how I feel and how much grief I get off the missus.'

'When you get back we'll square up the hotel bill with you.'

'Behave yourselves. You don't have to do that, mate. I'm having too much fun.'

'Sounds like it.'

'It beats working, that's for sure,' said Craven.

'How would you know? You never used to do any bloody work. Lazy wanker,' said Jimmy.

'Look lads, as nice as this is I need to get going. I have to make a couple of drive-bys to spook a certain South African mare. Can't sit around here chatting to you reprobates all day. Got things to do, you know?'

'You mean the strip-bar is open?' Will piped up.

'Piss off. Will keep you posted.'

'Bye, yer wanker,' they said in unison and the line went dead.

Craven was grinning so hard it looked as if his face might split in two. He started the engine and eased his way out to the junction with the dual carriageway. There was a gap in the traffic and he edged out.

He was still chuckling to himself when he slowed down to a crawl at a roundabout and then felt a shunt in the back and heard a crunching noise.

'You've gotta be fucking joking me!' he said, looking in his rear-view mirror to see the bonnet of the car behind tight up against his back bumper. 'You fucking idiot!'

He yanked up the handbrake and leapt from the car. The other driver was already out surveying the damage.

'What the hell are you doing?' the driver yelled at Craven. He was a man in his late twenties, wearing a beany hat. 'You jammed on your anchors.'

'I did not. I slowed down and you slammed into the back of me. Look at the state of that.' Craven pointed at his smashed tail light and dented wing. The other car was missing a headlight, its shattered glass lying on the tarmac.

'Like bollocks. You went to go and then stopped. I didn't stand a chance.'

Craven returned to his car, came back with his mobile and started taking pictures.

'Not sure the insurance company will see it that way,' Craven said. 'You went into the back of me which makes it your fault.'

'I'm not admitting anything, mate. In fact, did you roll back?'

'Now you're having a laugh, son,' he continued to snap away.

Cars were trying to squeeze by to join the other lane.

'Look mate,' the other driver said. 'Rather than hold up the traffic here, there's a layby about two hundred yards the other side of the roundabout. Let's exchange details there before we get run over.'

'I got your reg number so don't think of driving off.'

'Alright. Wind your neck in.'

They both got in their cars, filtered onto the roundabout and headed straight on before pulling over at a wide layby a short distance up the road. They were both shaking their heads when they got out of their respective cars.

'My headlamp is proper fucked,' the man said, squatting down by the side of his car.

'What's your insurance details?' asked Craven, ready to tap them into the notes on his phone.

'That's gonna cost me big time. And I don't get paid till the end of the month.'

'What's your name?'

'How am I gonna get to work?'

'That's your problem. Now what's your name?'

'Oh, erm, Joshua Thomas. What's yours?'

'Bradley Craven. Who's your insurance company?'

'Direct Line.'

'Same here. And your car is a…'

'A Volkswagen,' the man said.

Craven looked at the car and did a double take.

'It's a Skoda, mate. Not a VW,' he said

'Oh yeah, that's right.'

'This is your car?'

'Course it is… and I've got insurance.'

'Glad to hear it.'

A white Transit van pulled alongside and the side-door slid open. A man jumped out. The bloke driving the Skoda leapt on Craven and strangled him in a headlock. The second man beat him over the head with a cosh and they bundled him into the van. The men piled inside and there was the sound of heavy boots striking the metal floor and muffled cries for help.

After a while it went quiet.

The men bounded from the Transit, slammed the side door shut and banged on the side of the van. It sped away. Then they got into the two cars and followed.

Forty minutes later Craven was coming around. His temples throbbed and unknown to him he had a lump the size of an orange on the back of his head. His tongue was sticking to the roof of his mouth. He tried to move but his arms and legs wouldn't work.

He cracked open his eyes and found himself staring down at a concrete floor. He was secured to a chair under a single naked lightbulb. Everything hurt. He lifted his head and a searing pain shot down his neck. So he narrowed his eyes and tried to focus. Beyond the pale cone of light all he could see was darkness. The place reeked of stagnant water.

'Fuuuuck,' he wheezed.

A man came into the light wearing a black bomber jacket and jeans. His face was hidden by a ski-mask. Craven froze, taking a sharp intake of breath. He instinctively flexed his body but he couldn't move. The man strode over and grabbed him by the throat.

'Agghh. What do you want?' Craven croaked. The man slapped him hard across the face, making his head swim and his vision dance.

Craven yelled out

'I'm... I'm... a police officer.'

A second figure came into view, dark and brooding.

'An ex police officer.'

It was Malice.

Chapter 38

Breaking the news to a family member that their loved one had died was never an easy thing to do, and that is when they are of sound mind before they even receive the news. Telling Wendy Horton, on the other hand, was a terrifying prospect.

Pietersen rang the bell and watched the women dressed in blue tunics scamper around on the other side of the glass. She waited. After a couple of minutes, she rang again.

Senior Staff Nurse Lorraine Taylor came into view. She tapped a code on the inner door and unlocked the outer one. Pietersen opened her warrant card out of courtesy.

'Hi, sorry to keep you waiting,' Taylor said adjusting the spectacles.

'No problem. I'm glad Wendy is able to see me today.'

'Come in.' Taylor led her into the reception area.

'After last time I was unsure if she'd see me.'

'I know it's a frightening experience for people who aren't used to this environment but to us it's another day in the office.'

'It was pretty scary.'

'It can be.'

'I have bad news for Wendy regarding her husband, do you anticipate that will cause a problem?'

'You never can tell. Patients like Wendy who suffer with severe conditions are unpredictable. One day you can tell her the world is about to end and she'll smile and carry on with whatever she's doing, and the next you can tell her *Coronation Street* is on when she's expecting Emmerdale and all hell breaks loose.'

They walked down the long corridor with bedrooms on either side. This time Pietersen didn't want to look in through the open doors. The day room she had been led to was light and airy with a couple of two-seater sofas and an armchair. Vases of flowers decorated the sideboard and a trolley with a plate of biscuits covered in clingfilm was parked in the corner.

'I'll go and get her,' Taylor said. Pietersen though it best to remain standing, conscious of Horton's initial reaction when she clapped eyes on her.

The minutes ticked by. Then Wendy Horton appeared in the doorway, flanked by Taylor. Pietersen steeled herself.

'Here you go, Wendy, this is the police woman I told you about,' Taylor cooed.

'Have we met before?' Wendy smiled and took a seat.

'We have,' Pietersen replied, taking the seat opposite.

'I'll be just outside,' Taylor mouthed and left the room, leaving the door open.

'Oh, that's right. You came to talk about John. I'm sorry, my head has been a little on the fuzzy side of late.'

'That's fine. It's about John I've come to see you today.'

'Okay.'

'I've got bad news, Wendy. I'm sorry to have to tell you... John is dead.'

Pietersen braced herself to take evasive action. Horton folded her hands in her lap, staring straight ahead.

'Oh no,' she said. 'He was a lovely man and a good husband. How did he die?'

'I'm afraid, he was murdered.'

'Murdered? Now that's a shame,' she continued to gaze into the distance.

'The forensic evidence indicates it happened around the time he went missing.'

'Where was he?'

'He was buried on a plot of waste ground.'

'Are you sure it's him?'

'The dental records have confirmed it's John.'

'So that's why he never came home.' She snapped her fingers. 'Deep down I knew something bad had happened, he would never have just disappeared like that.'

'I'm sorry, Wendy.'

'It's not your fault. I'm kind of relieved to know for sure. It was the not knowing that drove me crazy, well that and the other stuff.'

'Once the coroner has released the body you can sort out the funeral arrangements.'

Horton's eyes began to tear up and she wiped her face with her sleeve.

'Do you know if he ever found the child?' she asked.

'Pardon?'

'Well, when I say child... they would have been a teenager by then.'

'Who would have been, Wendy?'

'John went off to find the son or daughter he'd never seen. He was ever so upset when he left, kept saying he was going to make things right.'

'Make things right with who?'

'The woman he'd had a relationship with, and the child. It was before me and John got together but...'

'Did he say who they were?' Pietersen said.

'No. He said the less I knew about it, the better. The scandal was going to ruin us. We had a comfortable life and John was high up in the education establishment. He said the disgrace would destroy everything he'd worked for.'

'What scandal, Wendy?'

'Someone was going to go to the press with what they knew. They threatened to expose John as a rapist and tell the world about his illegitimate son.'

Pietersen dipped her brow.

'Why didn't you tell us this before?' she asked.

'John said not to tell anyone. He said it had to be kept a secret but now he's gone... well... there's no point now. He said the fewer people who knew, the better. He broke down one day and told me all about it when the pressure got too much. I think it tipped me over the edge to be honest.'

'Let me get this straight — John went to find his illegitimate child and the mother because someone was going to expose him in the newspapers?'

'Yes, that's right. I thought you knew.'

'We didn't know Wendy, because you didn't tell us.'

'I thought I had.'

'No. Who was the person putting pressure on John?'

'What pressure?'

'You said someone was going to expose John in the press... who was it?'

'In the press? Why would John be in the press?' Horton screwed up her face and began wringing her hands together.

'Because of the illegitimate child and the rape.'

'Yes that's right. John said a woman accused him of rape and she had a child. It was a terrible thing for me to have to listen to, but he was in an awful state. He was at his whit's end.'

'Who was threatening to expose him?' Pietersen could hardly contain herself.

'John kept saying he would make it right. He was going to sort things out with the mother so whoever it was couldn't embarrass us. He kept saying he needed to get out in front of the story—not really sure what that meant.'

'Who was it, Wendy? Who was threatening John?'

'When he told me, I couldn't believe it. I mean... she had a child, just like that. Me and John tried for years to have a baby and nothing happened. We went to the doctors for tests and they said there was nothing wrong with me and nothing wrong with him. But we couldn't have one — why was that?'

'Wendy, I want you to focus,' Pietersen was leaning forwards in her chair. 'Who was the person putting pressure on John?'

'It's not fair.' Tears filled her eyes. 'We'll never have a child now. John's not here anymore. He went away and never came back.'

Taylor came into the room and took Wendy's hand.

'I think it's time to go back to your room now,' she said helping her to her feet.

Taylor led her away. Horton was muttering to herself as she went.

Pietersen pulled out her phone to make a call but could only reach Malice's voicemail. She clicked the hang-up button. What she wanted to tell him was not something to leave in a message.

She walked from the building and sat in her car, the revelations of the last half an hour playing havoc in her head.

Chapter 39

Malice was aware of his phone buzzing on the table. But he found himself a little too busy to take the call. He grabbed Craven by the jaw and yanked his head up.

'Who the f—?' Craven gasped.

'Or to give you your full title, Brad, *ex*-bent copper,' Malice said. 'And do you know how I know you're bent?'

'What is this?'

'Because so am I. And it takes one to know one.'

A firecracker went off in Craven's head.

'You work with Kelly,' he croaked.

'Well done. I was worried for a moment that the bump on your head might have done you permanent damage.'

'What the fuck is this about?' Craven flexed his arms against the restraints.

'You will notice, Brad, that while my colleagues have kept their faces hidden I have no such scruples. In fact, it's important that you know precisely who you're dealing with, and anyway I can't be doing with those masks — bloody itchy things.'

'I don't know you.'

'But we know all about you. And the question that's been bouncing around in my mind is, what does Bradley Craven find so interesting on our patch?. You've been here a few days so there must be some little tit-bit that's holding his interest. Is it a piece of skirt, Brad?' Malice released his grip. Craven stared up at him and said nothing. 'No, I think not. Are you looking to buy a second home here? No, not that either. So, what is it, Brad?'

'I don't know what you're talking about.'

'Oh, now there you go making your first mistake. And do you know what mistake that is?'

'No.' Craven shook his head.

'Taking me for a fucking amateur.' Malice seized Craven by the throat, forcing him back in the chair. 'Don't make that error in judgement, Brad, cos it's gonna get you hurt. Understand?' Craven nodded his head. Malice let him go. 'So, I'll ask you again. Why are you here?'

Craven let his head slump forwards.

'I got friends who will make mincemeat of you,' he snarled.

'Maybe, but as I look around the room,' Malice spun around with his arms outstretched, 'I don't see any of them leaping to your defence. You're all alone, Brad, and at this rate you're not going to be in a fit state to tell them.'

'Go to hell.'

'Ha, quite possibly. I'm not an unreasonable man and I can see you're upset with the way this is going. So I'm going to make it easy for you. Rather than playing twenty-questions I'll tell you why I reckon you're here and you can answer yes or no... Easy right?' Malice bent menacingly down in front of Craven and placed his hands on his hips. 'We've seen you cruising around in your car checking out the locality, calling into pubs, cafes, hotels and the like. Now we know that when you were a copper you were into knock off tobacco, spirits and counterfeit clothing and we figure that now you're more of a freelance operator you're looking for new markets. A new customer base. How am I doing so far?'

'Way off.'

'Don't think I am, you know. Are you still in touch with your two pals, Will and Jimmy? We know about them as well, and we think you're looking to branch out.'

'You couldn't be further from the truth.'

Malice slammed his boot into Craven's chest sending his crashing backwards. The back of his head bounced off the floor causing him to see stars.

'I fucking told you not to make that mistake again.' Malice was standing over him. 'You and your limp dick friends are looking for a new outlet and you're the scout.'

'I'm not. I swear to you.'

Malice shoved the sole of his foot onto his neck.

'I think you're lying.' He let his boot off and signalled to the two men. They righted Craven in the chair.

'I'm here because of Kelly,' Craven croaked.

'What, are you shagging her?'

'No, she planted evidence on us and I'm here to put the frighteners on her.'

Malice resumed his position bending down, but this time resting his hands on Craven's knees.

'What, Kelly?' Malice asked.

'Yes. That's why I'm here. I don't know anything about branching out.'

'Kelly Pietersen planted evidence.'

'Yes.'

'When?'

'She was working in anti-corruption and I was under investigation.'

'You're kidding me.' Malice started laughing.

'No, it's the truth.'

'Bloody hell. Kelly Pietersen is a bent copper too? You wait till I get back to the office. The amount of shit she gives me. I can't believe that.'

'It's the truth, I swear. That's why I'm here.'

'I can't get over that, Kelly-fucking-Pietersen… bent. What do you intend to do?'

'We don't know yet.'

'You're here to put the fear of God into her?'

'Yes.'

'That's it? Nothing else?' asked Malice, cracking a smile and shrugging his shoulders.

'Yes.'

Malice took a Stanley knife from his pocket and slid the triangular blade from the handle. Craven flinched when he saw the glint of stainless steel.

'Looks like I got you all wrong, friend. Looks like I should cut these ties and we can have a proper chat about Kelly-fucking-Pietersen.'

'Yeah, let's do that. She is a lousy piece of shit, that one.'

Malice plunged the blade into Craven's calf muscle.

He screamed.

Malice pulled it out and stabbed the knife into his thigh. He let out another squeal and lurched about in the chair.

'Do you know how many stab wounds it takes from a blade like this for a person to bleed out and die?' Malice held the blood-stained knife in front of Craven's face. 'No? Neither do I. But I reckon we're going to find out today.'

Craven was bucking and wrenching against his bonds.

'What the fuck do you take me for? Kelly Pietersen, bent? You're having a laugh.' Malice drove the blade into Craven's other thigh. 'Now you had better start talking sense while you still have blood left.'

'Aggghhhh!' Craven bucked back and forth, his whole body shaking.

'You're down here looking for a new territory and I'm not going to stand for that.' Blood was soaking through Craven's jeans. His mouth was open and his eyes were as big as pool balls. 'So, here's what we're going to do.'

'What... what the fuck... I'm bleeding,' Craven gasped.

'You are, but I think...' Malice stuck the blade into his other calf. 'You got a lot more left in you.'

'Aggghhh! Fuck!' Craven yelled.

'You see my market is just about saturated and consequently our top line isn't growing, but then we don't deal in the same goods you do. So, this is what's going to happen. You're going to work for me. How about that?'

'You're fucking mad.'

'I know. But I'm a good business man and I can see a great opportunity sitting right here in front of me. You and your tin-pot mates have product that I want and, as you love visiting us, you can be my man on the ground. How about that?'

'Fuck!' Craven was staring down at the growing map of red covering his legs.

'Because I think we're getting on rather well and we'd make a great partnership. Well, when I say partnership, you would very much be my whipping boy.'

Malice thrust the knife into Craven's upper arm.

'Jesus Christ!' he shrieked.

'Is that a 'yes', then?' asked Malice, pulling out the blade. He went to plunge it in again.

'Yes, yes, yes!' shrieked Craven.

'Yes what?'

'I'll work for you.'

'Doing what?'

'Supplying you with goods.'

'And…' Malice pushed the blade into Craven's cheek.

'I'll be your man on the ground.'

'Working here?'

'Yes, yes. Working here.'

Malice wiped the blade on Craven's leg before sliding it back into the handle.

'See that wasn't so bad now, was it? I knew we'd reach an amicable agreement in the end. You work for me now and that's fine. We'll sort out the finer details when you've stopped leaking claret over the floor. Suffice to say when you show up here, you report for duty to me. Is that understood?'

'Yes, yes…' Craven gasped for air.

Malice nodded to the two men in masks who descended on Craven. They cut him free from the chair and began to strip him to tend to his wounds.

Craven was sobbing.

'Don't forget to give him a shot of antibiotics.' Malice disappeared into the gloom. 'God knows where this knife has been.'

Chapter 40

Pietersen rushed back to the station and began annotating the investigation board. How the hell had that crucial piece of information not come to light before? She asked herself the question over and over and each time she came to the same line — 'Because John told me not to'.

She chewed the cap on the marker pen.

If Horton was being blackmailed, by whom?

'Pietersen! If you got a minute,' Waite barked from her office.

'Yes ma'am.' She dropped what she was doing and beetled off in the direction of her boss's voice. She found Waite sitting behind her desk. The look on her face wasn't good.

'You want a word?' Pietersen said.

'Yes, come in and take a seat.' Waite removed her glasses and motioned for Pietersen to close the door.

'Do you need an update on the cold cases?'

'No, I've just had an unusual call.'

'Oh?'

'Did you interview Brenda Copeland in connection with the murder of John Horton?'

Waite narrowed her eyes.

'Yes, ma'am. We pulled her in to answer a few questions. Why?'

'She hasn't made an official complaint but she said you and Malice were overbearing and that you were leading her with your line of questioning.'

'I can assure you we didn't,' Pietersen shook her head. 'There are a number of inconsistencies in what she told us, not least of which is she lied.'

'She said you tried to put words in her mouth; tried to trick her into saying things. The whole experience left her emotionally distressed.'

'That's not true, ma'am.' Pietersen stood up and shook her head.

'What bit of it isn't true?'

'I agree she was tearful at the end of the interview but we did not go over the top in any way.'

'So, she wasn't distressed?'

'She was upset, but—'

'Do you plan to interview her again?'

'Given the way the case in unfolding I would say that's inevitable.'

'You need to tread carefully.'

'We'll do everything by the book, I can assure you, ma'am.'

'That's what I want to hear.'

'If she hasn't made a complaint, what was the call all about?'

'It was ACC Beresford. Apparently, he's a personal friend of Copeland and is a huge admirer of her work with the church. He understands the need to follow up with witnesses and suspects, but is urging that we do so in a constructive and sensitive manner.'

'Constructive and sensitive? What does that mean?' Pietersen was struggling to hide the fact that she was pissed off. 'I can assure you our conversation with Copeland was entirely PACE compliant and at no time did we lead or coerce her in any way. How come he calls you? What about our chain of command?'

'Let me deal with that,' Waite replied. 'In the meantime, I can't afford to have either of you suspended pending disciplinary action. So make sure you proceed with the utmost care and attention. I don't want this blowing up in our faces because you're being overzealous.'

'But ma'am,' Pietersen snapped back, her jaw tensing, her neck beginning to flush red. 'That is not an accurate characterisation of what took place.'

'Where the hell is Malice, anyway?' asked Waite.

'He had a personal matter to take care of. He'll be back later.'

'Make sure you impress on him the seriousness of the situation. If he's in any doubt, I would be more than happy to impress it on him myself.'

'I don't think—' Pietersen protested.

'That's all, Kelly.' Waite held her hand up to signal the discussion was over. 'Leave the door open on your way out.'

Pietersen stomped out into the corridor and slammed the heel of her hand into the swing doors leading to the office. Malice stopped studying the board and spun around. His nerves were still on edge.

'Shit. Open the door, why don't you?' he quipped.

'Yeah, well, you're going to punch something when you find out what darling Twinkle has been up to.'

'Oh?'

'She's only been mouthing off to Beresford,' Pietersen thumped the back of her chair.

'Beresford? How the hell—'

'And he's been on the blower to Waite.'

'Kelly, you're not making any sense.'

Pietersen closed her eyes, took a deep breath and exhaled. She moved her hands from her shoulders to her waist as she breathed out. Then repeated the action.

'Okay,' she said, opening her eyes. 'That's better. How did you get on?' she sidled up to Malice.

'I'm fine.' Malice turned into her, keeping his voice low. 'Craven won't be showing his face around here again.'

'How can you be sure?'

'The less you know, the better. Trust me. He's gone back to his mates with his tail between his legs.'

'What did you do?'

'Let's say I asked him politely to leave.'

'I don't know what to say.'

'Then why don't you tell me about this lot.' He waved his hand at the board. 'I'm sure the last time I looked we didn't have the word 'blackmail' written on it.'

'I went to see Wendy Horton to break the news about John. While I was there she came up with a whole lot of new information we didn't know about.'

Pietersen spent the next fifteen minutes walking through her conversation at the hospital. Malice sat in silence, soaking it up.

'Bloody hell,' he said when she's finished. 'You have had an eventful morning. Who would want to blackmail Horton?'

'How about Maxwell?' she said. 'Horton confides in him what he'd done and tells him about the kid. Then at a later date they have a fall out and Horton tells him their relationship is over and tries to finish it. Maxwell goes into a rage and says that if Horton walks away, he will divulge his murky past.'

'That could work, but why would they wind up here in two separate hotels?'

'Because Horton wanted to make amends in some way and patch things up with Twinkle in order to minimise the impact of the story, should Maxwell go public. Maxwell follows him and tries to stop it happening.'

'Bloody hell, you have been busy. Did you think that up all by yourself?'

'Very funny.'

'Wendy is an unreliable witness,' Malice said. 'She could be making it up.'

'I thought that too, but take a look at this.' Pietersen handed over a sheaf of computer printouts. She ran her finger down a column of figures. 'It's the same every month up until June 2009.'

Malice studied the numbers.

'This is dynamite,' he said.

'It would seem to back up what Wendy Horton told me.'

'But how come they wind up being murdered?' he asked.

'We know Twinkle argued with both men at the church. What if she didn't want her past to catch up with her and killed them to keep it quiet?'

'Maybe it wasn't Maxwell, maybe …'

'I don't trust her.'

'Nor me. This is great work.'

Pietersen switched her head back to Superintendent Waite.

'Now for the bad news,' she said. 'I need to tell you why Waite has got out of her pram.'

'Is that why you were...' Malice cocked his head towards Waite's office.

'Apparently Copeland has a hot line to Beresford. Waite hauled me into her office to tell me we need to tread carefully. She's told the ACC that when we interviewed her we were overbearing and put words in her mouth. Waite said that in future we need to ensure our approach is constructive and sensitive.'

'And Waite supported the ACC?' Malice said throwing his hands in the air.

'Yup. All the way.' Pietersen puffed her cheeks out and nodded.

'For fuck's sake.' It was Malice's turn to lose it. 'As if the job isn't difficult enough without having the rug pulled from under you by those above. Come on, get your coat.'

'Where are we going?'

'To be constructive and sensitive.'

Chapter 41

Frank is staring through me with sad eyes. He looks like someone has let the air out of him. I find it strange how a ruthless killer can look so vulnerable. He's sitting one side of the bed with me on the other, Clem's hand is curled in mine.

I've spent the last fifteen minutes bringing him up to speed with the police investigation. I also stepped through the possible scenarios we could face depending on which way the case goes. But having a hypothetical conversation with Frank about events that may or may not happen was always going to be a challenge. He only deals in certainties — abstract planning is never his strong suit.

'There's nothing you need to do,' I told him when he reached information overload and began to panic. 'I want you to know what's going on. That's all.'

'Okay,' he'd replied. 'I don't have to do anything?'

'No, Frank, I'll let you know when you do.'

'That's good. Thanks, Twink.'

And that was it — briefing over.

I'm not sure how much he absorbed. His attention is focused on the man lying in bed with his eyes closed.

'He's going to be okay, you know.' I try to sound reassuring, for Frank as well as myself. I reach my hand across the bed.

'But he's been unconscious for a long time, Twink, and he's not getting any better.'

He links his fingers with mine.

'It's only been a few days, Frank. The good news is he's not getting any worse.'

'I miss him. It's weird not having him around to set up what we need in Winfield. Sherbet and the guys are fine but it's not the same without Clem.'

'You... you're doing a fantastic job. And when Clem wakes up he's going to be so proud of what you've achieved — the house is up and running, we've started talking to St. Juniper's and have our first OutReach meeting in a couple of days. Plus... you saved my life. That's quite a list of successes. Don't you think?'

'Yeah, I suppose so, when you put it like that.' He squeezes my hand in his bear sized paw. 'I don't know where I'd be without you, Twink.'

'I know where I'd be without you, Frank. In the bloody mortuary.'

For the first time since we arrived he cracks a smile.

'I need to go,' he says. 'Me and two of the lads are testing out a new patch tonight. We eyeballed it yesterday and there were tons of people milling around looking for gear, but nobody was there to sell it. I reckon it could be rich pickings.'

'Sounds like you've found us a gold mine. You stay safe.'

He comes around to my side of the bed and envelopes me in a massive Frank-style hug. I stand and go onto my tip-toes, kiss him on his cheek and then he slopes off. I can't stand the thought of going home. Dennis will be coughing and gagging over his meal and Zoe will want to talk about what's happened to Rebecca. The jungle drums are bound to be working at full speed. I got a call from Carol to say Rebecca had been suspended pending an investigation and that I had to drop by the office to provide a statement. She also said they were going to talk to Dennis. Thankfully it's only me and Rebecca who can understand him — at least I think that's the case. Zoe, for all her hard work and dedication, can't understand a single word. Given the circumstances that's just as well. I'm not worried about that, though. I'm more concerned with the bloody coppers and their constant poking around. Not sure what good Beresford can do but it was worth a shot. At the moment I can do with all the help I can get. Fuck knows I need it.

I don't know what concerns me most, the fact that they're asking questions about John and Tim or that they're getting a little too close to our drugs business. Not that they know that but it's still a concern. Having Clem out of action doesn't help, he'd know what to do.

The door behind me opens and in walks Malice and his side-kick. I puff out a frustrated sigh.

'Can we come in?' he says.

'Looks like you already have.' I let go of Clem's hand and straighten myself in the chair. 'Now let me guess, has the ACC sent you along to apologise? Or are you going to continue your campaign of harassment?'

'That depends,' he says.

'On what?'

'On the next few minutes.'

'Do you know how objectionable you are?' I scowl at him.

'Yup. Fully up to speed with that.'

'This is your friend from the church, isn't it?' Pietersen says pointing at Clem.

'Yes, he was involved in a road rage attack. But then if you were doing your jobs properly you'd already know that,' I say.

I stare at them and an awkward silence settles between us all.

'We know all about it,' he replies. 'That's why we know it's not been reported.'

'We've been busy.' I turn away and look at Clem.

'Your friend gets put in hospital and you don't report it to the police? Don't you think that's a little odd, especially when you have such a close relationship with a senior officer?'

'We've been more concerned with Clem's welfare.' I refuse to look at them.

'While allowing whoever did this to be free to do it to someone else?'

'This is a busy time for us,' I say. 'And I've had to keep things on an even keel.'

'Like looking after Frank for example? We passed him when we came in,' Pietersen says jerking her thumb at the door.

'They're close. We're all close and this is upsetting for us all.'

'The brothers match the description of the two men who threw John Horton and Tim Maxwell out of the church after the argument with you.' Malice has an edge in his voice that unnerves me.

'Not this again?' I slap my hands on to the bed.

'The witness gave a detailed description of the men and it matches Clem and Frank.'

'Really? What did the description say, 'two black men, one much bigger than the other'?'

'No,' says Malice. 'They recognised them from the OutReach programme, so we're fairly sure it was them.'

'*Fairly sure*? Your ACC is going to love that level of scrutiny.'

'We have further questions for you, Mrs Copeland. Not wishing to pressurise you in any way, but we would appreciate your help.' Pietersen asks.

'You've bent my ear twice now about events that took place years ago and I've been very clear in my answers. So, no. Actually, I would not like to help.'

'New information came to light today, Mrs Copeland,' Pietersen says. 'And we think you might be able to clear up a few points. Would you be prepared to do that?'

'No, love. I'm not interested. Because we go around in circles. You ask me a question and I answer it, then you tell me I'm lying and you ask me another. To be perfectly honest... now how can I put this without offending you... I'm fucking bored with the whole thing. Now if you don't mind I'm—'

'Brenda Copeland, I'm arresting you for obstructing a police officer ...'

Chapter 42

Malice was standing to attention in Superintendent Waite's office having what's affectionately known in the trade as a 'conversation without coffee'. She was normally a woman of pallid complexion, but not today. Today she'd chosen to adopt the colour red.

'Be sensitive, I said. Be constructive, I said. And you go and fucking arrest her.' Waite prowled around what little floorspace she had at her disposal.

'Copeland was refusing to co-operate with our investigation, ma'am. I had no choice,' he protested.

'I thought I'd made myself abundantly clear, but no! Apparently when I said, 'you need to tread carefully' you translated that into 'let's give it the full bull-in-a-china-shop treatment'. What the hell were you thinking?'

'Maybe I was thinking about solving a double murder case.' Malice snapped back.

'Don't get smart with me.'

'We need to interview her concerning the murder of John Horton and possibly that of Timothy Maxwell.

She's lied to us repeatedly and we have new evidence. We could make real progress here.'

'But there are ways of going about that.'

'And we're expected to form an orderly queue waiting for a convenient time when she deems us worthy of an audience?' Malice said, determined not to take this lying down.

'I don't think so, boss. I know you took a call from the ACC but with all due respect he's not at the sharp end of this investigation. I am. And that was my call given the circumstances. Taking her into custody was the right course of action whatever the fallout.'

'And that's my problem, Malice. You never consider the fallout. Get out.'

Malice stormed back to the office where Pietersen was sitting chewing her fingernails.

'I thought you might need this.' She handed him a cup of coffee.

'Thanks. It could have gone worse.'

'Not from what I could hear.'

'Are you ready? Clear on our lines to take?'

'Yes, and the duty solicitor has arrived. They're waiting for us.'

'Did you see the look on Copeland's face when the custody sergeant booked her in?'

'Yes. Like she was checking into a swanky hotel.'

'She didn't look in the least bit concerned.'

'There's something not right about this whole case. Let's do this.'

They gathered together what they needed and walked down to the interview suite. Pietersen opened the door to Interview Room 3. Twinkle was already sitting at a table. A man wearing thick rimmed glasses and a comedy comb-over was at her side.

Malice and Pietersen took their seats and he pressed the button on the recording device. There was a long buzzing sound. When it fell silent, Malice introduced everyone in the room and reminded Copeland she was under caution.

'You have significant bruising around your neck, Brenda,' Pietersen said. 'Would you like us to get that checked out?'

'No, I'm fine,' Copeland replied, conscious she'd had to hand over her scarf to the custody sergeant when she arrived.

'Do you want to tell us how you came by them?' Pietersen asked.

'I run the OutReach programme and we got into a minor scuffle with a lad. It was nothing serious, he didn't mean anything.'

'It doesn't look like it to me.'

'It's fine.' Copeland said, fingering the blemishes around her throat.

'I arrested you for obstructing a police officer in the execution of his duties, an offence which can carry a maximum one-month imprisonment and, or, a level three fine,' Malice said. 'You have not been formally charged with that offence but I do want you to cooperate with this enquiry, and that means answering questions. Do you understand?'

'I understand, that I am this far...' Copeland held up her hand with the tips of her thumb and first finger millimetres apart. 'Away from making a formal complaint against you Detective Sergeant.'

Malice looked at her, then puffed out a breath as he turned his attention to her solicitor.

'Do you agree to cooperate, Brenda?' he then said.

'Get on with it.'

'I want to start by returning to the—' Malice got no further.

'I'd like to start,' Copeland interrupted, 'by placing on record that this is the third time you've spoken to me in as many days, which in my view is excessive and bordering on harassment. My solicitor, Mr Jenkins here, has advised me that my best course of action is to answer 'no comment' to your questions. But I'm not going to take his advice because I want a public record of the ridiculous nature of this enquiry.'

'That's your prerogative, Brenda. Now if I might be allowed to continue?' Malice said. Copeland nodded and Jenkins looked like he'd received a sharp slap on the wrist. 'I'd like to return to the events of 1993 when you had an altercation with John Horton in a pub during which you glassed him in the face. You were found guilty of assault and some time before the sentencing hearing you suffered a miscarriage. We also know that during the investigation you accused Horton of rape, a claim you later withdrew. Why did you do that?

'How the hell is this relevant? It happened twenty-six years ago.' Copeland pulled at her hair.

'Please answer the question.'

'I told you all this before. John was away, studying at university and I suspected he was playing around. On my twenty-first birthday he bought me a jewellery set and we went out for dinner. When we got back to my digs, he wanted sex. I didn't fancy it, but that didn't stop him.'

'Was he violent towards you?' Pietersen asked.

'No. We'd gone to bed together and having bought me a nice gift plus a fancy meal he thought that gave him a fast pass to getting his leg-over. I was tired and full of wine and told him I wanted to go to sleep. He was having none of it and climbed on top. A couple of minutes later he was snoring his head off.'

'You reported this but it wasn't taken forward.'

'It was his word against mine and given the circumstances they didn't believe me. I'll ask you again, how is this relevant?'

'So he did rape you?' Pietersen said.

'Yes. I mean no, I mean... what the hell is all this about?'

'It helps to paint the picture of the relationship between you and John. You fell pregnant and told him about the baby.'

'Yes, that's right.'

'And you told us the row in the pub started because you confronted him about having sexual relations with other women.'

'That's correct.'

'Are you sure that's what the argument was about?'

'Yes.'

'Did you have the argument because you told John about the baby and he wanted nothing to do with it?' Malice joined in the questioning.

'No, that's not what happened.'

'Did you tell John he was going to be a father and his reaction was not what you expected. Instead of being delighted and supportive, he was more concerned about how it would impact on his studies and then, in a fit of rage, you smashed the glass on the side of the bar and attacked him?'

'That's rubbish.' Copeland flashed a glance at her solicitor.

'That's the reason why John did a runner after the verdict was handed down. He wanted to get away from his responsibilities. He had another life in university and having a kid was never part of the plan.'

'That's very interesting Detective Sergeant, but it didn't happen that way.'

'John never knew you'd had a miscarriage, did he?' Pietersen asked.

'I guess not.'

'You didn't tell him when he got in touch, trying to trace his estranged son or daughter?'

'How could I when he didn't get in touch?'

'I think he did. I think he tracked you down and you saw an opportunity,' said Malice.

'This is a pure flight of fancy.' Copeland turned again to her solicitor who was sitting stony-faced.

'You blackmailed John,' Malice continued. 'Threatening to re-ignite the rape allegation and his illegitimate child. You threatened to ruin his career and his marriage.'

'That's an outrageous accusation! I did no such thing.' Copeland jumped out of her chair. Her solicitor pushed her back down.

Pietersen slid a wad of printouts across the table.

'I am showing Brenda Copeland the bank statements for John Horton dating back to 2007 — item A003. They show cash withdrawals of two-hundred pounds made on the last day of the month. Twenty-one transactions altogether. The last one being May 2009. He sent you money every month because you threatened to expose him.'

'This is complete nonsense,' Copeland shoved the reams of paper back across the desk. 'There's nothing here that implicates me.' She was beginning to lose her nonchalant air.

'For twenty-one months you extorted money from him.' Pietersen pushed the paperwork back in front of Copeland. 'Then one day he shows up at the church — 19th of June, 2009. You fly into a rage and a heated argument ensues. Eventually your friends, Frank and Clements Mataya, eject him and Tim Maxwell from the premises. People have described the Mataya brothers as being your right-hand men in the OutReach programme. Others have described them as behaving like your minders. So, it fits that they would come to your assistance when you were confronted by Horton.'

'Don't bring them into this.' Copeland barked and pointed her finger.

'Are you denying they were there, or that they play the role of 'protector'?'

'I said leave them out of this.'

'What happened to John Horton and Timothy Maxwell after they left the church? What did the Mataya brothers do?' said Malice.

'John Horton was never at the church.'

'We think he was, and his surprise visit resulted in a blazing row. You were shouting and swearing at them — do you recall the incident now?'

'That didn't happen.'

'John showing up was not part of the plan, was it?' Pietersen leaned forward, trying to force eye contact with Copeland. She stared down at the table. 'You're known in the church as Saint Twinkle, people fall over themselves to hail your achievements from the rafters. You had just as much to lose if the truth about your past came out. The church has a track record of taking a dim view of women who get pregnant out of wedlock, especially those who extort money from a man for a child that never was.'

'This is a complete…' Copeland raised her head and glared at Pietersen; her eyes betraying every ounce of hatred she felt.

Malice pulled a photograph from a folder and laid it on the table in front of Copeland.

'I'm showing Benda Copeland item A011. This is the grave where we found the body of John Horton. He was killed by a blow to the head which caved in the base of his skull.' Copeland picked it up. It trembled in her grasp. 'Did the brothers kill John Horton after they escorted him from the church. Did you instruct them to murder him to keep him quiet? Or, did you deliver the fatal blow that took the life of John Horton?'

'I… I…' she mumbled, tossing the photo onto the table like it was red hot.

'We know you have a history of lashing out when events don't go your way,' Pietersen said. 'You yelled out in court that you wished John had one-hundred and ten stiches in his face instead of the ten he received. We know you're capable of violence. Did you kill John Horton?'

'I said about the stitches because I was angry.' Copeland clenched her fists. 'Angry that he'd forced himself on me and angry that he didn't want to know about the baby.'

'You lied to us?' Malice said.

Jenkins put his hand on her arm. But she yanked it away.

'I've had enough of this. I didn't blackmail John Horton.'

'I think that's exactly what happened, you saw an opportunity—'

'Neither did I kill him.'

'You had a strong motive to–'

'You know nothing about me!' Copeland leaned across the table and spat the words into Malice's face.

'You blackmailed Horton and when he unexpectedly turned up at the church you killed him.'

'I didn't do it… Dennis did!'

Chapter 43

Everything stopped in Interview Room 3. Malice, Pietersen and the duty solicitor did multiple double-takes. All of them looking like extras in a *Marx Brothers* sketch. Eyes wide, mouths open.

'Who?' Jenkins spluttered. He was way behind the curve.

'Dennis?' said Pietersen. 'Your husband, Dennis?'

'I don't know another one,' said Copeland.

'But you told us he'd been ill since…' Pietersen referred to her pocket book. '2005. You told us that his condition had deteriorated dramatically in the first couple of years to the extent whereby he required round-the-clock care. By 2007 he was virtually bed-bound.'

'Are you telling us that despite his debilitating condition Dennis was capable of blackmailing someone for almost two years and killing two men in 2009?' asked Malice, shaking his head in disbelief.

'I have no idea if he killed them or not,' said Copeland.

'But you said it was Dennis?' Pietersen asked.

'It was.'

'You're not making sense, Mrs Copeland.' Malice wiped at his forehead. 'How on earth could Dennis be able to do that?'

'Do you always lack imagination, Detective Sergeant?'

'Sorry?' replied Malice.

'I was asking do you lack imagination?'

'I'm afraid I don't understand.'

'I'll ask you love.' Copeland switched her gaze to Pietersen who bristled at the word *Love*. 'Does your partner usually have difficulty putting two and two together or is he having an off day?'

'I don't get what you're driving at.' Pietersen was equally as confused.

'Well he sure as hell isn't joining up the dots,' Copeland said tipping her head in Malice's direction. 'I reckon we've hit the buffers in terms of his mental agility.'

'Why don't you help us then, Mrs Copeland?' said Pietersen.

'I'm telling you my husband did those things. And you're challenging my version of events because you believe Dennis' illness would have rendered him incapable of carrying them out. Can you see a way in which my version of events could be true?'

Copeland sat back in her chair and folded her arms. There was a moment of silence as three people tried to get their heads around what they were being told.

'If Dennis wasn't that ill,' said Pietersen.

'Halleluiah! Go to the top of the class.' Copeland sprang from her seat, hands in the air. 'I knew you were brighter than him.'

'But at the time Dennis was four years into his illness and you were claiming incapacity benefit to pay for twenty-four-hour care. How can you say—'

'We lied about the severity of his condition in order to claim the benefit support,' Copeland interrupted. 'Do you have any idea what it's like caring for someone with a degenerative condition? Every morning you wake and ask yourself the same question, 'I wonder what he's going to be like today?' We needed help. I was working all night and caring for him all day. I didn't know if I was on my arse or my elbow most of the time. Do you know how long it takes to get assessed? And when you do, some kid turns up who's read every book there is on delivering critical care and has never so much as toileted a grown adult. And they tick their boxes before giving you the good news that the patient doesn't meet the necessary criteria. Like you should be delighted he's not as ill as you thought! Yeah, right. Fucking celebrate that, bastard. So yes, when we were assessed we exaggerated his condition. Not to put too finer point on it, we threw the kitchen sink at it.'

'You made it up?' Malice said.

'I didn't make up the fact that we were in desperate need of help. Or that Dennis was sick and going downhill. I didn't make up the fact that we were on the bones of our arses without two pennies to rub together. Dennis was going to get there at some point, we simply brought the date forward. I suppose now you're going to change tack and do me for benefit fraud?'

'We're more interested in getting to the bottom of what happened to John Horton,' said Malice.

'What did happen, Mrs Copeland?' asked Pietersen.

'Oh, please call me Twinkle. You're right. Horton and Maxwell showed up at the church. I'd been in contact with John since the day he'd reached out to me about the child. I told Dennis and all he could see was pound signs flashing before his eyes. So, he set about getting a monthly payment from John in exchange for keeping quiet about what had happened. All the time John was asking for photographs of the child and Dennis kept refusing. I told Dennis to stop. It was getting out of hand. It was obvious John was getting into a right state and becoming more and more desperate. Then one day, out of the blue, he turns up with Maxwell in tow.'

'What did he say?' asked Pietersen.

'He was demanding to see the kid. Kicking off big style. Clem and Frank had no idea what was going on, all they knew was this bloke was shouting at me and they booted him out.'

'The account we have states that it was you who was doing the shouting.' Pietersen referred to her notes.

'Yeah, well… maybe they're remembering what they want to remember. I can assure you there was shouting on both sides. John was really angry.'

'What happened next?'

'At around nine o'clock that night they showed up at our house, demanding I speak with them. I feared it might kick off again so I sent the carer home early to get a bit of privacy. Sure enough, the situation degenerated into a full-blown argument. John wanted me to forgive him about leaving me in the lurch and I told him to stick his apology where the sun doesn't shine. He said something about his wife being in a psychiatric hospital and how she was fixating about the rape and the baby. He said that if he went back and told her I'd forgiven him, she would get better. Given my own circumstances, I wasn't inclined to help anyone else recover. Least of all John's bloody wife.'

'How did Dennis get involved?' Pietersen asked.

'He was sleeping in the other room and the shouting must have woken him up. He was full of drugs and all over the place when he appeared in the lounge. We'd been doing some modifications to the down-stairs bedroom and there were tools lying about. He appears in the living room with a hammer in his hand. Before I could say anything, he set about them.'

'There was a fight?' asked Malice.

'Yes, of sorts. Dennis went berserk.'

'What did you do?'

'I ran.'

'Where to?'

'I don't know. I wanted to get out of there as fast as I could and spent the rest of the night wandering the streets not wanting to go back home. It was around five o'clock in the morning when I eventually returned.'

'What did you find?'

'Nothing. I came home to an empty house. John and his friend were gone as was Dennis.'

'What did you do?'

'There were blood stains on the carpet and on the couch. I set to with a scrubbing brush and got rid of them.'

'Is it the same suite and carpet you have in the house now?' Pietersen scribbled on a notepad.

'No, we got rid of them shortly afterwards.'

'Did you ask Dennis what he did or where he'd been?'

'Nope. He got back to the house around six and went straight to bed. At that time we had a turnaround for the carers at eight o'clock, so she didn't notice anything out of the ordinary. After all the excitement, Dennis collapsed. It was as though he'd used up a week's worth of energy in one go. He was out of it for days.'

'Why didn't you call the police?' Malice said.

'I figured Dennis had chased them away and wasn't too keen on the police asking awkward questions about why John was there.'

'Let me get this straight …' said Malice shifting in his chair. 'You never asked Dennis what had happened?'

'No, never. And he never spoke of it.'

'What do you think happened?'

'I don't think about it.'

'No, but if you did…?'

'Dennis always had a temper and it got worse as a result of his illness. He had so much pent up anger and frustration. Ever since you lot came around asking questions about John I've had a feeling that something bad had happened to them.'

'Did Dennis continue to blackmail John after they visited your house?' said Pietersen. Closing her notes and leaning forward.

'No. He said he'd come to an arrangement.'

'So, you believed they were still alive?'

'Of course.'

'What was the arrangement?'

'No idea. All I know is, he never mentioned John's name again.'

'Are you seriously expecting us to believe you don't know what happened to John Horton or Tim Maxwell?' Malice threw his pen onto the table.

'You can believe what you like. I'm telling you what happened. If you want to know more, you'll have to ask Dennis… good luck with that.'

Chapter 44

Bloody hell, this is dragging? I glance at my wrist, forgetting the custody sergeant had taken my watch when he booked me in. By my estimation, I've been here three hours. Twenty-one more to go. Then they'll have to charge me, release me or bail me to appear at a later date. They could go cap in hand to the top brass for a twelve-hour extension, but with Beresford in my corner, that's never gonna happen.

Tick tock, tick tock.

They took my fingerprints when I arrived and I had to endure a mouth swab, which was a first. It's a sorry barometer of my life that when I was allowed to make a call, I made it to a fucking care provider. I had to let Carol know what was happening so she could make the necessary arrangements for Dennis. When I told her, she went into a flat spin; kept asking me all kinds of questions I couldn't answer, none of which was about him. I tried to reassure her, but I don't think it worked.

I massage my fingers into my neck. My bruises are still sore to the touch. The whitewashed walls look like they could do with freshening up and the blue plastic-covered mattress has seen better days. My pillow has all the support of three layers of kitchen roll and I can push my fingers through the blanket, it's that thin. The camera in the corner of the cell keeps its beady eye on me. At least the stainless-steel toilet smells of bleach.

I settle back and pull the blanket around my legs. This is going to be my home for a while and the trick is not to allow my anxieties to run amok. The onus is on the police to prove I killed John, or ordered his murder. What I need to do is figure out my next move. It's unlikely they have any forensic evidence, or they would have nailed my arse to the front of the building by now.

All they have is a convoluted motive, a stack of unsubstantiated circumstantial evidence and an overactive imagination; hardly enough to clear the threshold test required by the CPS. I need to hold my nerve and run down the clock.

Tick tock, tick tock.

I'm imagining the scene in the incident room. Malice and Pietersen will be running around trying to work out what to do, with their boss yelling at them. I allow myself a little chuckle, thinking of the mayhem I've caused.

Their obvious course of action will be to speak to Dennis and conduct a search of the house. Plus they'll want to obtain his medical records. All of which should slow them down. They won't be able to obtain Dennis' permission to access his records and hopefully that will keep them tied up in red tape.

Tick tock, tick tock.

I'm worried about Frank. Sooner or later he's going to try to contact me and it won't be long before he's freaking out. I just hope he'll have the good sense to not do anything stupid. Though when that term is applied to Frank, the word 'stupid' covers a wide range of possibilities.

The hatch opens and a familiar face appears in the window.

'You asked for a cup of tea?'

Chapter 45

Malice and Pietersen were beavering away in the office, each one with a phone pressed to the side of their head. When their calls ended, they both stared at each other.

'Shit,' they said in unison.

'We need a letter from a senior officer requesting access to Dennis' records,' said Malice. 'Along with a completed DP2 form — whatever the hell that is. Only then can we get sight of them without his consent.'

'My call was no better.' Pietersen scraped back her hair and adjusted her ponytail. 'I spoke to a woman at the care provider and she confirmed he's unable to communicate.

We'd better get busy with the paperwork.'

'We need to search the house.'

'At least with Copeland under arrest we don't need a warrant.'

'You know this is a wild goose chase, right?' Malice said.

'I know. She's lying. I don't buy a word of it.'

'She did identify the murder weapon correctly.'

'Yeah, that could be a lucky guess or she might be throwing that in as a little teaser. She said that Dennis 'set about' Horton and Maxwell with the hammer. If that was the case we'd have found defensive wounds on the bodies. The post-mortem results said each man died from a single blow, there was nothing on their hands or arms.'

'Why would she throw her husband under the bus like that?' Malice said.

'He's a soft target and pointing the finger at him does make us jump through hoops.'

'The problem is... even when we look through his records what's it going to show? If the Copelands did exaggerate his condition in order to claim benefits — it's hardly going to say that.'

'We don't have a choice. Let's get the paperwork together and split up. I'll take the house and you pay the care provider a visit.'

Carol Tennant was waiting in reception, twitching. Her working week was going from bad to worse; first the revelation about Rebecca giving Dennis a handjob and now the police wanted to access his records. She was in full damage limitation mode.

Malice pushed open the door and she held out her hand.

'Carol Tennant, Director of Care.'

Malice shook it and opened his warrant card.

'DS Malice, I believe you spoke to my colleague on the phone earlier.'

'It sounded urgent.'

'Can we go somewhere private?'

'My office is on the first floor.' Tennant led the way up a set of stairs and passed a suite of offices. She beckoned Malice inside the third one on the right and closed the door. 'Please take a seat. Your colleague told me you wanted access to Dennis Copeland's records, which is fine.' She shrugged. 'But I'm afraid since the Data Protection Act came into force there are strict procedures we have to follow.' Tennant clasped her hands together on the desk, her head racing with possibilities and conjecture. 'Is this about the incident with Rebecca?' She could contain her anxiety no longer.

'Rebecca who?' replied Malice.

'She's one of the carers who looks after Dennis. Twinkle has made a serious complaint about her. I can assure you this type of thing is very rare, in all my years working in this sector I've never once come across anything like this.'

'What's the complaint?'

Tennant screwed up her face.

'It's not why you're here?' she asked.

'I'm sorry, I don't know what you're talking about.'

'Oh.' The tension eased from her shoulders. 'If you're not here to discuss the complaint then it would be wrong of me to disclose the nature of the incident.'

'I'm here because we want to see the care records for Dennis Copeland. I have the necessary paperwork.' Malice pulled two folded documents from the inside pocket of his jacket. 'I think you'll find them in order.'

Tennant scanned the pages.

'Murder investigation!' she gasped, her jittery disposition returning with a vengeance. 'I know you're talking to Twinkle down at the station, because she called me, but she didn't say anything about a murder investigation.'

'Mrs Copeland is helping us with our enquiries.'

'Is she involved?'

'I'm not at liberty to go into detail.'

'My God.'

Malice leaned closer.

'How well do you know Brenda Copeland?'

'Really well, we attend the same church together. She's a pillar of our community, an absolute diamond. I've known her and Dennis for years.'

'How long have you been providing care for him?'

'Since the beginning, so that would be... from 2005, maybe 2006. Twinkle looked after Dennis when he initially fell ill but then it got too much for her, we took over when his assessment came through. I've worked here for twenty-two years and have seen his condition deteriorate. Twinkle is a miracle... how she copes is beyond me.'

'How close are you to Dennis?' Malice asked.

'How do you mean?'

'Have you personally conducted a review of his care requirements or do your staff handle that?'

'I'm a Director in the business now but worked my way up. In the early days I was part of the team who looked after him and was very mindful of his worsening condition. As it changed we had to adjust the care provision to accommodate his needs.'

'Cast your mind back to 2009... how would you describe his illness?'

She raised her eyebrows.

'Umm... 2009... by then Denis had been sick for a couple of years and his health had deteriorated fast. From what I can recall he was largely bed-ridden apart from the time he spent in his wheelchair. He could just about feed himself but had to be helped with hot drinks. He was fully continent and his speech was okay… but it was starting to degrade.'

'Was he capable of getting out of bed unaided?'

'Oh no. His motor skills were poor. He needed help dressing and couldn't support his own weight. Though his cognisant abilities were intact.'

'So, in your opinion, Dennis wasn't capable of leaving the house under his own steam?'

'Absolutely not. Not in 2009. Can you tell me what this is about, why the interest in Dennis?'

'I can't tell you that, but it's why I want to see his records.'

Tennant read the two pieces of paper again.

'The paperwork looks to be correct,' she said. 'But it needs to be signed off by our compliance manager and she's away from the office.'

Malice bristled in his chair.

'I cannot stress enough how urgent this—'

'Please let me finish,' Tennant held up her hand. 'After your colleague called, I requested the records be retrieved from our archive. I'm afraid until the paperwork is complete, you can't remove the documents from our premises. However, in light of the gravity of the situation, you can look at them here.'

'Thank you. That's a start.'

'They're in the conference room next door.' Tennant got up from behind her desk and held the door open for Malice. They walked a short distance and entered a large board room with a massive table flanked by leather backed chairs on either side. Stacked in the centre of the table was a pile of storage boxes. 'These are his records.'

'Shit,' Malice muttered after he'd counted to twelve. 'I wasn't expecting this.'

'Every time a carer makes a visit, he or she fills in a day-sheet which details what they've done and the condition of the patient. Some carers write very little, while others write War and Peace. We compile the notes and store them.'

'Nothing is computerised?'

She shook her head, 'It's all done by hand.'

'Please tell me they're catalogued in date order.'

'They were.'

'What do you mean, *were*?'

'We've been in this building for a little over two years. Our previous office was in a shoddy state of repair because the parent company at the time wouldn't spend the money to renovate the building. It came to a head when several pipes burst and flooded the place. The records storage room took the brunt of it. We rescued what we could but some of the papers were destroyed.'

'Are all Dennis' records there?'

'Oh yes, they're all there, but not in a sensible order. We had to save what we could and maintaining the chronology was not the priority.'

'I'm particularly interested in June 2009.'

Malice removed the lid from the box nearest to him to find it stuffed full of papers, some in folders, others loose leaf. He pulled out a sheet. The ink in one corner had run from the water damage. He looked at the date on the top: 18 May, 2011. He pulled out another, 2 February 2007.

Bollocks.

Chapter 46

The door was opened by a woman dressed in a white tunic holding a cup of tea. Memories of her first encounter with Wendy Horton flashed through Pietersen's mind, and all of a sudden the thought of entering the Copeland's house took on an entirely different perspective.

'Can I help you?' the woman asked.

'Hi. My name is Detective Kelly Pietersen,' she offered her warrant card. 'Brenda Copeland is helping us with an enquiry and we have the authority to search her house. May I come in?'

'Umm... I suppose so. I'm Zoe, one of Dennis' carers. Do you mind if I call Twinkle first?'

'I'm afraid that's not possible.'

'The office said she was with the police and we had to be flexible with our hours.'

Zoe held her position, blocking the doorway.

'May I come in?' Pietersen tried again.

Zoe hesitated, then stepped aside.

'Yeah, of course. It's just me and Dennis, and he's taking a nap,' she said, tracking down the hallway to the lounge, Pietersen followed.

'How long have you been looking after him?' Pietersen asked.

'A few years now. I work the day shift. He's a lovely bloke. What's happened to Twinkle?'

'I can't say. Where's Dennis?'

'He's in the back room, I can show you if you like.'

'That would be good.'

The two women went out into the hallway and Zoe cracked open a door leading off to the left.

'Dennis has a room downstairs, for obvious reasons,' she whispered, stepping aside to allow Pietersen to pop her head in. The room was in semi-darkness with the curtains drawn. A large hospital-style bed with guard rails dominated the space. Around the walls were medical supplies, linen and towels stacked on shelves. A large bath had been installed in one corner with a second hoist hanging above it. Dennis was lying in the bed, wearing blue pyjamas, covered up his chest with a quilt. His face was the colour of uncooked pastry and he was snoring softly.

'He's not so good today, so he stayed in bed. The tablets knock him out when he's below par.'

Pietersen backed away.

'Do you mind if I take a look around?' she asked.

'No help yourself. I'll be in the kitchen. Do you fancy a cup of tea?'

'Coffee would be good.'

Zoe beetled off and Pietersen bounded upstairs. The bedrooms were neat and tidy; the beds looked as though they'd never been slept in. The main bedroom was at the front of the house, overlooking the road. She opened drawers, looked under the bed and rummaged in the wardrobe. Nothing but women's clothing, jewellery and shoes.

'I wish my place was as tidy as this,' she whispered to herself, as she went into the room across the landing. This wardrobe contained coats, scarves and the drawers were filled with bedding. She looked out of the window and saw a shed in the back garden.

That looks more interesting.

Pietersen went downstairs and passed Zoe preparing a hot drink in the kitchen. A rack of keys was fixed to the wall by the back door. She selected the most likely candidates and made her way outside. The third key she tried caused the lock to spring open. Inside was an oversized lawn mower, three-fold up chairs and a work bench.

'What have we here?' Pietersen donned a blue glove and shook an evidence bag from her pocket. She picked a hammer from the bench and held it up to the light. It looked old and well used. She dropped it into the bag and sealed the top.

When she got back in the house she found Zoe stirring a mug of coffee.

'Here you go,' Zoe nudged it across the worktop, her eyes widening when she clapped eyes on the hammer in the plastic bag. 'I'm going through into the lounge,' she said.

Pietersen placed the hammer on the floor in the hallway and followed her into the living room. She ran her eyes around the room, nothing jumped out as being out of the ordinary; a three-piece suite, a mantlepiece filled with photographs, a TV and a low coffee table.

'Is it because of what happened with Rebecca? I hear she's facing a disciplinary,' Zoe sat on the arm of the chair.

'Who's Rebecca?' Pietersen sipped her drink.

'She's the girl who works on the opposite shift to me. I don't know what went on but Twinkle was ever so upset the other morning. She left the house in tears when I arrived and the next thing I know Rebecca has been suspended. Everyone's talking about it.'

'No, it's nothing to do with that.'

'Dennis is really upset. He had a special bond with her.'

Pietersen was only half listening. Her gaze had landed on a photograph mounted in a silver frame on the window ledge. She sidled over and picked it up.

'Why is their relationship special?' she asked.

'Dennis isn't able to speak. He just grunts and snorts, or at least that's what it sounds like to me. But Rebecca seems to be able to have a conversation with him. He's going to miss that.'

'Sorry... say that again.' Pietersen looked at the picture, then around the room and back to the picture. It showed Brenda Copeland standing next to Dennis who was in his wheelchair. Behind them was a Xmas tree and the windowsill was crammed with cards.

'Don't know how it works,' continued Zoe. 'But she chats away with him. I'm completely lost, can't understand a word.'

'Rebecca speaks to Dennis?' Pietersen turned the frame over and prised open the metal clips securing the back.

'She does, but more importantly he talks back to her.'

'And he doesn't...' she removed the photograph and stared at the words scribbled on the back.

Twinkle, you lying cow.

'Sorry I don't understand,' said Zoe.

'Excuse me.' Pietersen walked out into the hallway and pulled out her phone. She dialled a number, Catherine Anders picked up.

'Hi Cath, it's Kelly Pietersen. I need a forensics team at the Copeland house ASAP.' She reeled off the address and returned to the lounge still holding the picture in her hand.

'Sorry Zoe. Tell me that again about Rebecca.'

Chapter 47

Malice drained the last of the coffee from a plastic cup and lined it up beside the others. The large table in front of him was piled high with paper and a stack of unopened storage boxes was sitting on a desk at the side. His temples were numb and his eyes were heavy.

The buzz from the fluorescent fittings above was the only noise. The place was deserted. He'd spent a couple of hours at the care offices trawling through the paperwork, getting himself worked up and frustrated. But more to the point… getting nowhere. Eventually Tennant had popped her head in to say he was free to remove the records from the premises if he wanted to. So, he bundled them into his car and had headed back to the station, where he'd been for the past four hours… getting nowhere.

He glanced up at the clock on the wall. It was close to eight p.m. The lights came on in the corridor outside and the sound of heels coming down the hallway got louder. Pietersen shouldered her way through the door, her arms ladened with two pizza boxes and a plastic bag.

'Dinner is served,' she said placing them on the desk before cracking open a can of coke. 'They didn't have that spicy one you wanted so I got something else.'

'Is it spicy?' Malice asked.

'Don't know.'

'This delivery service leaves a lot to be desired.'

'Get it your bloody self, next time.'

Malice flipped the lid off the box and tore off a slice of pizza.

'Thanks,' he said with his mouth full.

'What the hell is all this?' she asked, casting her eyes around the room.

'Visit reports. Every time a carer calls on Dennis they record it.'

'Shit, that's a lot,' she said, shoving the crust into her mouth and reaching for another. 'But surely all you need to do is—'

'They're not in date order. The reports are all mixed up.'

'Ah, hence the mess.'

'Exactly. How did you get on?'

'Good and bad. I found a hammer in the shed.'

'Nice one.' The end of another slice disappeared into his mouth.

'Your mate Anders took one look at it and said it wasn't the right shape. The one we're looking for has a rounded head whereas this one is square. She took it away for analysis all the same.'

'That was short lived.'

'Indeed. Then I spotted this…' she fished a photograph from her pocket. 'Take a look.'

Malice grabbed a napkin, wiped his fingers and pinched the picture.

'What am I looking at?' he said.

'Turn it over.'

Malice read the writing on the back.

'Christmas, 2007. Still don't get it.'

'During the interview Copeland told us that they had changed the suite and carpet after Dennis had attacked Horton and Maxwell.

'I remember.' He slurped from his can.

'She lied.' Pietersen handed over her phone with a picture of the lounge on the screen. 'I took that this afternoon. The suite and carpet are the same as the ones in this photograph.'

'Sharp observation. Have you got forensics to—'

'Not so fast, Tonto. A CSI team have given the place the full Luminol treatment. Given what Copeland had told us I was expecting it to light up with evidence of blood spatter.'

'And?'

'Not a drop.'

'The assault couldn't have taken place as she described.'

'Precisely. The lying cow.'

The sound of footsteps echoed in the outside corridor. ACC Beresford and Waite entered the room. Neither looked happy.

'I thought you two were still here. What the hell is all this?' Waite asked.

'Care records. We found that—'

'Why is Brenda Copeland being held in custody?' barked Beresford.

'I arrested her for obstruction, Sir, because she was refusing to cooperate with our investigation,' replied Malice, putting the remnants of his pizza back in the box.

'Is it any wonder she's not cooperating?' Beresford pointed a loaded finger at Malice. 'This is beginning to smell a lot like harassment to me.'

'I can assure you, it's not.' Pietersen chipped in.

'I understand you're questioning her regarding the murder of John Horton and Timothy Maxwell,' Beresford said.

'That's right,' Malice replied.

'What do you have on her?'

'Sorry, sir?'

'What evidence do you have?'

'We have an eyewitness account saying that Horton and Maxwell paid Copeland a visit at the church which resulted in a heated argument. The Mataya brothers had to escort the men from the premises. Many years previously Horton had raped Copeland and she fell pregnant but lost the baby, Wendy Horton said that her husband was being blackmailed by someone.'

'And you believe it's Brenda Copeland?' said Beresford. Waite was staring at the pizza.

'Yes we do, Sir.' Malice replied.

'Despite the fact that she's testified that it was her husband Dennis who was behind it.'

'Yes sir, but—'

'And that Dennis chased the men from the family home with a hammer.'

'That's right, but she's lying. We keep catching her out.'

'She's given you an account of what happened, hasn't she?' Beresford said.

'Yes but—'

'It puts Dennis in the frame, right?'

'Yes, but the woman at the care company said that he was incapable of carrying out those actions. These are the records. We are trawling though them to establish—'

'Even though Brenda has told you they had exaggerated the severity of his condition?'

'But I don't believe her, Sir.'

'Oh, so she's being held in custody on the basis that you don't believe her?'

'Sir, she's a serial liar. She said that Horton and Maxwell did not visit the church, then retracted that statement when we showed her they did. She said she'd never had any contact with Horton after the trial, but she had. She said they had changed the suite and the carpet in their house after 2009, which is a lie. It's still there. The list goes on and on and it's a pack of lies, Sir. At every turn she's spinning us a line.'

'So now we lock people up for lying?' Beresford sneered.

'Sir?'

'What hard evidence do you have that she was involved in the disappearance or death of Horton or Maxwell? Do you have a shred of forensic evidence that places her at the scene of the murders?' Beresford asked.

'No, Sir.' Malice replied.

'Do you have any forensic evidence that places her at the site where the bodies were buried?'

'No, Sir.'

'Any DNA evidence on the bodies?'

'No.'

'Her DNA on the murder weapon?'

'No.'

'You have no hard evidence of her being involved in any of this and you're holding her because, in your opinion, she's lied to you. Does any of that sound a little on the vindictive side, DS Malice?'

'I believe Copeland is involved in–'

'Holding her in our custody suite is going to achieve what… exactly?' Beresford butted in. 'Because from what I can see you should be burning your energies looking into Dennis Copeland, not his bloody wife.'

'The Director of Care confirmed that Dennis wasn't capable of carrying out those actions.' Malice reiterated the point, but knew it would fall on deaf ears.

'And if he was pretending, that's precisely what she'd say?' Beresford was having none of it.

'These records will show—' Malice waved his hand at the boxes.

'I have no idea what you're trying to prove, but it doesn't feel right to me. Do you know what the press will do to us if this gets out?' Beresford slapped his hand against one of the boxes.

'The press?' Pietersen jumped in.

'They're going to say that with drug and knife crime going through the roof we're spending our time locking up people who are highly regarded members of the community. We're locking up a woman who is referred to as a fucking Saint. Now either charge her, or release her. And from what I've heard, only one of those actions is going to fly, because if you pursue the other we'll be the laughing stock with the CPS.'

Beresford marched out of the room. No one spoke.

'Get it sorted,' Waite finally found her voice as she followed him out.

Malice tore off another slice of pizza when they had both disappeared.

'Ouch!' said Pietersen. 'What are we going to do?'

'Carry on the line of enquiry implicating Dennis, I suppose.'

'We don't have a lot of choice.'

'You get off home. I'll clear this lot away in the morning,' he said, getting to his feet.

'Where are you going?'

'To give Saint Twinkle the fucking good news.'

Chapter 48

I'm standing in reception, staring out at the car park. Finally a set of headlights come around the corner and her car pulls up outside. I shimmy through the revolving door and jump into the passenger seat. She looks at me and reaches across to take my hand.

'Thanks Carol. I didn't know who else to call. They said I could have money to get home on the bus or a travel warrant… but how would that work? There's no bus stops anywhere near where I live. I didn't know what to do.' I burst into tears. Carol is a sucker for the waterworks treatment. She wraps her arm around my shoulder.

'It's fine. If you can't phone me, who can you call?' she says.

'It was horrible.' I choke back the tears. 'They kept asking me questions which I couldn't answer. Then they put me in a cell and left me there.'

'It must have been frightening.'

I peel myself away from her embrace and wipe away my tears with my sleeve.

'I kept getting confused,' I croak.

'You did the right thing, let's get you home.'

'I just want to see Dennis and lie in my own bed with a cup of tea.'

She straightens herself in her seat, checks her mirrors and pulls away.

'We'll be there in no time,' she says.

I dry my eyes with my sleeve and stare out the window.

Malice had a face like a smacked arse when he opened the cell door. And he nearly choked when he uttered the words 'you're free to go now'. I pretended I hadn't heard, forcing him to say it again. They stuck in his throat even more the second time.

'Aren't you charging me with obstruction?' I'd said to him, getting to my feet.

'No, you cooperated... which is all we wanted in the first place.' He'd waited at the door to escort me to the custody sergeant. The look in his eyes said it all. What he really wanted to do was step into the cell, shut the door and beat the shit out of me. But that's not allowed under PACE.

I took my time, savouring every second. He handed me over at the desk and did a swift disappearing act. Seeing him so angry almost made my day... almost.

'The police came to see me,' Carol says.

'Oh?'

'They wanted to see Dennis' care records. The problem is they're in a right state. Remember that flood we had at the old offices when we had to clear everything out in a hurry, well they got all muddled up.'

That's a shame.

'They asked me questions about Dennis as well,' I say. 'But to be honest I couldn't understand what they were driving at. It was very confusing, and they kept twisting my words.'

She puts her hand on mine.

'It must have been awful,' Carol glances across and gives me half a smile. I give her one back. 'Did they mention anything about Rebecca and the complaint?'

There we go! Your main worry is the reputational damage to your firm.

'No, they didn't,' I reply.

As much as I'd like to twist the knife, I can't be bothered.

'That's a relief. What questions did they ask?'

'Do you mind, Carol... I don't want to talk about it? My head is spinning and I just want to get home.'

'Of course. Listen to me rabbiting on with my twenty-questions when you've had a dreadful ordeal.'

We travel the rest of the journey in silence, which suits me fine. Carol is a lovely woman, but she does tend to prattle on about jack-shit. We come to a stop outside my house.

'There's a new girl on tonight,' Carol says as I open the car door. The night air rushes in. 'Give me a call tomorrow, I'd like to know you're okay.'

'I will,' it's my turn to squeeze her hand. 'Thanks for tonight.'

I walk across the road and open the front door. By the feel of it, the new girl has the heating turned up to maximum. It's like a sauna in here.

'Hi.' She appears from the lounge. A young slip of a girl with short brown hair and a stud in her eyebrow. 'I'm Lizzy. You must be Twinkle. I've heard so much about you.'

'Hi, Lizzy.' I sip off my coat and amble through to the kitchen to put the kettle on.

'There's tea in the pot,' she says. 'I just made it.'

'Okay, thanks. How's Dennis?' I pick a mug from the cupboard, pour from the teapot and add a dash of milk.

'He's been good this evening, the last I checked he was asleep.'

'I'll pop my head in to say goodnight.'

I take my tea and head to his bedroom. Sure enough, Dennis is breathing deeply; a soft rattle coming from the back of his throat. I pull a chair up to the side of his bed and move the red call button which is laying on top of the bedding. I press the mug against the inside of his forearm. It takes a couple of seconds before he jumps, his eyes wide.

'Agghhhh,' he gurgles. I keep the mug tight against his skin. His eyes flash about the room and he begins to jerk around. 'Gggraaa.'

I pull the drink away.

'Hello, Dennis, I wanted to say goodnight.'

'Kkkuuuhh.' He's choking his words out. His fingers claw at the quilt cover looking for the call button. I smile at him.

'I also wanted to tell you that I've figured out a way to fix the little problem we had earlier. You know... when you were telling lies to Rebecca.' His body goes into spasm. Fuck knows what he's trying to do. 'I've kind of killed two birds with one stone. She won't be coming around anymore. And pretty soon, neither will you.'

Chapter 49

Pietersen raced up the stairs to the office. She'd slept much better and had woken before her alarm, her head fizzing with what needed to be done. She bolted down the corridor until she came level with the conference room. The view through the window made her stop. The lights were blazing and Malice was sitting at the boardroom table with his head resting on folded forearms.

'You're kidding me,' she muttered.

Malice sat bolt upright at the sound of the door opening and looked around the room. He rubbed his eyes.

'Please tell me you haven't been here all night?' Pietersen asked.

'Umm... I've not been here all night.'

'Bloody hell, Mally. When I left you were going to see Copeland, then pack up to go home. Christ, this place stinks of pizza.' She closed the lid on the box and opened two of the windows.

'I wanted to have one more crack at this lot before I left. The next thing I know it's twenty-past four. What's the time now?' He rubbed the ache from his neck and shoulders.

'Just after seven.'

'Oh, shit.' Malice stood up and stretched his arms in the air. His neck cracked when he moved his head from side to side.

Pietersen looked at the piles of paper strewn across the table and floor.

'You feeling okay after what Beresford said last night?' she asked.

'I want to think he's doing what he considers right, and he's looking out for the good of the force overall. But all I keep coming back to is he's a meddling prick who has Waite by the short and curlies.'

'Yeah, it was pretty rough. Where did Beresford get his information from? Case details like that don't make their way up the chain of command that quickly.'

'That's easy. He got them from the horse's mouth.'

'How come?' Pietersen gathered up drinks cans and napkins and put them in the plastic bag. She opened a third window.

'He went to the custody suite to stick his nose into the sergeant's business at the same time Copeland had asked for a cup of tea. He took it to her and must have got an earful in the process.'

'Who told you that?'

'The custody sergeant. I think it gave him the shock of his life when the ACC showed up.'

'I've been thinking, I reckon it's worth getting a CSI team to go over Copeland's lounge again. She obviously didn't want us looking closely at the suite and the carpet. I reckon it's worth another shot. Maybe we missed something.'

'There's no point,' Malice said, brushing pizza crust from the front of his shirt.

'Why's that?'

Malice handed her a dog-eared and water damaged sheet of paper.

'Take a look,' he said.

'Fucking hell… sepsis.'

'Where the body's immune system over reacts to an infection.'

'I know what it is.'

'It would be a waste of time sending a team back to the house. It never happened.'

'So she was lying,' Pietersen said, studying the notes written on the sheet. 'Again.'

'You can't trust a word that comes out of that woman's mouth.'

'Not sure how far it moves us forward. Beresford was adamant we're skating on thin ice with Copeland. All this does is trap her in another lie. We need hard evidence. The further we dig into this case the more I'm convinced Copeland was involved in both deaths. We need more than what we have. We need something that places her at the scene.'

Malice's phone rang, it was Anders. He listened to what she had to say then hung up.

'That was Catherine,' he said. 'She's found something interesting.'

Malice pushed open the door and allowed Pietersen to walk into the lab before him. He gritted his teeth and pulled a face. He didn't like visiting the labs. They reminded him of the dentist.

Catherine Anders strode over to greet them.

'You're up early,' Malice said.

'Did you sleep in that shirt?' Anders replied, looking him up and down. 'Is that pizza?'

'Funny you should say that,' quipped Pietersen.

'What have you got?' Malice brushed at his shirt.

'Let's go in here, I have something that might make your day.' Anders said leading the way.

They trooped into an office with a huge TV on the wall. Anders powered up her laptop and the decomposed remains of two bodies came up on the screen.

'The one on the left is Horton and that's Maxwell,' she said, pulling an electronic pointer from her pocket, and shining the red dot on the image. 'We have the full report back now on both bodies and can confirm there is no clear evidence which could lead us to the identity of the killer or killers.

'We can also confirm from the decomposition of the clothing, that they were buried around the same time. This is not a case of one being buried one year to be followed by the other a year later.' She clicked the mouse and the picture changed to show a closeup of the impact sites in the skulls.

'The same weapon was used to kill both men. And I'm sorry, Kelly, My gut proved to be right… the hammer you found yesterday is not the one that was used.'

'Bugger,' Pietersen said under her breath.

'This is confirming what we already know,' said Malice, trying to scratch a stain from the cuff of his shirt.

'Yes, but this is new. We went back to the burial site to ensure we'd gleaned everything we could from the scene. When we dug deeper we found this…' she clicked the mouse again and a different picture came up on the screen. This one showed two strips of material, a number of wooden fragments and a small rectangular piece of metal with holes drilled at the corners. A rule was positioned at the top of the photograph to give a sense of scale.

Malice walked up to the TV.

'What is it?' he said.

'We found this in Horton's grave about four inches below where his body was lying, which is why we missed it the first time around. These...' Anders stood up to join him and pointed at the screen. 'Are strips of leather. One has decomposed but the other is in reasonable condition. You can see here there are knots tied in it. The fragments have a defined radial curve around the edges which leads me to believe they are wooden beads.'

'It's a bracelet,' said Pietersen.

'That's right. This...' Anders pointed to the metal rectangle. 'Is either a pendant or an adornment of some kind. It's possible the leather was threaded through the holes and tied around the wrist. I believe what we're looking at is the remains of a bracelet which was dropped when Horton was buried. The piece of metal has the remnants of a ceramic design on one side.' The picture on the screen changed again to show a magnified image. 'Even though it has eroded over time, under the microscope you can still see the definition and colours. There are three horizontal bands: The top one is black, the middle one is red and the bottom one is white. You can also see that in the centre of the top band is a red hemisphere, with what look like flecks of black.'

Pietersen was also on her feet, staring at the screen.

'Is there any significance in the design?' asked Pietersen.

'There could be, but only you will know that.' Anders replied. 'This is the Malawian flag.'

'Fuck me,' Malice said.

'I'll take that as a yes, then.'

'The brothers…' Pietersen whispered.

'The good news doesn't end there.' Anders brought up a graph. 'We found skin cells embedded in the leather and on the back of the metal from which we were able to extract trace DNA. The results came back this morning… anyone fancy a guess?'

Chapter 50

I've got a banging headache this morning. I suppose with everything that's going on, it's no surprise. I must admit, despite my bravado, I didn't much enjoy my time in the cell. But then I suppose that's the point. I pop a couple of tablets and wash them down with a hand full of water from the tap. I shower and get myself ready for the day. There's so much to do and my head is a jumble of conversations.

Lizzy seems nice enough. She's keen and happy, which they all are at the beginning. Give her a year and she'll be as jaded as the rest. I walk downstairs to find her in the kitchen. She hands me a coffee.

'Thanks. Do you have any plans for today?' I ask her.

'Not really. I need to do a food-shop later, but other than that I think I'll take it easy. What about you?'

'I've got a list as long as my arm, I need to get going. I'll say good morning to Dennis before I head off.'

I enter his room, leaving Lizzy in the kitchen. His head lolls to the side when he sees me come in. He fixes me with watery eyes. If looks could kill.

'Morning,' I say, standing at the side of his bed. 'I'll be out for most of the day because there are some people I need to see.' I lean down and put my face next to his. 'I need to talk to them about you,' I whisper. 'We have lots to chat about and you're the main topic of conversation. Or to be precise, the main topic is how to get rid of you.'

He flinches and starts to grunt.

'We've got it all worked out,' I hiss in his ear. 'And pretty soon you won't be here. You'll be in a hospital somewhere under lock and key. Hopefully in a remote location where it's way too far to visit. You've been a bad man, Dennis. When you killed those men, you did a wicked thing.'

He slobbers a response.

'Now, *I* know you didn't murder them. And *you* know you didn't murder them. But the police believe you caved their heads in with a hammer and buried the bodies. They're lapping it up. So... when they come around, they're here for you. I just wanted to let you know.'

I straighten up and hold the cup of coffee above his face. My hand trembles. He screws his eyes shut and blubbers.

'Oooo, it's gonna spill,' I chant before pulling the mug away. 'Not today, Dennis, not today,' I chuckle as I leave the room.

'Is he awake?' Lizzy calls from the lounge.

'He is now.' I place my drink on the hall stand, pull my jacket from the hook and head out the front door. 'See you tonight,' I call out.

I sit in my car and call Frank. It's my third call this morning and he's not picking up. I hope he hasn't got himself into trouble, that boy can be a one-man civil disturbance on occasions. His phone clicks through to the answer machine.

Bugger!

I want an update on how things are progressing at Winfield. Given what he told me we should be up and running on a couple of new patches by now, and we have a meeting with Bertram later today to introduce the OutReach programme to the parish committee ahead of the formal launch.

I check the silk scarf around my neck in the rear-view mirror. The bruises are fading but they're still tender to the touch. I wonder how Malice is feeling this morning. After my performance with Beresford I would have thought he'd have given him a good kick in the shins. It's good to have friends in high places. Even if they are tossers.

I start the engine and join the traffic on the main drag into town. The sun is already doing a grand job of making the day come alive, I switch on the radio and enjoy the music. It's the 80's hour and I sing my head off on my way to the hospital. Seven songs later I'm parked up and making my way into reception.

The lift is packed with glum faced people, the weight of the world sitting on their collective shoulders. I get out at my floor and wind my way through the labyrinth of corridors to Ward 8C. I nod good morning to the staff clustered around the nurses' station and push open the door to the side room.

The bed is stripped and the room empty.
What the...

I step into the room and squint at the bed in a bizarre action of making sure I'm not seeing things.

'Can I help you?' says a voice behind me. It's a nurse I've not seen before.

'Umm ... yeah ... I've come to see Clem.'

'Can I ask who you are?'

'I'm his... I'm a friend. A close friend. I've been coming here every day since he was admitted. Where is he? Has he been discharged?'

She edges into the room and allows the door to close behind her.

'I'm afraid Mr Mataya suffered a stroke and—'

'When? When did this happen?' I splutter.

'In the early hours of this morning.'

'Is he okay? I mean, where is he now?'

'We rushed him into ICU where we could treat him better.'

'Intensive care! How is he?' I ask again.

'I'm sorry to have to tell you but he's unable to breathe on his own and is on a ventilator.'

I shake my head.

'What does that mean?'

'He's not showing any signs of brain activity. I'm sorry.'

'Why wasn't I called?'

'If you are not a next of kin we wouldn't contact you. I believe his brother is with him.'

'No, no, no. This can't be happening. He'll be alright. I know him better than anyone. He's strong. He'll pull through this.' My legs feel weak and I slump onto the edge of the bed.

'I'm sorry to be the one breaking the news.'

'No, he's gonna be okay. I know it.' I rush from the room in search of ICU. 'He's got to be okay.'

Chapter 51

Malice knocked at Waite's half-open door and strolled in — then immediately wished he hadn't. She was tapping away at her keyboard, cursing at herself with her glasses balancing on the end of her nose. Malice had seen her like this before and it was never good.

'I swear to God if that performance improvement team dream up another fucking graph which I'm expected to explain to the boss, I'm gonna get myself sacked for gross misconduct,' she snarled at the PowerPoint slide, not looking up.

'I'll come back,' Malice said, turning to leave.

'No, come in. I could do with a diversion. I mean, take a look at this,' she spun her laptop around to face him and removed her glasses. On the screen was an intricate chart titled: Rolling KPIs. 'The question for today is: Can you explain the dip in performance that occurred over the weekend of the 21st?'

Malice stared at the graph, none the wiser.

'Umm... which date?' He prodded the screen with his finger.

'And I don't suppose an answer of 'no I fucking can't' will win the day.'

'Are you sure you don't want me to come back when you're less tied up?'

'No, you're fine.' She slammed the lid shut and slumped back in her chair. 'What is it?'

'I need you to do something.'

'Oh?'

'I need you to keep Beresford on side.'

'Fuck, not that again. And why would I need to do that?'

'Because of this.' He produced a sheet of paper and laid it on the desk. She picked it up.

'Shit.' She fumbled with her glasses, reading it a second time.

'Exactly. He has a bee in his bonnet about this one. I don't want him trampling over the investigation, getting in the way.'

'Does he know about this?' She waved the sheet of paper in the air.

'I came to you first.'

'Okay, I'll tell him. But I can't promise anything.'

Malice snatched it from her hand and headed out the door.

'Good luck explaining your graph,' he said.

'Piss off.'

I find ICU and burst through the double doors. The nurse who looks like she's been on shift for a week jumps out of her skin as I hurl myself at her desk.

'Clements Mataya, he was brought here in the early hours of this morning.' I'm breathless, the bloody lift was taking ages so I ran all the way. 'Can you tell me where he is?'

'Who are you?' she asks.

'A close friend.' I'm out of breath. 'I've been visiting every day since he was admitted. The nurse on the ward said he was on a ventilator. I can't believe it. He was okay yesterday. She said Frank was with him.'

'If you'd like to follow me.' She gets up and walks me over to a side room. Clem is lying in bed. The yellow blanket is gathered around his waist, leaving his chest bare. He's wired up to all manner of machines and has a blue corrugated tube down his throat. His chest is rising and falling in time with the sound of the machine.

Frank is sprawled with his face buried in his folded arms on the bed. He raises his head when I come in the room. He jumps up and comes rushing over.

'Twinkle, they said Clem is dead. But he's not, look at him. He's alive.'

'Are you okay?' I say, stealing glances over to Clem.

'No, I'm not okay. I've been freaking out. They called and said for me to come to the hospital because Clem had taken a turn for the worse. I get here and he's wired up to all this shit,' Frank points at the equipment. 'I saw him move, Twink... so he can't be dead, can he?'

'Try to stay calm.'

'I tried to call you but there's no signal. And I didn't want to leave Clem so I was stuck. I didn't know what to do.' He wraps his arms around me and lifts me inches off the floor. I struggle for him to put me down.

'Let me find out what's happening.' I turn to the nurse who's standing next to us.

'Can we talk outside?'

'Sure.' We go into the corridor. A few other nurses who have congregated at the desk stare over.

'This is a terrible shock, I was here yesterday and he was stable.' My eyes are pricking with tears.

'Mr Mataya suffered a stroke. We're unsure if it was connected to his injuries. The probability is they did play a part. It caused the blood supply to his brain to block.'

'Will he get better. I mean what can you do?'

'I'm afraid he no longer has any brain function.'

'But Frank said he saw him move.'

'That can happen as a response to a spinal reflex, which doesn't involve the brain.'

'You mean he's brain dead? How can you tell?' I say, my voice growing in volume.

'His eyes are fixed and dilated and he has no gag reflex. All together we've performed six tests and they were done twice to avoid any misinterpretation. I'm afraid the only thing keeping Mr Mataya alive is the ventilator. If we switch it off, his breathing and heart will stop.'

'Oh my God.' I cover my face with my hands. 'But they said upstairs he was stable, they told me over and over again, 'there's no change'. No one said anything about the possibility of him having a stroke.'

'I'm sorry, these things are unpredictable.'

'There must be something you can do?'

'I'm sorry.'

'So, there's *nothing*...' the words dry in my mouth. She shakes her head.

'Take all the time you need. I appreciate this has come as a huge shock.'

I walk back to the room in a trance. Frank looks up, his face streaked with tears. I rush over with my arms outstretched and he gets up and envelopes me in another hug. With my face pressed into his chest all I can hear is the sound of him sobbing.

The door behind us opens. I turn, expecting to see the nurse entering the room. But it's not her. It's that bloody Malice with his South African side-kick.

'What the hell do you want?'

'Brenda Copeland, I'm arresting you on suspicion of murdering John Horton and Timothy Maxwell.'

Chapter 52

The part of the station that housed the interview rooms was a place for measured questioning and even tones. Not today. The corridors were filled with the roaring echoes of Brenda Copeland.

Malice and Pietersen entered the room and took their seats while Copeland tramped around the room.

'Oh, here we go,' she said. 'I wondered when you two would arrive. Every time you show up, that Judy Collins song goes off in my head. You know the one, *Send in the Clowns*.'

Jenkins — Copeland's solicitor — was staring at his notebook with a look on his face that said 'I don't want to be here.'

'Please sit down, Mrs Copeland,' Pietersen said. 'Then we can make a start.'

'Make a start! You did that days ago when you began to harass me. How many times is this now? Cos I've lost count.'

'Please take a seat,' Pietersen said again. Copeland pulled the chair away from the table and dumped herself in it.

Malice pressed the button on the recorder and it emitted a long buzzing sound. When it stopped, Pietersen took the lead by introducing the people in the room, repeating the charge against Copeland and reminding her she was under caution. The formalities dispensed with, she consulted her notes.

'On the 19th of June, 2009 you were visited by John Horton and Timothy Maxwell at your church. You had a conversation which escalated into an argument. That's right, isn't it?' Pietersen eyed Copeland who was staring into the middle distance.

'No comment.' She'd obviously decided to heed her solicitor's word on this occasion.

'This argument got so bad that witnesses have said you were swearing and cursing at the men.'

'No comment.'

'In fact, such was the ferocity of the row the men had to be escorted from the building by Clements and Frank Mataya. That's right isn't it, Mrs Copeland?'

'No comment.'

'John Horton believed he had fathered a child with you and when he got in touch you saw an opportunity to blackmail him. You said that if he didn't give you two hundred pounds a month you would expose his illegitimate child and resurrect a rape allegation. That's correct isn't it?'

'No comment.'

'You strung John Horton along for twenty-one months, letting him believe he had a son or daughter. All the while you pocketed the money. You had as much to lose as him if the truth came out. You'd built yourself up a formidable reputation in the church and a scandal of that nature would not look good. Blackmailing John was the ultimate solution. It kept him quiet while maintaining your integrity. And it put over four thousand pounds in your handbag. Didn't it, Mrs Copeland?'

'No comment.'

'When we put this to you last time you said that it wasn't you who was blackmailing Horton but your husband, Dennis Copeland. You went on to say that Dennis' illness had been exaggerated in order to pass a medical assessment and claim help and benefits.'

'No comment.'

'You said that Horton and Maxwell came to your house and the argument continued before Dennis 'set about them' with a hammer. You went on to say that Dennis chased them from the property and didn't return until six a.m. the next day. And you didn't know what had happened to Horton or Maxwell. That's correct, isn't it?'

'No comment.'

Malice placed the photograph taken from the house in front of her.

'For the purposes of the tape,' he said, 'I'm showing Brenda Copeland item A006 which shows a picture of the lounge taken at Christmas 2007.'

Pietersen continued her line of questioning.

'You told us that the suite and carpet had been changed after Dennis attacked the men. But this photograph shows that's not the case. Why did you say that?'

'No comment.'

'Is it so we wouldn't bother sweeping the room, looking for traces of blood?'

'No comment.'

'Because there are no traces of blood, are there, Mrs Copeland?'

'No comment.'

'A man wielding a hammer and setting about two other men... you would expect to find blood at the scene. Don't you think?'

'No comment.'

'There's no blood because it didn't happen. Dennis couldn't have committed the attack because he wasn't there, was he?'

'No comment.'

Malice placed a piece of paper on the table. It was dog-eared and water-damaged.

'I'm showing Mrs Copeland item A008,' he said. 'It is a handwritten visit report dated 17th of June, 2009 from one of Dennis' carers at the time. It states that Dennis was admitted to hospital having developed sepsis and the provision of home care was suspended, pending a review at the hospital. The next entry states that the care package had resumed six days later on 23rd of June, 2009. He spent a total of five days in hospital being treated for blood poisoning.'

'Which means, Mrs Copeland...' Pietersen said. 'He couldn't have done it,'

Copeland looked at the visit report, scrutinising the notes. Beads of sweat broke out on her forehead. Eventually she pushed it away and said, 'No comment.'

'Did Horton and Maxwell come to your house at all, or is that a complete fabrication?' asked Malice.

'No comment.' Copeland wiped her face with her hand.

'What happened to them after they left the church?' he said.

'No comment.'

'Did you kill John Horton and Timothy Maxwell?'

'No comment.'

'Did you order the Mataya brothers to kill them?'

'No comment.'

'When we excavated the graves where the bodies were found we uncovered this...' Pietersen showed Copeland the photographs of the bracelet. 'I am showing Mrs Copeland item A009. It was buried along with John Horton. Do you recognise it?'

Copeland fixed her gaze onto the picture. The years fell away. She swallowed hard.

'No... no comment.'

'Despite being in the ground for ten years, we were able to extract a DNA sample which produced a positive match with an individual on the database.'

'No...' Copeland didn't finish.

'That person is you, Brenda Copeland. Your bracelet was found in the grave of John Horton. You most likely lost it when you were burying the bodies after you killed them. That's right isn't it?'

'No comment,' she said wringing her hands in her lap.

'You murdered John Horton and Timothy Maxwell and buried their bodies. You dropped this bracelet and it found its way into the grave.'

'No... no I didn't.'

The solicitor put his hand on her arm.

'The evidence tells a different story,' said Pietersen.

'I didn't do it... it was Clem.'

Chapter 53

For the second time in two days everything stopped in Interview Room 3. Malice, Pietersen and the duty solicitor collectively did another Marx Brothers impression.

'Clements Mataya?' Malice spluttered. 'The guy who's lying in the intensive care unit?'

'Yes,' replied Copeland.

'Oh come on, Brenda,' he said, failing to keep the incredulity out of his voice. 'First you tell us it's Dennis, now you say it's Clements. Do you honestly expect us to believe any of this?'

'It's not up to me what you believe,' she replied.

The solicitor once again placed his hand on his client's arm and whispered in her ear. Copeland looked at him as if he'd just told her she had dog shit on her favourite shoes.

'I need to reiterate,' said Pietersen. 'The DNA found on the bracelet buried along with the body of John Horton is a direct match to yours.'

'I gave the bracelet to Clem,' said Copeland.

'What?' Malice and Pietersen said in unison.

'He brought it back as a present from a trip he'd made to Malawi. It was at a time when him and his parents were not getting on very well... you know what families can be like. His parents did the dirty on him and buggered off back to Malawi, leaving him here in the UK with his brother Frank.'

'Why would he buy you a present?' Malice asked.

'Me and Clem were, how can I put this, more than just friends.'

'You were in a relationship?' Pietersen said.

'You could say that. He'd given me the bracelet as a token and said whenever I feel down, I should put it on and it would be like we're together. So, I did, for years. Then Clem came back from visiting his parents and he was distraught. They basically said they didn't want to know him anymore. He was in a dreadful state. I gave him back the bracelet so when he was down he could do the same. I said he needed it more than me.'

'How did it wind up buried in the grave with John Horton?' Pietersen asked.

'John and the other guy came to see me in the church. There was a terrible row. He was accusing me of keeping the child from him and blackmailing him for cash. I told him there was no child and that it was Dennis who'd been the one strong-arming him for money.'

'Dennis? But I thought we'd established he—'

'All you've established is he was in hospital on those dates. We were still pretending he was worse than what he was. As I told you before, when John got in touch, Dennis saw pound signs. When John turned up at the church it kicked off big time, Clem and Frank showed them the door.'

'What happened after that?' asked Malice.

'Clements was furious when he found out what had been going on. You were right when you said my reputation in the church could be ruined. And Clem's good name was closely linked to mine. If it all went pear-shaped for me it would for him too. Clem made Dennis give him John's contact number and set up a meeting to smooth things over. He said he wanted to meet with them somewhere private, somewhere no one from the church would see them together. They met in a disused factory near the Claxton estate.'

'When was this?' Pietersen said.

'The same evening as the argument in the church. I kept pleading with Clem that there had been enough upset already but he was adamant he was going to sort it. I thought he was going to punch Dennis when he found out, but he stormed out of the house instead.'

'What happened at the factory?'

'John and Tim Maxwell tried to turn the tables. John demanded the money back and wanted compensation or he would go to the police.'

'But that makes no sense,' Malice said.

'It made no sense to me at the time either. I'm just telling you what happened. The meeting didn't go well and Clem wasn't falling for any of John's bullshit. At some point the argument became physical and Clem picked up a hammer that was lying on the ground and hit John on the back of the head. Maxwell rushed over to help and Clem struck him on the side of the head. Clem is a strong bloke and both men died instantly. He decided to hide the bodies, came back the next day and buried them under the bike shed. That's when he must have lost the bracelet.'

'How do you know all this? Were you there?' Malice said.

'No. Clem told me. I said that if we were going to have any kind of future together, I had to know.'

'Why didn't you report it to the police?'

'I wanted it to go away. The rape... the miscarriage... Dennis... the lot. Clem gave my life direction, he gave it meaning, and I was not about to throw all that away.'

'Clements is lying in ICU and the diagnosis is he's brain dead,' Pietersen said.

'I know.' Copeland burst into tears and began rocking her shoulders back and forth. 'I know!'

There was a knock on the door. Pietersen got up and stepped outside the room. Two of the people left behind were trying to digest what they had just heard. The third person was thinking, what next?

After a few minutes Pietersen returned to her seat.

'Mrs Copeland, as part of our investigation we've conducted a search on your second property. The one out of which you run the OutReach programme.'

Copeland stopped rocking. She sat bolt upright.

'Don't you need a warrant?' she said.

'As you are under arrest, we don't.'

'I don't think that's right?' She turned to Jenkins, who gave her a withering look before he nodded.

'We were looking for the hammer used to kill Horton and Maxwell.'

'You didn't find it. As I said, Clem used one that he found in the factory.'

'That's right. We did however find traces of blood on the walls, on the carpet and the furniture. Do you know anything about that?' Pietersen said, fixing her with a stare.

'I ... umm ... no.'

'Our forensics team have said some of the blood is relatively new, while other traces are old. Do you know anything about that?'

'Erm... no... I mean, I own the house but I'm never there. I'm the landlord and that's it. I don't know what goes on there.'

'You have no idea why we would find blood spatter in the house?' Pietersen asked.

Copeland's mouth was open but it was clear nothing was going to come out. Malice shot a look at Pietersen and smiled. She smiled back.

Malice clicked the top of his pen and closed his notebook.

'Interview suspended at 13.05.'

Game over.

Chapter 54

Three days later

Malice peered up the road to see the rain washing in waves across the puddles. The light from the streetlights above gave the water an orange tint. He pulled his coat collar around his neck and pressed the bell again. Hayley opened her front door, dressed in her pajamas. He gave her his broadest smile.

'Sorry it's late. Is Amy still up?' he said, rolling the bike back and forth.

Hayley stared at the bike.

'Can't say I'm pleased to see that again. You'd better come in.' She walked down the hallway into the lounge and switched off the TV. 'Amy, your dad's here,' she called out.

There was a scampering of little feet as Amy came flying down the stairs.

'Daddy!' she screeched. Malice knelt down and she flung her arms around his neck. There was a strong smell of toothpaste.

'Hey, Sweet Pea, I brought this back,' he said, leaning the bike against the wall.

'How did you do that?' She climbed off him and reached for the saddle.

'I went to see Tristram and asked for it.'

'He came to see me today,' she said, running her hands along the handlebars. 'I thought he was going to be mean to me, but he said sorry then ran away. It was a bit scary.'.

'It worked out okay in the end,' Malice said. 'You go and finish getting ready for bed, I need to have a chat with mum.'

He got up and ambled into the lounge. Amy scooted up the stairs on all fours.

'What really happened?' Hayley said, sitting on the sofa, nursing a cup of tea.

'I asked for the bike back and they said no. Then things got a bit awkward and I pulled out my badge. I told them they didn't want the kind of trouble I could bring raining down on them.'

'Did it end well?'

'Well enough.' Malice settled into the armchair opposite. 'How have you been?'

'I got a visit from Carlton today. He came and found me when I was picking up Amy.'

'Oh, that's a turn up. What did he say?'

'He told me that the Hester boy had confessed to taking the bike and that he'd handed it back.

'That's progress I suppose.'

'He then went on to give me a load of bollocks about how the school has to be extra vigilant when dealing with issues like this.'

'Did he now?' Malice chewed his lip.

'He also said the way you had behaved was unacceptable and likely to inflame, rather than resolve, the situation.'

'Cheeky bastard.'

Hayley stared down at the carpet. Her foot began bouncing up and down. She tapped her ringed finger against the cup.

'I said that I felt the way he'd handled things was unacceptable and that you were right… he was a dick.'

'Bloody hell.' Malice threw his head back and laughed. 'He won't have liked that. Nice one, Hayley.'

'I said it loud enough so the ear-wigging cows who were milling around the gate could hear it first-hand. I thought if I'm going to be the talk of the playground, it may as well be for something I've done, rather than something you've done.'

Amy clattered down the stairs and burst into the lounge.

'My school bag's packed and I've got my clothes out for tomorrow,' she chimed.

'Good girl,' Malice got up from the chair and swept her into his arms. 'I'm going to say goodnight because I have to go.'

'Ohhh.'

'I'll see you again, real soon.'

'Daddy?'

'Yes.'

'Did you have a think about that smart watch?'

Malice flashed a glance at Hayley who looked down into her cup. In his mind's-eye he could see the box still sitting on the windowsill.

'When you asked mummy about it, what did she say?' he replied.

'Mummy said I would have to wait for Father Christmas to see if he might leave one under the tree.'

'I think Mummy's right, don't you?'

'Yes, maybe.'

'Go on.' He lowered her onto the floor.

'I'll be up in a minute,' Hayley said.

'Okay.' Amy scurried out of the living room.

'There you go, Mally, that wasn't difficult now, was it?' Hayley said, getting up and walking to the kitchen.

'No, I suppose not.'

'Do you want a coffee?'

'No, I have to dash. I'm already late.'

'Same old… same old… always late for something.'

'I'm glad we got it sorted,' Malice made his way to the front door.

'Me too. She loves that bike.'

'Well… she needed a new one.'

'Go, before we fall out again.'

Malice hunched his coat over his head and ran across the street to his car. He piled into the driver's seat and sped up the road, then came to a halt at the junction on the edge of the estate. He revved the five-litre engine of his Mustang while he was sitting at the traffic lights waiting for them to turn green. The throaty roar made him smile. The lad in a hot-hatchback in the lane next to him dipped his throttle and the tuned exhaust rattled and popped in response. The look on the young man's face said it all.

Come on, old man, let's see what you got.

Malice shook his head, reached into his jacket pocket and produced his warrant card. The lad held his hand up in a sign of surrender and stared out the windscreen, avoiding further eye contact.

The lights changed and Malice pulled away with all the acceleration of a pensioner on a Zimmer frame. The souped-up boy-racer trekked along behind.

Malice smiled to himself. He was in danger of having had a good day and he couldn't remember the last time he'd experienced such a phenomenon. His workload hadn't left him shredded at the end of his shift, he'd left the office at a reasonable time and Waite had called in sick. Result! Plus he'd had a conversation with Hayley that had not left him reaching for the paracetamol and to top it all he'd also been invited to dinner by a woman. Which was a novelty.

His phone rang. He hit the hands-free button.

'Where are you? I've got the takeaway keeping warm in the oven.'

'On my way, Kelly. I got pulled onto a call when I was about to leave work. I won't be long.'

'Might have guessed.'

He could hear the clatter in the background of plates and cutlery being laid out.

'Thanks for the invitation, by the way,' he said.

'Don't get too excited. You're the only person I could think of who was available to help celebrate my birthday. Which, right now, probably makes me the saddest woman in the country.'

'Even if I was the last resort, I still appreciate the thought.'

'No problem. Have you got me a card?' she asked.

'Not exactly…'

'That's a no, then.'

'It's more bottle shaped than card shaped.'

'That's good enough.'

'Anyway, it's a double celebration.' His grin widened.

'How come?'

'I'll tell you more when I get there. Let's just say it involves our favourite pathological liar, the CPS and another charging decision.'

'You're joking?' Pietersen shrieked.

'Nope. That's what the call was about. I have a bottle of fizz on the passenger seat to toast her good health.'

'Christ, at this rate Copeland is going to be in prison for the rest of her natural life.'

'The CPS have reviewed the blood spatter found at the house and agreed we can charge her with conspiracy to murder. The lab came back with three different DNA profiles, all of which match missing persons.'

'And don't tell me… each missing person was enrolled in Copeland's OutReach programme.'

'Well done. You should be a copper.'

'That's brilliant news. Now the trial can go ahead.'

'Yup.'

'Get your arse over here. I could do with raising a glass of bubbles to that.'

Malice disconnected the call and drove at the designated sixty-miles per hour on the dual carriageway, resisting the temptation for floor it. In no time he was pulling up outside Pietersen's flat. He locked the car and made his way up the steps into the lobby area, then took the lift to the third floor. He walked down the hallway clutching the bottle until he reached No.10 where he stopped dead.

The door was ajar and there were splinters protruding from the doorframe where the lock had been forced. His senses went into overdrive. He tapped the door with his fingertips and edged it open. The smell of Chinese food filled the hall and he could hear the sound of the TV.

'Kelly!' he called out. There was no reply. He crept into the lounge gripping the neck of the bottle. 'Kelly!' he called again.

Nothing.

The sitting room was empty. He picked up the remote, switched off the TV and stood in the lounge listening. The only thing he could hear was the sound of next door's television drifting through the wall and a low hum coming from the next room. He sidled into the kitchen to find the oven on low. Her phone was sitting on the worktop.

'Kelly,' he called out. 'Where are you?'

He dashed to the bedroom and shouldered open the door. It was empty. The same with the bathroom.

'Kelly!'

He glanced down to see a red smear on the floor. It was blood.

'Kelly!' His head began to spin.

Malice caught sight of his reflection in the hallway mirror.

Written on the glass in lipstick were the words:
Come and get her.

Chapter 55

Pietersen regained consciousness to find herself in what felt like a tumble dryer. The hum of road noise filled the confined space and blackness swamped her. She tried to move, but she couldn't. Her arms were secured tight behind her back and tied to her ankles. Her legs were bent double and her back was arched. Lying on her front, she struggled to breathe.

When she did manage to steady her breathing, her head began to clear. She could remember opening the door to her apartment, expecting to find, Malice. Instead it was William Maddocks and James Bailey.

Maddocks had slammed his foot against the door and then his fist in her face. The hallway light passed overhead as she toppled backwards under the weight of the blow. She'd landed star-fish shaped on her back, a cacophony of flashbulbs popped and fizzed in her head. Rough hands rolled her on to her front and she felt the air rush from her chest as both men knelt on her body, crushing her flat to the floor. The front door slammed shut.

She'd let out a scream and a fist crunched into her head again, smashing the side of her face into the laminate floor. That was the last she could remember.

She managed to roll onto her side to alleviate the pressure on her chest when the car lurched over a bump in the road and bounced her into the air. She came down hard on her shoulder and winced. The ball of material rammed into her mouth was in danger of sliding down her throat. She could feel the knot of whatever was holding it in place pressing hard against the base of her skull. With every movement she could hear the crackle of thick plastic, lining the floor below her.

The vehicle veered off to the left, shoving her into the corner of the cramped compartment. Then it slewed the other way and her head struck something hard. She tried to heave air into her lungs through her busted nose. Everything hurt.

Suddenly, the car came to a stop.

She heard doors opening and closing and the sound of muffled voices. The boot lid flew up and a burst of light from a torch burned her eyes. Two faces stared down at her. The men grabbed hold and heaved her over the lip. She dropped onto her back, knocking the wind out of her. Pietersen snorted snot and bloody mucus through her nose. Maddocks and Bailey reached down, hooked their arms under hers and heaved her across the floor. The pain in her shoulders was excruciating.

She tried to take in her surroundings but all she could see through the gloom was high breeze block walls and concrete. Then she was being dragged down a narrow corridor until they reached a metal door at the end. One of the men kicked it open.

They dumped her onto the floor and fed a thick rope around her chest and under her arms. She could hear the sound of a ratchet clicking and slowly she began to be hauled into the air. In her hog-tied position, it wasn't long before she was swinging clear of the ground.

Maddocks laughed. He reached out and spun her around. Faster and faster she twisted in the air like a bad circus act. The room hazed in and out of focus and her stomach cramped.

She was aware of laughter filling the small room. Maddocks stepped forwards, snaked his arm out and smacked her right shoulder, speeding up her rotation. Her head lolled around and her eyes rolled back. Then her guts heaved and vomit spewed through her nose and she began to choke.

'Wow, check this out,' Maddocks leapt out the way to avoid the nasal spray of puke, splashing in arcs on the floor.

Pietersen went into spasm, thrashing around at the end of the rope. Her stomach cramped again, sending another plume flying through the air. She was drowning in her own sick.

'That's epic, man,' yelled Bailey, whooping and waving his hands.

He grabbed hold of Pietersen to stop her spinning and flicked open a knife. The blade sliced through the rope holding the gag in place.

'Watch your feet,' he yelled as he yanked the ball of cloth from her mouth. Pietersen coughed a hail of vomit through the air. Her chest heaved and she coughed again. A second plume of bile hit the deck.

'She wouldn't be much fun at the fairground,' Maddocks sniggered.

'Not sure she's much fun anywhere,' Bailey replied.

Pietersen was retching while trying to control her breathing. Her vision was coming back and she could see both men standing in front of her, slapping each other on the back and cackling.

Maddocks leaned in and grabbed her by the throat.

'Not much fun, are you bitch?' he pulled his arm back. Fist clenched. Pietersen shut her eyes and tried to force her head down.

'Steady on, Will. There's plenty of time for that.' Pietersen heard a man's voice off to the left.

'Yeah, you're right.' Maddocks let her go and stepped aside. She opened her eyes to see a blurry figure hobble into view, dragging his left leg.

'I don't walk so good since your boyfriend had a chat with me. The doctors say it will get better with time, but for now let's just say I'm not going to be winning any races.'

The man put his hand on her forehead, lifting up her face. Brad Craven was dressed in jeans and a crisp white shirt. A gold chain graced his neck.

'I... I don't know what you're on about. I don't have a boyfriend.' Pietersen choked on her words, her vision oozing in and out of focus.

'No, and that's the trouble with you, Kelly. You never know about anything, do you?' Craven said, letting her head drop.

'Go to hell.'

'Like the time you knew nothing about taking money from that shop when you raided it. Or the time when you knew nothing about planting the marked bank notes at our houses.'

'That didn't happen,' she spluttered, trying to cough up the last of the vomit from her throat.

'And I suppose you didn't know anything about this either...' Craven unbuckled the belt and let his jeans drop. His legs were a patchwork of bandages and plasters. Some were stained red where his blood had seeped through. 'Your boyfriend cut my legs up. He did it while giving me some cock-and-bull story about him being a bent copper and wanting me on his payroll. He must have thought I was born yesterday. I just told him what he wanted to hear and he let me go. The man's a fucking amateur.'

'I have no idea what you're talking about.' Pietersen spat on the floor.

'Maybe you do, maybe you don't, but it doesn't matter in the long run.' Craven pulled up his jeans, grimacing as the material brushed past his wounds. 'Sooner or later he's gonna come running and when he does, we'll be ready.'

'Ready? Ready for what?' Pietersen said, as she slowly rotated.

'To welcome him in the appropriate manner. We need to show him the hospitality of the North. Isn't that right, lads?'

Bailey laughed.

'Too right,' Maddocks said.

'You'll have a long wait,' Pietersen croaked.

'We got plenty of time. It's nice having you around, Kelly. You wouldn't believe how long me and the guys have been looking forwards to this.'

'I'm going to—'

'No, you won't, Kelly, take a look around. You're trussed up like a turkey at Christmas and you can shout and scream till your lungs pack in. No one will hear you. Now… as much as I would like to stand around chatting all evening, I have things to do.' Craven nodded to Maddocks who removed a syringe from his inside pocket.

'If you hold still, it won't hurt so much.'

Chapter 56

Malice screeched to a halt and leapt from the car, slamming the door so hard the vehicle shook. He paced around in a circle, punching the night air with both fists.

'Fuck!' he yelled to no one.

Curtains twitched in the houses across the road, their occupants not used to late night outbursts. He'd been driving around for the last hour looking for Pietersen; a fruitless task because he had no idea where she was or what vehicle she might be in. But he tried anyway. After all, he had to do something.

The indicator lights flashed orange and he trudged down the street to his ground floor flat, ramming the key in the lock. The front door chipped paint from the wall when he shouldered his way inside. His coat bounced off the hooks on the wall and landed on the floor.

'What the fuck have I done?' he muttered to himself. His head raced with a plethora of possibilities. 'Think, man, think.'

He pulled his laptop from his bag and powered it up. The light from the screen cast a blue hue around the room as the Force's logo came up. A few clicks later he typed in the name Bradley Craven.

A mugshot of the ringleader appeared. The same face that Malice had seen contorted in agony when the short triangular blade had sliced into his flesh — a brief moment of pure enjoyment which he was now regretting.

It should have been his fucking throat.

Malice navigated his way through the system until he found an address. James Bailey was next, followed by William Maddocks. With the information scrunched up on a Post-it and thrust into his pocket he went to his bedroom and threw a handful of clothes into a holdall. Then changed out of his slip-on shoes in preference for sturdy lace-up boots.

A few minutes later he was back in his car and heading over to where his parents had lived. Skirting around the housing estate he drove alongside a row of domestic garages. Every one of the doors could have done with a lick of paint.

Malice parked up and stepped into the night air, leaving the engine running and the headlights blaring. He fished a small key from his pocket and unlocked the one with No.44 scratched into the metal. The door mechanism complained when he twisted the handle and heaved open the up-and-over door.

Shimmying between his dad's old Rover 75 and the inside wall, he made his way to the back of the garage where there was a workbench and some tools. It had been fifteen years since his father had passed away. The car had been the old man's pride and joy. Maybe that's why every time Malice had come to sell it, he couldn't bear to part with it.

The boot lid flew up and the interior light came on. Inside was a kitbag and a rolled up blanket. He ran the zip down to reveal ropes, a hunting knife, two crowbars, rolls of gaffer tape and various other goodies.

He lifted it out and made his way back along the wall, squeezing into the driver's seat. In the glove compartment were three fat envelopes and a mobile phone. The happy consequence of killing Lubos Vasco and his men. Malice pulled them out and flicked through the contents of the envelopes — twenty thousand pounds should do it. The wad of notes and phone went into the side pocket of the bag.

He went back to the boot, lifted out the rolled up blanket and laid it on the work bench. Beneath the layers of material was Hester's shotgun. He looked around and found what he was looking for — his dad's hacksaw. That would make it much more user-friendly.

Ten minutes later Malice was back in his car, running through a checklist in his head. Then he reached into the bag and peeled a twenty-pound note from the stash - his stomach rumbled. He would need to stop for food on the way. It was a long drive to Leeds.

Chapter 57

With five universities and a thriving social scene, Leeds has enjoyed a staggering rate of expansion since the turn of the century. And with such growth comes opportunity. It has become a magnet for new business and a hub for the financial and banking sectors as well as, of course, a hotbed of crime.

Craven drove through the city, past the Parkinson building, and headed towards Hyde Park. He was feeling good. The last twenty-four hours had gone to plan and even though the injuries to his legs and the two stab wounds to his upper arm were hurting like a bastard, he allowed himself a smile.

The wide streets gave way to narrow roads, lined on both sides by rubbish bins. Most of which were on their sides spilling their feted contacts onto the pavement. He turned into Harold Grove and made his way between the rows of terraced houses and double-parked cars.

The street was situated to the north west of the city and was one of ten densely packed streets, all of which were entertainingly called Harold: Harold View, Harold

Mount, Harold Terrace. It was an ideal location. The area was frequented mostly by students and as such it was a place used to the occasional whiff of something dodgy.

Craven found a gap at the kerb and pulled over. He walked up to No.47 and unlocked the heavy metal security gate, then did the same with the two mortice locks on the front door. When he purchased the property, the added security measures were a great addition for what he had in mind, though it told you everything you needed to know about the neighbourhood that they were already in place when he bought the house.

He went inside to be greeted by an overpowering smell of Indian food and Jakub Gorski — who was standing in the living room surrounded by boxes and crates of glass bottles stacked to the ceiling.

'Hey, Brad.' Gorski zigzagged his way through and offered out his hand. 'Good to see you.'

'I wanted to drop by, see how you were doing,' Craven pumped his hand.

'We're doing okay, but this place is shit. When can we go back to bulk processing?' Gorski was a forty-year-old Polish national who had found himself unemployed from his supply chain role when the manufacturing business, for which he worked, went into liquidation. With no work at home he found himself in the UK washing cars to make a living before deciding there was more money to be made putting his expertise to good use by importing and distributing fake spirits from Europe. That's when he teamed up with Craven.

'Jakub, I keep telling you this is a pilot. We need to start small to test the market and refine the product.'

'Don't lecture me on how to scale up production and launch product,' he snapped back.

'I'm sorry. I want to be extra careful, that's all.'

'I know that Brad, but have a look will you?' he waved his hand around the room jam-packed with materials. 'It's the same upstairs. The place is rammed and the one-thousand litre bulk container is under a tent in the back garden. We're having to decant the bastard by hand and it's killing us.'

'It's only for a short time while we sort things out. I've got people interested here in Leeds plus Birmingham, Manchester and Liverpool. And they loved the samples we gave them. Don't worry, my Polish friend. When this takes off we're going to need a much bigger premises.'

'If you say so. Come on, let me show you what we have.' Gorski shuffled from the living room into the kitchen. Craven followed him to find a young Asian chap hunched over three huge pots bubbling away on the stove and a massive chopping board covered with spices and diced vegetables. He had a pair of head phones clamped over his ears and didn't look up. Craven glanced at Gorski and shrugged his shoulders.

'What's all this about?' he said.

'It's better that the house smells of curry and besides we have to feed the blokes.'

'He's here every day?' asked Craven.

'Yup. He makes good food.'

'Yeah, but curry every day?'

'They seem to like it.'

They walked to the back of the kitchen and down a steep set of narrow stairs to the basement. As they descended, the aroma of curry was replaced by the smell of strong liquor. Gorski pushed open a door to what used to be the third bedroom. The room was devoid of furniture; crammed instead with a filling station, a cork-wrapping machine and a labelling unit plus a huge steriliser. Thick polythene sheets covered the walls and ceiling while four LED flood-lamps gave the stainless steel machinery a clinical feel. Six men turned around to see who had entered the room, but immediately got back to work when they clocked who it was.

Dressed in white paper boiler suits, each man was wearing safety goggles and a face mask. When the alcohol vapour condensed onto Craven's eyes, he wished he was wearing the same gear. An extraction unit hummed above their head, doing a crap job of sucking the fumes from the confined space.

'Bloody hell,' he said, wiping the tears away on his sleeve. 'That stings.'

'See what I mean? This is less than ideal,' replied Gorski.

Craven picked a bottle from the crate at the end of the line, turning it over in his hands. 'This is good, very good. The labelling is excellent. How's the specific gravity?'

Gorski lifted a clipboard from a nail in the wall and studied the columns of figures.

'The alcohol content is around forty-three per cent but we have had some variation,' he said.

'How much?'

'Plus or minus three points. But it's getting better. We're averaging around one hundred bottles per hour which explains the quantity of materials upstairs. The labelling machine is a pain in the arse and slows us down. But I have my best crew on it.'

'This...' Craven held the bottle up. 'Is going to make us a lot of money.'

'I agree. But we need to scale up.'

'Not until we've ironed out the wrinkles.'

'Fancy a taste?' Gorski took a small stainless-steel cup the size of a shot glass and placed it under a nozzle. He opened a tap and filled it with clear liquid. Then he picked up a bottle with the words TEST written on the label in Sharpie pen and poured a drop into another cup. He handed both to Craven who held the first one under nose before taking a sip. 'There's no point testing the aroma down here,' Gorski laughed.

Craven drank from the second cup. 'Wow, that's amazing! I defy anyone to tell the difference between that and the real stuff.'

'It's good, yeah?'

'Better than good. That's superb.' He took another swig.

Craven was an astute businessman with one eye on his current interests while the other was focused on breaking into new markets. For a long time, he'd noticed the explosion of gin sales following the repeal of the Gin Act in 2008. That was where the smart money was heading. Craven intended to be at the forefront of bottling premium counterfeit Gin at a knock down price and selling it through a network of bent establishments — from night clubs to corner shops, he reckoned there was a ton of money to be made. But he didn't have the skills or inclination to set up his own distillery. The gin was distilled on a farm on the outskirts of Koszalin and shipped to the UK under a multitude of false papers. For Craven it was simple. He had a track record of doing it with vodka, why not gin?

'The numbers stack up,' Gorski said taking the bottle from him. 'This brand retails at forty pounds for a seventy centilitre bottle and we pay eighty-six pence per landed litre. The bottles, labels, corks and foil wrapping came in under budget and the distribution costs are the same as before.'

'Only this time we'll be filling the lorries with more expensive product.'

'Exactly. When we start to ramp up, this is going to be a goldmine. We have the next shipment due in a few days.'

'I need to speak to you about that.' Craven gestured for them to move back upstairs, a welcome relief for his smarting eyes. They emerged into the less abrasive atmosphere of the lounge. 'I want you to use a different transport route for the next batch.'

'What?'

'And keep it to yourself.'

'But everything is arranged.'

'Then fucking re-arrange it. If there's a couple of days difference in delivery dates we can live with it. The next set of outlets aren't expecting to get their goods for a while.'

'Why the hell would we want to do that?'

'I like to keep people on their toes — including you.'

Chapter 58

Pietersen felt around with her bare feet. When they'd snatched her from her flat she wasn't wearing shoes. Her toes poked gingerly around the corners of the room, occasionally finding vomit on the floor. It was a ten feet by six feet empty box. She couldn't even see the walls, the place was so dark.

She'd come round lying on her side with her hands secured behind her back and had immediately retched. From her nausea, dry mouth and sweating, she reckoned they had injected her with some kind of opioid. She could remember the sudden feeling of euphoria — despite her predicament — as the drug raced around her system. Then everything went black.

Her ears pricked up. There was a sound. A door opening.

There's someone coming!

Pietersen edged her way to the back corner and lay on the floor. She curled into a ball, tucking her chin into her chest.

A strip of light appeared under the door and a shadow danced across it. The sound of two rusty bolts drawing across echoed around the room. Pietersen had one eye cracked open to see the door fly open and a pair of legs strode in.

'Wakey, wakey, rise and shine. It's another new day filled with hope and anticipation. Well, not for you, but anyway...' It was Maddocks. He walked over to where she was lying. She could see his polished black brogues and the hem of his suit trousers. He'd either been to work or was on his way there. 'Come on, sleepy head it's time to get up.' Pietersen didn't move. 'Wow, this place stinks of puke. I've brought you a bottle of water and a pack of biscuits.' The shoes were a couple of feet from her head. He reached down and jabbed her shoulder. 'Hey, wake up, bitch.'

She cracked open her eyes and groaned.

'Whaaaat? Where am...?' she slurred.

'Have you had a nice trip?' He shoved her with the sole of his shoe. 'Did the nasty injection give you a hard time? Tell you what, I'll leave these over here for you to have when you're feeling peckish. I would advise you to eat something, because in a couple of hours you're gonna get your next shot and we don't want you dying on us now do we? Who knows... by the time your boyfriend turns up we might have made you into a full-blown junkie.'

He placed the water and biscuits in the corner by the door.

When he turned, Pietersen's head caught him full in the face. She drove with her legs, bulldozing him backwards. He brought his hands up to his busted nose.

She stomped her right foot into the side of his leg with all her might. A loud crack reverberated off the walls as his knee gave way.

'Aggghhh!,' Maddocks screamed, falling backwards. She stomped again and caught his shattered leg with a glancing blow. He twisted to the side, snorting blood down his front.

Pietersen launched into him, hammering her knee into his head. He tried to duck away, but a second blow caught him in the temple, smashing his skull against the wall. She crunched her knee into his jaw.

Her leg was pumping like the piston of a steam hammer.

Eventually he stopped trying to avoid the blows and his arms flopped to his sides.

Pietersen kept on going. The back of his head thudded against the plasterboard.

Exhaustion overcame her and she collapsed on top of him, her heart pounding against her chest. She rolled away, gasping for air. Maddocks was slumped in the corner. A starburst of blood smeared across the wall behind him.

The room was spinning and she could feel her knee beginning to swell against her jeans.

She got up and hobbled out the door. There was no time to waste. She had to get out of there if she was going to survive.

Chapter 59

Malice held his breath while he dialled the number. The clock on the dashboard read 8.10 a.m. — twenty minutes before team briefing. He was banking on her being in a flap with no time to talk.

'You never call me at this time. What's up, Mally?' Superintendent Waite answered.

'Sorry, boss but I won't be in today. I got a family emergency on my hands.'

'Okay, when will you be back?'

'Maybe a couple of days, maybe earlier.'

'For Christ's sake, you don't make life easy. Do what you need to do and keep me posted. Is there anything urgent with the Copeland case?'

'No ma'am, all of that is taken care of.'

'Okay I'll see you—'

'Oh, and one more thing… Kelly called to say she was sick today. Thought I'd better let you know.'

'Bloody hell. What's wrong with her?'

'Flu or something…'

'Great. I need to dash, got a meeting at half-past.'

The line went dead.

Malice unwrapped a breakfast bar from the box he'd purchased in the service station and stared out of the window. Straight ahead was No.8, Beaconsfield Crescent — a well-kept detached property with a flashy Jaguar sitting in the drive.

His wife has a nicer car than him.

He saw the bedroom curtains open and a willowy woman with blonde hair nudged open the window. She fussed with the ornaments that were sitting on the windowsill then disappeared from view.

Malice munched on the bar and swigged water from a bottle. To get this right he needed to be in three places at once. He'd weighed up the options and had chosen this one first.

The front door opened and a man appeared wearing jeans and a white shirt. He opened the garage door and went inside. Seconds later he came out carrying a black kitbag and tossed it onto the back seat of the Jag. He jumped into the driver's seat and reversed out of the drive before swinging around in the road and screeching away.

The vehicle passed the end of the road where Malice had been sitting in his car for the past four hours. The driver had a dark stubbled chin and was wearing sunglasses. His arm was draped over the sill of the side window, a cigarette dangling between his fingers. Malice wondered if the stab wounds to his legs were causing any problems.

Pietersen ran headlong down the passageway to the door at the end. Her heart was racing and every part of her ached. The concrete tore at the soles of her feet as she lurched from side to side, trying not to fall down. At any second she expected to see the shape of Bailey or Craven silhouetted against the light at the end.

She barged through the door and entered a vast building with a sky-high roof held aloft by metal girders. The floor was a patchwork of different colours where machinery and equipment had once been bolted to the floor and workbenches and lockers were dotted about. Light flooded in through huge windows in the roof. The acrid stink of burned wood and grease hung in the air.

Pietersen scanned the disused warehouse and saw what she was looking for. Secured to a wall was a strip of galvanised cable tray, one of the few metal fittings the scavengers had missed. She hurried over and knelt down with her back to the edge of the tray, feeling its jagged edges with her fingers. She jammed the rope binding her wrists against the metal and began to work her hands up and down. The edge of the steel bit into her skin. She kept going.

Up and down. Up and down.

Come on!

She bit her lip when she felt the warm trickle of blood on her hands.

Up and down. Up and down.

The muscles in her shoulders screamed for her to stop as she forced her arms apart, trying to avoid the serrated edge of the tray.

Suddenly the rope gave way. She was free.

She scampered across the floor on all fours and hunkered down behind a bench to check the damage. A series of ugly slashes criss-crossed the inside of her wrist and her feet were a mess. She picked chippings and debris from the broken skin.

Think, think.

She had no phone, no money and wasn't going to get far, running away with no shoes. Her body shook as the exertion began to take hold. She was thirsty and hungry.

Think, think.

Bailey or Craven could show up at any minute and when they find Maddocks, they're going to be all over this place like a rash.

Ideas crashed around in her head. None of them good. She popped her head around the side of the bench — all clear. So she crabbed her way across the warehouse floor and headed back through the door leading to where she'd been held. It was a huge risk.

Her feet began to burn as she hurried down the passageway to the room at the end. Maddocks was still hunched in the corner. Pietersen put her fingers to his neck — he was definitely dead. She rifled through his pockets and found a set of keys, then fumbled with his shoe laces. In less than a minute, the bolts on the door clanked shut and she was running back to the open space with the pack of biscuits and water in her hands. Maddock's shoes clip-clopped on the concrete.

Craven was looking forward to today. The sun was shining and he had eighties music to sing along too. The prospect of torturing Pietersen was the cherry on the top. Oh, and of course not forgetting the chance that her boyfriend would turn up at some point to save her. The more the merrier.

He cruised down the road and pulled into a parade of shops. He might have a packed to-do list but there was a full race card on at Haydock and he couldn't miss out on that. He shoved open the door to the bookies to be greeted by a group of guys all with the same idea.

'Eyes down for a full house, lads.' A man sporting a hoody and a baseball cap called out. 'The unluckiest man in West Yorkshire has just walked in.'

A peel of laughter went around the room.

'Sod off the lot of you,' Craven replied, slapping him on the back. 'I'll be quids-up today while you boys are crying in your beer.'

'You don't want to bet on that, do you?' another one said.

Craven laughed, then strutted up to the counter and handed over his completed betting slip along with three hundred pounds.

'Fuck me. There's enough there to choke a donkey,' the hoody-man yelled out.

'That's what your missus says when I pop round.' Craven was in his element. He took the receipt and stuffed it in his wallet. 'Can't stop around here chatting to you tossers,' he said over his shoulder as he walked out.

He got back in his car, filtered into the flow of traffic and wound up the volume to belt out *Living on a Prayer*. He turned right at a roundabout onto the A64. A multitude of destinations were written on the signpost. One of them read: Sleaford.

The driver of the Ford Mustang three cars back watched him turn... and followed.

Pietersen was crouched amongst a clump of bushes, surveying the front of the building from fifty yards away. She was cramming biscuits in her mouth and washing them down with water. The sugar coursing through her bloodstream was making her feel human again.

Maddocks' coat was around her shoulders, his keys in the pocket. From what she could tell she seemed to be on the outskirts of an industrial estate which butted up against a main road. Most of the surrounding units were empty and boarded up, with signs everywhere announcing 'Security Patrols'. But so far there'd been none.

Earlier, when climbed through a gap in the fence she'd walked around pressing the key fob. Maddocks' car was parked against the kerb in a side road. The tyre wrench from the boot was laying in the grass beside her. Now all she had to do was wait.

Her knee was throbbing. She rolled up the leg of her jeans to find it turning an angry shade of purple. The gravity of her situation was sinking in. It was tempting to take Maddocks' car and drive… just drive… but where would she go? She could run and hide, but for how long? Craven would catch up with her one day. She had no choice. She had to stay and finish the job.

A car came into view.

It cruised by and came to a stop near to where Maddocks had parked. The door opened and Craven stepped out. He reached into the back and brought out the kitbag. Pietersen gripped the wrench and watched him ease his way through the hole in the fence and disappear into the building.

Thank God there's only one of them.

She dashed into the open, keeping low. As she approached the fence, she caught sight of someone in her peripheral vision, moving fast.

He was running towards her carrying a sawn-off shotgun

Chapter 60

Pietersen crouched down when she reached the perimeter fence. The man skidded to a halt next to her.

'What the fuck are you doing here?' she whispered through gritted teeth.

'I waited outside Craven's house and followed him. Shit, are you okay?' Malice panted while gripping on to the shotgun.

Pietersen touched her busted nose. It hurt like hell.

'I'm fine,' she winced.

'Bloody hell.' Malice grabbed her hand and turned it over to expose the gashes on her wrist. 'What did they do to you?'

'I said I'm fine.' She jerked her arm away. 'We don't have much time. When Craven gets to the room where I was being held, all hell is going to break loose.'

'Come on. We need to get you away from here,' said Malice, looking around to check their escape route was clear.

'No way, Mally.'

'What do you mean?'

'It has to end here.'

'What are you talking about?'

'I don't have time to explain. This is my problem and I'm gonna sort it. Where the hell did you get that?' she said, pointing at the shotgun.

'I took it from a kid who nicked my daughter's bike.'

'What?'

'Never mind. Come on.'

Malice jumped up, glancing over his shoulder. Pietersen dropped the tyre iron and snatched the gun from his hand. She cracked open the barrel to reveal two cartridges.

'This is more like it.' She shoved him to one side and eased through the gap in the fence.

'What the f—' Malice said.

Pietersen dashed across the yard and into the warehouse, clutching the gun. She was racing for the door at the end when she heard the roar of a man's voice coming from the passageway.

She reached the entrance and ducked to one side. The sound of heavy boots echoed down the concrete corridor. Craven was swearing and cursing as he went, his lop-sided gait giving his footsteps an irregular staccato sound.

Pietersen could see Malice at the far side of the building and waved for him to get back.

The noise coming from inside the tunnel was getting louder.

Craven elbowed his way through the door and Pietersen smashed the butt of the shotgun into the side of his face.

He staggered sideways.

'I fucking warned you,' she yelled at the top of her voice.

She levelled the weapon and pulled the trigger. The gun went click.

Fuck!

She checked the safety and tried again.

Click.

Craven recovered his footing and spun around. He bellowed when he clapped eyes on Pietersen and lurched at her.

She dipped to the side and swung the gun in an arc, bringing the barrel down hard on his shoulder. His legs buckled under the weight of the blow. He would have let out a scream, but the wooden stock thudded into the back of his neck. His eyes rolled back and he slumped face down onto the concrete.

Pietersen threw herself on top of him but Malice wrapped his arm around her body and dragged her off. The gun scudded across the floor. She broke free and launched herself at Craven again, rolling him over and throwing punches at his face.

'Fucking hell, Kelly!' Malice heaved her to her feet and they both fell backwards, landing in a heap. He clamped his arms around her until she stopped struggling.

'Leave it. Leave it,' he yelled.

He looked across at Craven, who was lying on his back, staring at the roof.

Malice crawled over and pressed his fingers into his neck.

'He's dead.'

'Good,' she snarled.

'What about the others?'

'Maddocks is lying in a room down that corridor.'

'Is he...?'

'Dead? Yes.'

'Let's get him out of here.' Malice gripped the collar of Craven's shirt with both hands and dragged him across the floor and down the passageway towards the room at the end. Pietersen got there first and slid the bolts across on the door and pushed it wide. Malice hauled Craven inside and dumped next to Maddocks. 'Fuck me, Kelly. You did a proper job, I'll give you that.'

'They were never going to stop. And with what you did to Craven, you were next on the list.'

Malice unzipped the kitbag lying on the floor.

'Shit. They had some nasty treats in store for you,' he said, bringing out a blowtorch, a drill and a bottle containing a yellowy liquid. He took the top off and smelled it. 'Petrol. Ouch!'

'Who knows, that could have been meant for the both of us,' she said, sinking onto her haunches with her back against the wall.

'What about Bailey?'

'Don't worry about him. He was always the third wheel in the operation, more of an errand boy than anything else. Without Craven and Maddocks he's nothing.'

'So, we don't need to find him?'

'No. He'll piss his pants when he finds out his mates are missing.'

'Let's get the hell out of here. We'll take this with us, my prints are on it.' Malice held up the kitbag and made for the door.

'I can't.' Pietersen put her head on her knees.

'What? Come on. Let's go.'

'My DNA is all over this room. Not to mention all over them.' She pointed at the bodies lying on the ground. 'You need to leave.'

'What?'

'Leave the bag and go back to the car.'

'What are you gonna do?'

Pietersen got to her feet, dipped her hand into the bag and lifted out the bottle of petrol. Then she riffled through Craven's pockets for his lighter.

'Go back to the car and wait,' she said.

'Are you sure?'

'Go.'

Malice gave the room one last look before marching down the passageway. He picked up the gun and made his was across the warehouse and out into the yard. His car was parked a couple of streets away.

He slumped into the driver's seat and stared out the window. After a while he could see Pietersen walking up the road towards him, carrying the kitbag. She was limping and had discarded the jacket.

She opened the door and eased her aching body into the passenger seat

'Now we can go,' she said, pulling down the sun visor and flipped open the mirror.

'I told Waite you weren't in work because you had the flu.'

'Might want to think of something else.' She ran her fingertips over her broken nose and bruised cheek.

'Are we all done?' he asked.

She slapped the visor back in place.

'Yeah, all done.'

Malice gunned the engine and sped away from the industrial park. Pietersen twisted in her seat to look out of the back window. Faint wisps of black smoke were rising into the sky above the warehouse.

Chapter 61

Seven weeks later
HM Prison Holloway

I gave it my best shot, but it's difficult to argue with the science. Like all good lies, keeping things close to the truth almost won the day. It was fun while it lasted.

It's unlikely they will make the murder charges stick. All the bracelet does is put me at the scene of the burial, it doesn't mean I killed them. To convict me of murder, I reckon the police would need my DNA on the hammer, which is going to be tough because I threw it into the reservoir.

It was one of our favourite picnic spots and we brought it along wrapped in clingfilm. And when I say I threw it into the water, it was Clem. I tossed it about five feet and Clem laughed his head off. He retrieved it from the shallows and launched the hammer halfway across the reservoir.

I remember it was a beautiful day and we ate quiche and sandwiches and sat in the sunshine. I was lying in his arms watching the clouds drift by.

'That one looks like a dog with a ball,' Clem said, pointing a finger at the sky.

'Rubbish. It's a kid on a bike,' I'd said.

We played cloud shapes for ages, enjoying the silliness and the close feel of each other's company. It was strange to think there was a murder weapon lurking beneath forty feet of water in such an idyllic location.

When recounting what had happened to Horton and Maxwell to the police, I kept as close to the truth as I dare. It was a simple case of substituting me for Clem.

After the argument at the church, we'd arranged to meet John and Maxwell at the abandoned factory. The discussion got heated and they kept pushing and pushing. John wanted to see the kid that never was and Maxwell was banging on about the money and how I had to pay it back or they would go to the police. They were shouting at each other as much as they were shouting at me. I remember my foot touched the hammer, laying on the floor. And in that moment I thought… *I've had enough of this.*

I hit John so hard I thought his eyeballs were going to fall out of his face. He went down like an ironing board. Then, out of the corner of my eye I caught a glimpse of Maxwell. In hindsight I think he was rushing to John's aid but I thought he was coming at me. I swung my arm with every ounce of strength I had. Sometimes I lie awake in bed and can still hear the crack. He was dead before he hit the ground.

That was it. All was quiet. Problem solved.

I can't believe I lost my bracelet when we returned the next day to dispose of the bodies. I can remember one morning realising it wasn't in my jewellery box but Clem told me not to worry. He said he'd buy me another when next he returned to Malawi. He never did.

I'm on remand pending my trial. You would think they'd have got their bloody act together by now. I can only assume they're trying to piece together the blood found in the house. To be honest, I'm not sure how many people were killed in that room. The newest sample they found must be Joseph but I'm struggling to remember the names of the others.

My legal counsel argued that because of Dennis I should be granted bail, but that fucking Rebecca had to stick her oar in. The police produced a statement from Dennis which he supposedly dictated to her. It said how I'd lied about the blackmail and how he'd never heard of Horton or Maxwell. He also went on to list a catalogue of times where I'd abused him and referenced some of the physical evidence in the visit reports.

My solicitor argued that this was a vindictive act on Rebecca's part, given the serious claim lodged against her. And anyway, how did the police know this wasn't her words and not his? Turned out they'd videoed him giving the testimony and when she read it back to Dennis at the end, the bastard blinked twice for yes. Which kind of went against me.

I bet Beresford is beside himself. After all, he's nailed his constabulary colours to my mast and I've fallen from grace in spectacular fashion. Serves him right, the twat. As for the rest of the church, I'm sure they will be praying for my salvation, and Ketchup will be crying in the font now he doesn't have the OutReach programme to crow about.

I miss Clem every day and it hurts that I wasn't with him at the end. They say that there's a soulmate in life for everyone and he was mine. I worry about Frank. God knows what he's doing now. He could be locked up as well for all I know, or dead. I ring his mobile most days and it clicks through to voicemail. I fear the worst but it could be as straightforward as the silly bugger hasn't charged it up.

I've resigned myself to serving a custodial sentence. I'm not sure for how long but when I get out I have a party-pot of seven hundred and thirty thousand pounds waiting for me. And when I spend that, I know where Clem's cash is stashed. Though I'm hoping I can somehow get that money to Frank… if I can ever get hold of him. They wouldn't let me out for the funeral. I presume Frank had to make the decision to pull the plug which must have destroyed him.

I sometimes think about Dennis and thank my lucky stars I'm in here and don't have to look after the sick bastard anymore. Fuck knows what's happened to him. Maybe Carol's moved him into the new offices so she can keep her sympathetic eyes on him. She's such a sweetie.

As I sit on my bed in my cell, it strikes me that for the right kind of person there's a lot of money to be made when you're banged up in prison. A synthetic cannabinoid called Spice is the drug of choice, and it's selling like hot cakes. It's more prevalent in male prisons but I am all about equality and it's about time the girls had some fun.

It's known as the 'zombie drug' for good reason, the effects can be unpredictable. On the few occasions I've seen it in action it reduced one person to a vegetative state for much of the day, while another attacked a prison officer before throwing herself off the landing onto the safety netting.

The latest wheeze is to soak paper in the stuff and send it to inmates in the mail. A single sheet of paper can go for three hundred pounds. All you do is cut it into strips and sell it to people who are into vaping. They tear off a piece and stuff it into the burner and away they go. It's wicked. If I could get hold of Frank we could get this off the ground.

And another business opportunity is mobile phones. Tiny things, which would cost twenty pounds on the outside goes for ten times that much in here. I never knew they made them so small. It's a gold mine ready for the taking.

I knew I would fit straight in when I learned there was a church. I've already floated the idea that we could set up a self-help group whereby those who don't want to be involved in the drugs scene can come along and be 'saved'. Seems to me a straightforward way of identifying a new target market.

The only problem is the wing is ruled by Trudy, or Queenie as she likes to be called. Apparently she's serving a life sentence for murdering her husband, but due to her unruly behaviour she's serving a sentence long enough to have killed his entire family. I think she likes being here. I'm slowly becoming her go-to woman when it comes to fixing things. Fuck knows why, I've only been here the strike of a light and I'm already streets ahead of the rest.

The chances are I will serve my sentence here. There aren't that many women's prisons. If I play the 'Dennis' card and say I want to be close to him in case anything bad happens I can't imagine them moving me.

Fingers crossed that when I'm released God will have done what he should have done years ago and have taken the fucker. Not that I believe in God, though I believe in the sentiment, and let's be fair, it's the sentiment that counts.

    Most of the inmates have cottoned on to me being called Twinkle. Some of them give it the Twinkle Twinkle, Little Star routine which drives me mad. My uncle's version rings in my head each time. The version he made up to keep me quiet after he raped me.

> *Twinkle, twinkle little lies,*
> *How I see them in your eyes,*
> *Keep the truth inside your head,*
> *And hope that no one winds up dead.*

    Living a life full of lies has served me well but as for the part where no one dies, it's fair to say, I've allowed that one to slip.

    I'm already thinking Queenie lacks vision and is letting the younger ones run rings around her. Sooner or later she'll be history and if I can hasten her demise I'll be ready and waiting to fill the gap. People are queuing up to knock her off her perch and I'll have fun giving them a helping hand. After all, everyone walks around with an invisible set of user-instructions hanging around their neck. The trick is working out how to read it.

    It's my one and only skill but then I've reached the conclusion … it's the only one I need.

Acknowledgements

I want to thank all those who have made this book possible:

My family, Karen, Gemma, and Holly for their encouragement and endless patience. Plus, my magnificent BetaReaders, Nicki, Jackie and Simon, who didn't hold back with their comments and feedback. I'm a lucky boy to have them in my corner.

My fabulous ARC Group who have shouted about my books and made me blush with their unwavering support.

Also, my editor, David Lyons, my proofreader, Brigit Taylor, the fabulous Emmy Ellis @studioenp and cheriefox.com who designed an amazing cover.

My wider circle of family and friends for their endless supply of helpful suggestions. The majority of which are not suitable to repeat here.

And last but by no means least, you the reader, for making this all worthwhile.

How to get in touch

I love hearing from readers. If you want to get in touch please use the links below. Subscribe to my Readers List on my website to receive further details of new releases, promotions and events.

Website: robashman.com

Email: info@robashman.com

Facebook: Rob Ashman Author

Twitter: @RobAshmanAuthor

Printed in Great Britain
by Amazon